Niall Williams

Only Say the Word

PICADOR

First published in Ireland 2004 and in Great Britain 2005 by Picador

First published in paperback 2006 by Picador
an imprint of Pan Macmillan Ltd
Pan Macmillan, 20 New Wharf Road, London NI 9RR
Basingstoke and Oxford
Associated companies throughout the world
www.panmacmillan.com

ISBN-13: 978-0-330-43396-9
ISBN-10: 0-330-43396-2

www.niallwilliams.com

Grateful acknowledgement is made for permission to reprint
lines from 'Known World' from *Electric Light* by Seamus Heaney,
copyright © 2001, published by Faber and Faber Ltd.

1 3 5 7 9 8 6 4 2

A CIP catalogue record for this book is available from
the British Library.

Typeset by Intype Libra, London
Printed and bound in Great Britain by
Mackays of Chatham plc, Chatham, Kent

NIALL WILL
Ireland, with
the author of
which has sol
bestseller.

FOR YOU, OF COURSE

Only say the Word
And I shall be healed.

Prayer before Communion

One

I do not know what words to write. There have been so many words written already. So many endings and beginnings. I have lost my faith.

Yesterday I sat at this table for hours and wrote nothing but your name. I wrote it in the four corners of the page, as if by doing so I might conjure you at its centre. I wrote it while waiting to begin, but how can I begin without faith? I have gone through days when I was certain I would never sit down again and try to write anything. I have despised myself for the weeks and months of unlived life spent creating those books of mine that stand on the shelf above the fireplace. What was first a refuge became the place where I was most comfortable, where I could forgive God His own oversights and blunders and make the plots come out all right. But what now? I seem to know no other way of living except to sit each day before the white screen and listen for the words. I do not want to invent a meaning this time. I don't want to pretend there is a God or that the innocent die for reasons secret and profound.

And so I sit here, and feel your absence and wonder how to begin to live without you.

Begin.

Kate.

The blankness of the page is like a hurt. I write your name on the paper to put you back into my life. As though words were real things. As though when I write your name you are here.

Kate.

*

Autumn progresses. The rain is ceaseless now, and yet seems hardly to fall, a soft grey, wrapped like a shroud about all west of the Shannon. Leaves of sycamore blacken and curl their edges. When the wind picks up the rain, they come slanting across the cottage window in stricken flight. All the last blossoms are faded now, and crimson geraniums are stalks of brown seed and yellowed leaves. Everywhere the countryside is tattered, wind-wild. You can feel that somewhere in the deeps of the earth something is slowly souring which once was sweetening.

Across the valley small herds of cattle move and stand and move again for shelter. Between the showers huge blackbirds come and alight in your garden. I raise my hand from the table and they do not fly off. They wait there, as though burdened with some significance, when I know they have none.

Rain comes again and streams down the window.

*

I have read Margaret Atwood say that all writing is an attempt to bring back the dead. To journey into the past and bring back what is vanished. Something like that. Some act of resurrection. But tonight while the salt wind off the Atlantic makes rattle the cottage windows all such claims seem unreal and beyond me.

All I can do now is tell the truth. Tell how it is. Do not make a story.

If only I could do that.

The world slips away from me here. I do not watch the television news now. When I walk outside in the night and look up through the whirl of wind that pulls the clouds across the stars, I think of the God that I once believed existed where now there is only absence and emptiness, the deep and the darker blue as the stars vanish.

I come in and go through the cottage in the half-light, gathering up Jack's clothes or Hannah's books and magazines. I make tidy little stacks. I think I am doing very well, but then something of you breaks through. I see one of your paintings. I feel a tightness close at the base of my throat and I think, I cannot do this. I do not believe in a heaven or any hereafter. In books I have written, I have pretended that I did.

4

Once, I imagined all the dead souls reunited as in a dance and the mending of all loss. But here tonight I know I do not really believe this, and my forehead films with a clammy sweat and nausea twists in my stomach.

The house is utterly still. The children sleep. Night fills the valley.

*

Tell the truth. The truth begins with me sitting here trying to tell it. I sit at this long table that overlooks the garden and this valley in the west of County Clare. Truth. The ocean is not far. Truth. It is the autumn of the year two thousand and one. This is the place where in the wet green stillness I try to write stories. I have written many, and poems too, but none that seem real to me now. None that capture the ice-fire of grief that is in me now. All seem so artificial and unreal and I wonder what is the use of all my books now?

The children are home from school. I hear them moving about restless with the empty time. Hannah comes and asks me when will I be going to the village. She needs shampoo. Ten minutes later Jack who was eight years old two days ago stands at the doorway and asks why we do not live in America. They have better television in America, he says.

I want to tell him that television is not important. I want to take him inside my arms and hold him here beside me and say I know how things are for you. I know the harrowing the world has already made in the soft places of your spirit. I know your fears and pains and because I am your father I cannot know them for an instant without wanting to make them pass.

But the words, or perhaps the means to say them, seem stolen from me, and instead I say I will try and get better stations on the television. 'I don't like it here,' Jack says, and turns and goes off.

Help me.

Begin.

Begin with the image of a woman with blonde hair diving into a blue pool in high summer. The pool is at the end of a long lawn that runs down from the big house. The house is in Westchester County, New York, near the town with the Indian name of Wapaqua, where the woman and her brother grew up. Now it is the house where her divorced mother is to live alone, for that summer the woman is to marry and her brother is to leave for a life in California. The woman dives into the pool and a man stands and watches her. It is the hour when evening is falling quickly and the shadows of the hemlocks and cedars are lengthened and blue. The heat of the day is passing but still trapped somehow in the falling of the dark and so the air is thick and heavy, and the perfect strokes of the woman as she swims length after length are a kind of coolness that is lovely and soft and easeful. She swims with remarkable beauty and it is as if the water is her true element and while within it there exists for her nothing but the motion of her body and its fluency. And at that moment when the evening has just become night, from up at the house her mother stands and turns a switch and at once the pool is a blue and golden dazzle, lit from beneath, and the swimmer like a fabulous creature fallen from above.

But all of that is so much later.

Instead, here is a boy. He is a boy as thin as a stick. He is a boy happy in the world still who lives along a country road outside the small village of Dun in the west of County Clare. His hair is

6

fair, his nose saddled with freckles. His eyes are green. He has a brother five years older than himself and a sister, Louise, an infant.

His father is Tom Foley, a big, quiet man who works in the post office of that village. He operates the switchboard and connects the calls that link Dun to the world. He is a man measured in everything he does, a man who never raises his voice. His day is filled with the quiet interrogative '*Yes?*' he repeats over and over as he answers a call. '*One moment now, please,*' he says two hundred times a day. And then, without the slightest inflection of victory or pleasure, '*You're through now.*' In a black Morris Minor he travels the two miles between the house and the post office. Though he is not yet old his hair, once a dark brown, now grows in silver wings over his ears. His eyes are a soft grey like flannel. When you look into them deeply you can see tiny flecks there, minor speckles that might be tears in a cloth revealing something of what lies beneath.

There is a crinkled picture of him on the steps of some building in Dublin beside the stout and grave-looking figure of the boy's grandfather who died two years later and never met his grandchildren. In the photograph Tom Foley's expression is youthful and even what was once called dashing. He wears a white shirt and a narrow tie beneath his dark jacket and looks out from the picture with an open face almost smiling. In his eyes there is optimism and hope and valour. But in time all these have vanished. Few traces of that youth remain. The man he has become sits in the empty post office, leaning forward and balancing his forehead in his right hand as if holding there memories of that time long ago. A man of few words, when the bell rings above the door, his head rises, and, summoned back from far away, he says the name of the man or woman in soft greeting.

The boy's mother is from Dublin. Her name is Marie. She is slim and fine-boned with long black hair turning silver and worn up at the back of her head. She is older than her husband. He met her one rainy night in Liverpool when he thought he was on his way to join the British army. She was in Findler's Lane crying on

7

the ground. Though it is a secret, shared only with Tom, earlier that day she had given birth to a girl that had died. She thought it punishment for sin, despite the fact she had planned to have the child and raise it a Catholic and had told God as much many times in the nine months previous. Tom Foley squatted down in the puddle beside Marie and within an instant had chosen love over war and decided to bring her back to Clare.

When he first brought her to the village, they lived above the post office and she worked with him behind the counter. She tried to know all the Marys and Annes and Bridgets of Dun and the parish beyond. For a season she attempted to win them, to smile and ask of their children, to know who had a son gone for a job in Dublin, whose daughter was sickly and who was hoping for a position in the bank. But it was of little use. Marie was an outsider in that place. Her clothes were too fine, her make-up too elaborate. The people did not warm to her, nor she to them, and after a while she stopped going downstairs to the shop. Soon Tom bought a cottage out in the countryside and Marie did not have to be in the post office or sell the newspapers there on Sunday mornings when he was gone to Mass.

Now, years later, she is beautiful still. Her beauty is older and has a sorrowful quality sometimes when she stops in her kitchen and is held on the thorn of a memory, or the loneliness of her life rushes in on her. But she breaks free of this and her silver-black hair falls to her shoulder and she turns swiftly and her green eyes capture you when you look at them. 'Now, what's next?' she says. She cooks thick dark stews that sit all day on the turf range and fill the house with rich savour. In summer she must have flowers brought into the house, and goes out along the roadside and plucks foxgloves and snaps branches of honeysuckle to bring inside. In the house she works diligently, making neat warm towers of ironed clothes and calling the boys to take them to their rooms upstairs. Her sons quietly obey.

Matthew, the oldest, is tall and earnest, and is in his school the brightest boy at maths. When his father comes home to his dinner, Matthew sometimes has to walk the infant Louise in her pram and does so without complaint, pushing the navy blue carriage with the white rubber wheels along the bumpy road at the top of the valley, past the yellow meadows. Sometimes the younger-brother-that-is-I, Jim, runs some of the way after him and catches up and makes foolish faces, but Matthew does not mind. He goes on ahead and I run back home. I lie down in the wild grass at the side of our house and sometimes read comics or *Boy's Own*. My mother comes and stands by the front door. After his dinner my father sits in what is now called the television room and watches the news of our country. When the news is over he will turn off the television to save electricity and smoke a cigarette and then open the newspaper he has already read. He rereads it carefully, every word, and when he is done he adds it to the soft yellowing stack that rises alongside his chair.

When Matthew returns I jump up to meet him and he raises his finger to his lips and makes a shushing sound to tell me our sister is asleep. I hold up my two hands and flap them by the sides of my ears to make him laugh. I twist my face about and come close to the pram, but he does not laugh and waves me away before skirting by the old hay barn to the back door. He does not come back out. I already know he won't. I know he will drink a glass of milk and my mother will come out to the kitchen and thank him and take Louise and carry her upstairs. Then Matthew will go in and say goodnight to my father though it is still bright, and he will say he has some work to do upstairs for school.

I lie outside on the grass. It is May. The sky, like a blue sleeve darned with flies, is too bright for sleep. There is the first tangled scent of the meadows thickening, of wildflowers new-bloomed, of woodbine and fuchsia, the warm smells of the animals in Mick Hehir's bog meadow. I am a week from my First Communion. My thoughts are pure things and are like so many white birds floating about me as I lie there. I do not go off to play elsewhere or to seek company in one of the farms down the road. I am some-how empty and filled at the same time, and I think I am aware

that this is a time I will remember later on in my life. I lie there
with no shoes on and read and turn over and look at the sky as if
it were a window. I do not know what I am looking to see. My
eyes are too poor to detect the coming stars. I believe in God up
there. I think of Him in His vast terrain where He can run in
gigantic strides across it. But then such thoughts dissolve and I
am thinking of nothing. I am a boy lying on the grass in the May
evening in the turning of the world. My father comes to the front
door to call me in for bed.

'Jim,' he says softly. He says nothing more, and I rise and
go in.

For the first time, I have a room of my own. Matthew is next
door and sits studying at his table. I say goodnight to him and he
turns and looks at me briefly and the look is one I cannot translate and so I make a face to see will he smile and he does and I go
to bed.

I cannot sleep. My mind runs. I think of that day and the one
before and the Communion coming and fuse one thing into
another until the air is threaded back and forth with the long thin
webs of a small boy's thoughts. It is too warm for sleeping, but I
am meant to sleep. I must not turn on the light, and so instead
take one of my library books and hold it up by the window to
read in the half-light that falls there. It is a child's version of the
story of Marco Polo. From the words and pictures of its pages
another world comes and fills the bedroom with sailing ships and
strange names and spices I have never tasted. I read because I
cannot sleep and then I cannot sleep because what I read is more
real than my own life. At some moment my eyes fall from the page
and yet it is as if I am still reading on and within the story. I roll
back and forth in my bed so it rocks softly. It is a ship sailing out
to sea from Venice.

*

My mother is a devout woman. She has a sister who is a Sister, a
nun in the missions, and a small statue of the Virgin in her room,

and in summer she fills a vase with hedgerow flowers to stand beside it. She prays when she wakes up in the morning. One of the prayers is in Irish and to my boyish ear seems all the more holy for that. God understands all languages, I have decided, even made-up ones. And in that year of my First Communion I test His comprehension with my own invented vocabulary. I kneel by my bed in my pyjamas and mouth soft plosive sounds, weird vocables of devotion, untranslatable by all but Him. *Hayem guam tagus eefa nunc qua inta novi* God. Through the wall I can hear my mother murmur, and hear too the small sounds of my sister in her cot beside the big bed. My mother's prayers float over her as I imagine they did once over me although I cannot remember. I know not to disturb her and to get dressed and go downstairs and have my breakfast with my brother. Though I carry a small grudge at this, a short fat wedge of resentment at my sister taking all the prayers, I do what is asked of me without complaint.

I know that Louise has arrived in our family unexpectedly, as a blessing, my mother has told me. 'A wonderful, wonderful blessing.' I know that in some unspoken way the family was finished when I was born, that although my mother longed for a daughter she had come to accept there would only be Matthew and me. But I do not know then of her own private sense of grief and atonement, or the anxiety that wormed in her for the nine months she was waiting, wondering if this would be a girl, and the final sign of forgiveness.

When my mother comes down she wears a bright dress and is made up, her hair brushed so the black waves of it fall softly. The baby is in her arms sleeping. My mother moves about with Louise cradled there. She whispers that Matthew was just the same, waking at every hour of the night and asleep again as soon as he was in her arms.

'Yes. You were. Do you not remember?' She is smiling over at him.

Matthew looks down at his toast intensely as if a mathematical puzzle is drawn there.

'You don't. I know you don't. But you were. You didn't know night-time from daytime.' My mother turns to tell me. 'He wanted to sleep all afternoon and I would have to shake water on him to try to get him to wake up. Then he'd wake up for a few minutes and next thing you know his head would be down and he would be asleep again.' She laughs as she tells it and I laugh too but Matthew does not. 'Your sister is just the same.'

'Was I the same?'

'You were the best boy,' my mother tells me. 'You knew what was right.'

My father comes into the kitchen and is clean-shaven, wearing a white, ironed shirt that makes his own spirit seem ironed out, flattened.

'Tom, here's your tea,' my mother says and pours it thick and dark from the pot the way he likes it.

My father sits down like a man made of cloth. He makes no noise.

'Morning, Matthew, Jim,' he greets us, but does so in such a way it would seem an intrusion or disturbance of some kind if we were to do more than just nod in reply. It is as though he is a conduit only, connecting the line to someone else but not to him. He looks above the net curtain at the weather. The sky is overcast and rain is coming. A little flickering of response happens around his mouth, a tightening, which may be a net to catch his words.

My mother comes to the table.

'Bless us, O Lord,' my father says, 'Jim?'

And I say the prayer I have learned and then we sit there, ordinary, without event, in the plainness of time, sipping our tea and eating our bread.

On a sunlit day I make my First Communion. I hold the perfect circle of the host in my mouth and feel I am like a candle lit. The holiness of the world astonishes me. I am so deeply grateful for all things created and not least the simple life of our family. From the church I walk up the main street of the village with my hands held flat together but a tiny space in between them, as though cupped between my palms is the delicate airlike wonder of my soul. I am a big boy now. I can take over some of Matthew's chores and free him for his schoolwork. I bring in turf for the range. I gather kindling in the grove beneath the high whoosh of the sycamores. I ask to take Louise in her pram, and my mother hesitates but then allows it. I do not truly want to take her but I want to spare Matthew.

I push the pram out along the upper road at the top of the valley. But soon Louise is crying and I run faster, bouncing the pram over the road, and faster still when she does not stop. We fly along, hedgerow and fenceline a blur. Her face is a small red knot as her cries continue. I extend my arms and lengthen my stride. 'Stop it,' I tell her, 'Lou, stop; stop, Lou. Lou-Lou,' and shake the pram in a sideways motion even as we race forward. But she does not stop. She wails as if some precious thing is broken. And still I try and push us forward, fast forward, thinking perhaps to outpace or outdistance the pain or fear or that we will arrive in a place, a pocket of air or countryside, where sanctuary is. I run on, half wild now with panic. When I slow at all, Louise cries louder still. Cows turn in the field. I talk to her in what I think are the tones of my mother's voice. But it is no good, her face looks boiled, and I turn the pram around and I am running with it back toward home when I see my mother out in the road with her arms folded across her chest, waiting anxiously for our return. As I arrive in front of her Louise is bawling still. My mother's face is grey. She reaches in and lifts the baby in her arms and as she does feels the pillowcase soaked through.

'She wouldn't stop,' I am breathlessly saying. 'I tried . . .'

'Shush shush,' my mother says, but whether to me or my sister or both I cannot say. She is already turned and heading back into the house and I am standing there with the empty pram.

And in that same passing of time, the same even measurement in which one moment seems identical to the next but is not, our life is struck and falls apart.

One morning in the season of Advent that year, I wake and a

frost has fallen. The dawn, if it has broken, brings no light. In the distance the few street lights of the village are still burning and hide the last stars and make a pale amber glow. I wake and look out of my bedroom window at the garden and can already feel some fracture in the world. I stand at the window in my pyjamas. I press my nose and my lips to the glass and see my breath come up and cloud and slowly fade, and for no reason that I can yet shape, I do not want to move away from here. I think Christmas is not coming, as if there has occurred a strange anomaly, a flaw in the workings of calendars and chronometers. The stillness of the house is like an enormous being that sits in every room but mine and swells out and takes up all the air. I am afraid to go out and face it. I stand there a long time as everything of that morning enters me, frozen whitened ground, the church spire, the stilled village, twisted knotted clumps of blackthorn hedgerow, thin white webs hanging, the grey birdless air. There are lights on now in Keane's and Dooley's across the valley; where I can see it, the road glitters and Hehir's fields are a greyish white. The frost is not quite snow but is yet like a drapery. It should be festive and cheery on this morning, and my brother should be at my door and we should be thinking of what presents will come soon and how later we will go outside sliding along with arms waving. But it is not like that. My breath mists against the glass. When at last I move I move as if in a trance and, opening the door of my room, I feel a heavy weight fall upon my heart. Behind her bedroom door my mother is softly crying.

I hear a moaning that is soft and continuous, and in its rhythm I can picture my mother rocking back and forth and back and forth again. I wait there. I am afraid of thresholds, afraid that I will not be able to go forward to what awaits me, and afraid that once I do the world will be changed forever and there will be no way back. Matthew is still sleeping when I go to wake him.

'Matthew? Matthew?' My voice is quiet. My hand shakes him.

When he first raises his head he seems to be looking at a dream. It is a moment before he props himself up on an elbow.

'What time is it?' he asks me.

'Mammy's crying.'

Matthew knows more of the secrets and formulae of how the world works and knows that I should go back to bed.

'Go on,' he says, 'go back and go asleep for another bit.'

'Mammy's crying. I heard her.'

He looks at me and he rubs his eyes and then he gets out of the bed and we walk together across the landing to stand outside my parents' room, where he can hear the crying too. For a time we say nothing outside the closed door. It is painted in white gloss paint and shines. The handle is a silver bar like a blade and, along with everything in our house, has been cleaned for the coming of Christmas. My brother looks at me. 'We should go back to our rooms,' he whispers. Then my hand is reaching out and opening the door where the crying is louder and where my mother rests on the edge of the bed with Louise in her arms. My father is in his pyjamas, sitting in the chair upon which he normally hangs his clothes. His head is low on his chest. There is the smell of cigarettes and then the small thin plume of one burning in an ashtray beside the bed. I watch it as if something is revealed in its slow steady expiration.

My father does not move at first. When he does the motion of lifting his head to look at us seems to require a great energy and when his eyes meet ours some last vestige of hope that this might not be true snaps away. His chin rises and trembles and his face seems to fold in upon itself as if he weeps inwardly, his hands clutched to his knees all the time. My brother and I stand there for what seems forever. My mother does not look at us. She sways with Louise. On the floor at the bottom of the bed scattered in bright boxes are the yet undelivered toys of our Christmas.

Louise has died in her sleep. She has passed through a portal in the dark and stopped breathing in the night while my mother was not six feet away and the statue of the Virgin turned toward the cot. My mother holds her and tries to clutch the heat in the infant body that is fading with every second and the soul is already long departed. My brother and I are struck wordless and do not know if we should walk out of the room and go back to our beds. Neither of us is crying. We feel strangely affixed to the scene and yet entirely removed from it, as though it happens through some veil that falls between us and our parents.

At last I step away from my brother and walk around the end of the bed toward my mother. Her eyes are wet and swollen and closed, her cheeks raw. I do not know how but I want to be able to help her to stop weeping. It is as if I imagine myself to be an agent of healing, as if something like grace is flowing through me and if I can reach her and touch my hand against her face it will in some way be the beginning of repair. I do not understand the feeling in such terms yet, although that is what it is. I want to touch my mother's face. That's all. When I get close enough and she does not open her eyes and has no sense of me being there in the frosty dawn light by the empty cot where Louise has died, my father speaks.

'Jim,' he says. He says the word like it is glass he must swallow cleanly. He tilts his head back and his eyes appear in water. 'Jim, stop.'

My mother does not open her eyes.

My father reaches and draws on his cigarette and the tip of it flares red and his right eye shuts as if he has been wounded there. 'Come here,' he says.

He raises his hand from his knee and holds it out toward me. Matthew is still standing inside the doorway. My father holds out a hand to him in turn, but Matthew does not move. I go to my father. He puts his hand around my back, his large strong hand, and holds me to him where I feel the damp and smokiness of his pyjama shirt against my cheek. His head comes down to rest on the top of my head. He says nothing. My brother stays apart from us. After a time he goes out of the room.

When my father lets me go, he holds me back from him. I see all that is inexpressible in his face and see too the raw feeling that is already retreating into the deeps of him. It is moving away even as I am trying to take hold of it. Then it is gone completely and his eyes reassume a look of dark pools.

'Go downstairs now,' he says to me. 'It'll be all right.'

I know that it won't be. Even as a child I know that nothing in our life will ever be the same again, but I nod to him.

'It'll be all right,' he says again. 'Little Louise has gone to heaven.'

My mother is weeping and rocking with the baby in her arms.

'Go on now,' my father says more loudly.

But I do not go. I do not want to move away from that spot for already I can sense that this is only the beginning of the pain. The moment I move, the future begins and with it the dull procession of mourners out from the village and from the villages and houses far away across the countryside, the thousand handshakes, the black stream that will come and go from our front door and print a smudged stain up through the garden along the immaculately frozen path. From this moment – to which my mind will so often return in the years to come – will come all the rest. So I stand in the room and do not go when my father tells me to. He tells me again, but I won't move. I stay rigid with my hands by my sides. Perhaps my father speaks to me again. Perhaps he raises his voice, I do not know. For then his arms are about me and he is lifting me up and carrying me from the bedroom and I am crying out and kicking and thrashing and telling him to stop and to put me down. But he does not. He lifts me higher until I am over his shoulder and we pass out through the doorway and across the hall and I am screaming out and crying for him to stop but he carries on, as if he has rescued me and I am to be delivered across a threshold where suffering and death cannot reach.

Today, while the children are at school, the man comes and clambers over the roof, installing the television channels. I wait in the sitting room and, through the chimney, hear him moving about above me. Pieces of song, I think I catch. Then he knocks at the back door to lay the line inside.

'Perfect signal up there,' he tells me. He has a round genial face and thick curling hair.

'It's for the children.'

'Oh, they'll love it, no fear about that.'

He has a long coil of white cable to bring into the house. I follow him like an idiot as he walks about the kitchen studying for the best site to drill.

'By the window, I suppose?' he says.

'Yes, that's fine.'

The drill chews into the old wood of the window.

'It's to be a surprise,' I say, when he has the hole bored.

'Lovely, for a birthday or something is it?'

'Yes,' I lie, 'that's right, for a birthday.'

'They'll love it. The kids all love it, sure. Won't take them ten minutes —' he gestures with his thumb on an invisible remote — 'they'll have the controls down pat. My own? Would you stop, you couldn't get it out of their hand.'

I nod and smile and not for the first time have the feeling I am making a colossal mistake. I go and wait in the front porch while he brings the cable in and pins it high along the walls.

He calls me after a while to come and see the demonstration. There is a blue screen and a list of twenty channels. They scroll and another twenty appear, and then another.

'You got a good package,' he says. 'All the channels?'

'Yes.'

'Reception's good, isn't it? Very clear.'

'Very.'

'And that's an old television now.'

'It is.'

We watch the screens turn over. He thumbs on a channel of news and neither of us says anything as a woman in a green dress tells us of the weather in South America. It is a wet spring in Peru.

'There is another television in my daughter's room.'

'Well, you need another box for that.'

'I see.'

'You do.'

We watch a satellite image of clouds moving over southern Chile.

'Unless,' he says, 'you want me to split it and run the same signal. She'd get the same programme you're watching here.' He pauses and scratches at the back of his head. 'I wouldn't be doing it, though. It wasn't me who told you about it or did it, you get me?'

'I do.'

I am his assistant then, following, holding the cable, steadying the chair. We go through the front room where your paintings hang and he stops and looks at them and, thinking I am the artist, tells me they are very nice. When he has the job done, he switches on the set and, as the picture comes through clearly, it is a kind of quiet victory for him.

'Thank you, I am very grateful,' I tell him, giving over the cheque and the twenty in cash for himself.

'She'd need the channels if she's anything like my daughter,' he says. 'Fashion TV, MTV, you name it.'

I don't tell him it is for Jack. For cartoons. What kind of father would I seem then?

'Must be a bit lonesome for them out west here all the same. Growing up, I mean. I'm back in town myself and coming out here today

19

you'd notice the quiet of the countryside, so you would. There's many houses closed up altogether, isn't there? Jeez, there is.'

He sees something in my face, some sensitivity to this, and stops there and brings back his best smile to say, 'Well, good luck with it, anyway. I hope they'll be happy.'

Afterwards, for the rest of the morning and the beginning of the afternoon I am filled with nervous anticipation, waiting for the time to collect the children. For a while I lose all misgiving and doubt and forget about arguments for and against television and think only of the surprise and the possibility of joy. I know this is the prime characteristic of my parenting now, the overwhelming desire to bring happiness to my children, and am aware too that I feel this because I want to remedy what I could not save from breaking.

At three o'clock I wait for Jack. He comes down the slope of the small schoolyard shouldering the bag that is too heavy for him. He is neither smiling nor sad, but looks as though he has been washed all day in some pale mild tedium. Some of the children walk out with others. Some are jostling and laughing and shouting things. Not Jack. He gets in and buckles the belt.

'Well, how was today?'

'Fine.'

'Fine?'

'Yeah.'

'Good man.' We drive. 'You're a great man, do you know that?' I glance over at him.

'Yeah,' he says, his eyes not leaving the road in front of us.

'Do you have much homework?'

'I have sums. And I have Irish.'

'That's not too bad. Let's go and wait outside the school for your sister.'

'I'm hungry.'

'I know. I'll get you something. Don't worry.'

We drive down through the village and I stop and run in with Jack and stand over the freezer as he picks up and puts down different ice creams before making his choice. When we go up to pay for it,

Pauline Brady says to Jack, 'Who's a lucky boy, getting an ice cream straight after school?'

But what I hear her saying is: who is the hopeless father feeding his son an ice cream instead of a dinner?

We stop outside the secondary school and wait the twenty minutes for Hannah. I am split between excited anticipation at the prospect of the children discovering the satellite channels and knowledge of how absurd it is, my idiocy in imagining that something so trivial could cure anything. When Hannah comes, she is part of the great surging crowd that spills from the school on the bell. She throws herself into the back seat of the car and lets out an exhausted sigh. I wait, but she says nothing.

'Well?' I ask her.

'What? Go on.'

'Hello, Dad. Hello, Jack,' I say.

'Sorry. Hi, Jack. Hi, Dad.'

We head home. Cyclists waver along the way.

'Good day?'

'Oh, you know.'

I watch her face in the mirror. She looks drawn.

'Yes. Sure,' I say.

There are the few houses on the edge of the village and then a straggling few, and then there are only the hill fields and the cattle standing by the wire. I stop the car out the front of the house.

'I have a surprise,' I say. 'I want you both to go in and try and find it.'

Jack smiles the smile that nearly breaks me.

'A surprise?' he says.

'Yes. It's for both of you.'

They go in then, and I wait, and a few moments later, Hannah comes out and says, 'I can't believe you got them. You got the channels.'

'I did.'

'Are you sure about it?'

'What do you mean?'

'Well . . . oh, nothing.'

I go in with her and Jack is already sitting in front of the Disney Channel or something like it.

'How is that, Jack?' I ask him. 'Good?'

He nods and smiles, and then the smile slips away and he sits there quiet and contented and in a place where I think maybe he is safe for a while now.

For hours after Louise has died I pray for a miracle. The boy I am believes in miracles. Vivid in my mind then are the stories I have been told in school of healing and resurrection, the image of Lazarus walking anew up the dusty streets that were to be the route of his funeral. I go to my room and kneel and pray in my own invented language, then again in English, and, after that, I say the one I know in Irish. I say them so that Louise might start to breathe again. I think it is possible, if only I know the correct number and combination of Our Fathers and Hail Marys and Glory be to the Fathers.

But the hours pass and daylight falls into the room with cruel and relentless progress. I know from the terrible hush of the house that my sister is still dead. With the clear vision with which a child sees the world in the year of his First Communion, I come to understand that Louise has died because I did not love her enough. It comes to me as simply as that. I was a poor brother to her. I see her tiny face explode with tears and hear her cries again as I ran along the road with her in the pram. On my knees in the bedroom I think of the times I wished she had slept and had not taken my mother or my brother away from me. I think of the times Matthew had to take her for walks, and the secret resentments that lurked in me crawl horribly to the surface and I know that that is why she died. I did not really love her.

Though the funeral passes and the world resumes the air of normality once more, it is not so. Inside our house there has come an airborne disease that rots our spirits and leaves us empty and fearful in the corners of life. We do not speak of it. We do not ask my mother about how or why Louise died. We return to school after the holidays and hear the stories of what other boys found at the end of their beds on Christmas morning. None of our teachers speak to Matthew or me about our Christmas. When I come home from school one afternoon I find pieces of the statue of the Virgin in the field at the back of the house, but I do not ask my mother about it. There is no air for such discussion.

My mother's green eyes have changed, their quickness and light vanished. It is as if she sees the world with only the merest acknowledgement. All the while, a part of her is staring inward at some terrible truth. It is a truth I do not know or understand. I am only a boy who feels his mother grown distant. My father, I think, is aware of this, aware that with each day she is moving further and further from all of us, but it seems he can do nothing to reach her and catch her hand before she goes. He had thought he was her rescuer. Tom Foley had believed that life was a simple construct, happiness a thing that could be built if you were careful and not frivolous or indulgent. He became middle-aged when he was twenty-five, and shouldered the burden of providing happiness for my mother, supposing that it could be achieved by paying the bills on time, replacing slates in the roof, the leak in the tap, keeping cardboard files with meticulously ordered papers on insurance and savings. He asked nothing for himself. When he went to work, and sat all day in the little cage of the switchboard, he went with the tacit understanding that there was an agreement, a contract between himself and God, that he would perform his duties and God would perform His, and thereby guarantee our family's happiness.

In the aftermath of death my father feels cheated. He does not speak to us about it. He smokes cigarettes, smokes them until they are stubs burning in his fingers, as though what he hungers for is the taste of ash. He goes to work in the post office, connecting the calls of others and making none himself. In the evenings when he comes home, my only contact with him is when I bring him my homework in English and Irish and maths to show him everything neatly done and correct.

I watch him closely. His cigarette burns. His eyes move very slowly over every word I have written. When he has finished he folds the exercise copy closed. He keeps it in his hand for a moment.

'You're a good boy, Jim,' he says, and he looks at me. His chin lifts and trembles. I watch the workings of his mouth and his eyes as he struggles to control what is rising and readying to flow inside him, and he looks away. 'If we do our best,' he says, 'if we do our best, then . . .' For an instant he cannot continue. He is not entirely convinced of his longest-held conviction. He tilts back his head as though to keep in what is always on the point of spilling. To mask this, he coughs and makes a loud performance of it. 'If we do our best, Jim, that's all anyone can ask of us.'

'Yes, Dad.'

He draws on his cigarette. His cheeks are flooded with colour now, blood rising from some source untapped inside him.

'You do your work and you'll do fine,' he says. 'You watch your brother, and one day you'll be going off to the university.'

It is his credo: you will go to the university in Dublin, you will get a degree and a good job. For these too are thresholds and if my brother and I can pass over them he will feel we are safely delivered. I look at his eyes and then cannot. He hands back to me the copy with my correct grammar in English.

And just so we live on, enduring in a kind of quiet, secretly bearing our wounds.

My brother Matthew becomes a genius at maths. By the time he is fourteen he can do abstract calculations in his head and for the Christian Brothers at the school in town he is living proof of the capacities of the trained human brain. The figures with which he covers the pages of copybooks are small and neat and, when I go to his room and look at them, all the problems seem part of one long seamless conundrum whose formula is capricious and difficult beyond understanding. The better Matthew gets at maths the more silent he becomes. The other subjects at school do not matter to him. He writes answers on poetry in one line. He writes out his French verbs in a small neat hand and makes them, too, seem like mathematical tables. He brings home prizes of ballpoint pens and compass sets and a slide rule. They lie on the table beside the cups and plates I have set ready for tea when my father comes home. He picks up whatever is there and looks across at Matthew, who is unable to meet his eyes.

'That's a very nice pen,' he says. 'What did you get that for?'

Matthew does not look up. He seems burdened by the attention, as if it revolves around a misdeed he has committed and of which he is vaguely ashamed.

'Trigonometry test,' he says at last. He says it as if it is a foolish thing without merit.

Whether my father senses this or because he considers it unnecessary he asks Matthew no more about it.

'Very good pen,' he says.

He does not know trigonometry and butters his bread and sips the tea and the word *trigonometry* is suspended briefly in the air over us.

Increasingly, as time passes, Matthew seems to live with us but not among us. He cannot play football with me in the back field. He has work to do in his room. He comes down the stairs for meals. The Christian Brothers have told my parents that he is scholarship material. They have given him work in applied mathematics and advanced physics and he is able for it, they say. He has a brilliant future ahead of him.

One day he arrives home with his school report. It is the late afternoon and our mother is sitting in the kitchen. She has come from the back room where now on her sewing machine she has started making dresses for children in Africa. She is sitting at the table as if expecting someone, but it is not us. We come in and she starts like a creature frightened, and her eyes move quickly and her hands rub on her apron. '*Right*,' she says, standing up, her smile thin and brittle. Matthew puts his report, in its brown envelope, on the table and crosses to the sink to pour a glass of water. I stand and want to see my mother open it and be happy and proud.

'It's his report, Mam,' I say. I already know it is a very good one. I know the reports are usually sent in the post because the boys are not trusted to deliver them but that Matthew is an exception.

My mother blinks a few times and is like a bird rising with several flutterings to a different branch.

'Yes, his report,' she says, and opens it. 'Well, well.'

The single page wavers in her hand. Matthew stays by the sink and studies the net curtains. I watch my mother's face, how her eyes try and focus on the list of subjects and grade A marks. I know that through her must rise some pride and joy, but after the death of Louise any such feelings are instantly kept in check. It is as though she imagines she is being spied upon, and must not betray happiness or joy in her children lest they be taken from her. She holds the page shaking slightly in her hand, she touches the tip of her tongue to her lips, but before she can speak Matthew moves from the sink and walks out of the room and up the stairs.

I know that this is wrong. It is like the pieces of an image have been badly assembled, and that from such the picture can only get worse. I know this is not how it should be, but know too that I cannot find out how to repair it.

Matthew is gone upstairs. I come up later after him and knock on his bedroom door. There is a pool of lamplight on the table and within it he is stooped over pages of figures. He does not look around at me. I wait, afraid that I might disturb him and he might lose his place so that some path or portal in the great formulae will be closed to him forever.

He rocks slightly on his chair.

'Yes, what?' he says at last. He says it some moments before he lifts his head to look at me. He says it not impatiently but in a manner that is matter-of-fact and suggests that for all intrusions there must be a clear and valid explanation.

I have none.

'That was a good report,' I say.

He looks at me.

'Mine won't be as good as that.'

'It doesn't matter,' he says and turns back to the sheets of his calculations. I want to stay there and to think of something brilliant to say to him, but nothing will come. After a time I go across the little hallway to my bedroom. I have read all the books that are there, some of them several times. Outside the night is falling into the fields and the few street lights in the village are flickering on. I sit down at the small desk where I am to do my homework, but instead I open my spare copy called *Roughwork* and in it I begin to write a story. It is a story about a father who comes home one evening from his work at the post office and announces to his sons and his daughter that they must have a party for they have a genius living among them. The mother laughs and smiles. She dances around the kitchen with the little girl who is called Lou in her arms.

*

And so I too make my escape. In our family we are each like boats slipped from the moorings, out in deep waters, and utterly separate or tangled in our own nets of grief and loss. We live together in the house but are each alone. The only time I am with my father is on Thursday evenings when he takes me to Ennis to the county library while a woman called Connie covers for him on the switchboard. After our tea my father gathers the previous week's reading and stands at the door of my bedroom.

'I am going to the library,' he says. He knows already that Matthew will not come, that there too many sums unsolved, and I think he fears that if he asks me outright he risks my refusal to go. So instead he does not ask, he softly announces and stands waiting. He lets his eyes look sideways at the birds on the wallpaper for the briefest moment and then he turns to go and hears my scrambling to be after him.

I go with him in the green Ford Cortina that has replaced the Morris Minor. From the cautionary nature that has become his, my father has me sit in the broad back seat lest there be a crash. I am behind him, seatbelts are not yet common and I think if he hits something on the road I will fly forward and crash my skull into his. To save us then, I dig my head back into the red leatherette and try to create backward force as the car accelerates along the bumps and curves of the boggy road to Ennis. There are no street lights and few other cars. Briefly we light up the dark and then leave it behind us once more.

When we get to the old ivy-covered building of the library my father stands at the desk and returns what we have borrowed. He tells me to go ahead, and I disappear between the stacks but watch while he turns, puts on his glasses, and, with what seems to me almost infinite resignation and weariness, walks to the section called Non-Fiction. He moves like a man with a mission; as though he must work his way through every volume the library has on Ireland, as though if he can read his way through the centuries of its history he will come at last upon that very moment itself, that *now* in which his own life can finally be explained. In imitation I resolve to read all of the children's classics and, in due course, everything in the building. And in time it is there, in that building, that I come to feel most at home. I am twelve years old, then fourteen, and fifteen, and I am still going to the library with my father and working my way through the shelves. I know the smell and feel of everything in that place. I take down volumes I have read before just for the strange pleasure to be had in holding them. It comes to seem that in so doing I can keep contact with the person I was a week, a month, a year before, and there is comfort in that.

As we drive home through the dark a short stack of books sits beside me in the back seat of the car. On the front passenger seat are my father's histories. As we leave the town and are out once more along the winding rain-road to the west, he turns his head slightly to his left shoulder and asks, 'What did you get this week?'

There is an oily skein of rain across the windscreen and the wipers pass back and over but do not remove it. The road is barely visible. There are no houses or street lights and the bogland and poor fields on either side are gone and the car that holds us might be falling through space. I look down at the books as if I do not remember, but in fact am already enjoying them in a kind of anticipatory pleasure.

'*Waterloo, The Red Badge of Courage, The Last of the Mohicans*.'

There is a pause. The wipers jerk up and over again and clean away nothing.

'*The Last of the Mohicans* is a good one,' my father says.

We drive on. There is no more conversation than that, but that alone is enough for me. I do not realize then that he himself has never read *The Last of the Mohicans* or that his approval of it is random and simply a way of speaking to me. I lift it to the top of the pile and know that I will begin with that one the moment I reach my bedroom.

And so we go on. I go to school and return. I suffer silent terrors of my teachers. My stomach is a cage of butterflies all the day. I fear making the slightest mistake and do the same sums over and over to be sure that they are right. Figures seem uncertain and softly mutable. What exactly is seven-eighths multiplied by nine-tenths? I do the calculations and check the figures and then shortly afterward feel I have almost certainly missed something in the computation. In class the teachers almost never pick on me for answers. There are twenty-seven other boys squirming and showing the crowns of their heads when the teacher asks, but never is mine the name that is called out. I think it is because of Louise. Because of Louise I am made of thinner, more delicate stuff now. My porcelain spirit is not to be tested and though I know the answers and know that day after day I am never questioned my breath still comes shallowly and I think if I open the lid of myself, butterflies will emerge.

In the yard we line up for games of football and the captains pick the teams. They are fellows swarthy and stalwart and the world bounces off them. They have bruises on their shins and their ears have been pulled by the Brothers and their hands leathered. I have stood on cold March days and watched the diminishing of the line as boys were called to one side or the other and they crossed the small space that is a threshold of sorts and I remained behind. A Brother has told someone I am not to be tackled, and this word has gone forth around the school, so I drift off through the yard and put my hands in my pockets and soon do not bother to stand in the line at all. Sometimes I see my brother Matthew with some of the older boys, the maths men, the angular fellows, too long for their trousers, with square glasses and tufted hair. He seems at one among them, is changed from the brother I have at home. In the yard he speaks in quick-fire bursts, makes barbed comments on the idiocy of the teachers and does not notice me at first. When he does there is something in his look that tells me not to approach. And so I don't. I realize that something about me is strangely shameful or embarrassing, that when others are in my company they feel awkward and ill at ease. This is not because I am forceful or loud, it is because I am quiet.

And so we still go on. In the evenings when the four of us gather for tea it is as though thick curtains are drawn about each of us. We sit and eat our toast and jam or currant loaf and afterward Matthew and I go upstairs for our homework. My mother goes to the back room where she works the Singer sewing machine making dresses, and my father sits and reads about the country or stops to watch the evening news. There is nothing more than that. I copy the example of my brother and stay at my desk until bedtime. I do my work quickly so that I can read a book and soon here are Uncas and his father, the noble and grave warrior Chingachgook, whose quiet composure lends him an air of ancient wisdom. They stride through the forest of my bedroom and stand and listen for the wingbeat of eagles. In the world of my imagination I am drawn into the trees. I am a boy grown thin and weak-eyed and could not climb the high wooded paths or sheer rock falls in the land between the Hudson and the Potomac

– but within my bedroom I can. I follow Hawkeye the Deer-hunter through that green landscape of pure wilderness and am deep beneath the leaf canopy where lances of sunlight make freckles of the flies and other insects travelling the silent air. I am an Indian running through the undergrowth in buckskin leggings. Moccasins on my feet snap softly the slender twigs. Blind birdsong is overhead. In a blue clearing a hawk flies. I match the pace of the Mohicans and hurry in the wake of the fierce Magua. I meet the fair-haired Alice and the dark-haired Cora where they are escorted on slow horses under the high dark arches of the forest. Here are trees I have never seen, boughs of saxafrax and leaves of sumac, their scent thick and sweet. I say the sounds of them in a whisper, and they appear. The girls are captured and must be rescued. They will be, I think, and then say it out loud. *They will be, by the last of the Mohicans.*

And outside, though rain is falling in the dark night of County Clare, I do not think of that. I do not realize yet that the fierce hold of the book is partly its plot of rescue, or that deep in my mind is embedded the thorn of a sister lost. That is still ahead of me. Still ahead too are all those books I will write where I am urged by some inner prompting to fix the plot of the world and prove to myself that God exists. I read, and sometimes read in a kind of whisper as if to one younger than me. But while the words pass I do not think of our home or of Ireland or the time in which I am living. I think only of the story in the book. The seasons outside, the wet and the partly dry, come and go and are both entangled so that the passing of time is itself without structure or shape, but a long grey dream without seam or end.

*

When my brother Matthew is eighteen he achieves a perfect score in mathematics in his final examinations and wins a scholarship to university in Dublin. It is August when we get the news. The meadows are golden and alive with the traffic of haymakers all the long hours of daylight. In years to come the making of hay will be abandoned and replaced by the baling of silage in black plastic, but in west Clare then it is still a season of men in rolled shirtsleeves and two-pronged hay forks. Boys, girls, and women too are abroad in the meadows. In the pressing heat some wear sombreros or battered straw boaters or simple kerchiefs knotted in the corners, forking the hay into what are nearly the last trams of that century. In the middle of the morning little clusters of people sit like white dots in the distant fields and throw out their legs or lie back and have flasks of tea and buttered sandwiches. As the sun burns, the boys of summer grow thick-armed and brown and wear the swagger of princes of that parish.

But not so my brother Matthew. In the months that have followed the exams a slow worm of lassitude has entered my brother. He cannot rise from bed in the mornings. My father knocks on the bedroom door as he goes out to the post office, but Matthew does not respond. Despite the blaze of brilliant sunlight framed behind the curtains, the boxroom remains in shadow. No window is opened and the air is a slow moving parade of dust and dead numbers. Textbooks have not been put away and are scattered about along with notes and sheaves of calculations for problems solved and unsolved. In his bed my brother lies awake. He cannot bring himself to get up. He knows that on their farms the Dooleys and Donnellans and Keanes could do with his help. He knows that Mick Hehir and Breda down the road want him. But he does not go. He turns over to the wall and another hour passes. In the aftermath of the efforts of the exams he is emptied of life. My mother comes and asks him if he is unwell but he answers only a single word no and turns over again. And still the worm eats away at him. It progresses through his spirit steadily so that even when he rises and comes into the kitchen in the middle of the afternoon there seems little of him there.

I ask him if he will come outside with me. 'They are saving hay down in Cleary's meadow.'

His eyes are slow to respond. He is looking down at the floor.

There is a tiny movement of his tongue on the inside of his lips as if testing his answer.

'They have extra forks,' I say.

'I don't feel like it,' he says, and drifts off back to his room.

In the daylight hours Dun is empty with everyone gone to the fields or the bog. Even in the post office my father has little to do, and few calls are connected to anywhere. He sits behind the little mesh screen at the switchboard and waits. Sometimes he reads his books about Ireland. Sometimes tourists come in looking for directions to somewhere else. Meanwhile, the days drowse on. I go out and ride to neighbours' bogs in the back creels of tractors. I spend the day stooping amidst the ten thousand sods of turf, by bog cotton and cuckoo flower, and become brown and freckled, welted along my arms by a million midges. And in the drift of time there on the bog, when an hour may be a minute or a day long, when all runs together into a cloth of gold and blue and brown, my family disappears from me. I do not think of my sister dead or my brother in his room or the strange distance that seems to exist between us all. My eyes burn red and water with pollen, but I help in the bog and am happy to be there in that dream-place where time seems not to exist and nothing much is said as the sun crosses slowly above our backs.

And in the evenings of that same summer, before Matthew leaves for university, I come home in the back box of a tractor and am dropped off at the crossroads. The dust of the turf is in the creases of my skin, brown face powder on my cheeks and rimmed beneath my eyes like liner. I come into the house and wash myself and eat cold meat and salad and there is something serene in me. My limbs are aching, and a weariness is in my bones, yet I am stilled and at peace, gifted the perfect faith of innocents. I think, *things will be all right*. Somehow we will manage.

The rest of the evening is mine now and the anticipation of it is like something deep and delicious inside me. I go up the stairs to my room and on the steps my feet are not my own and I am not going to my room. I am travelling with Mr Pumblechook to the old brick house with the iron bars. For reasons peculiar to his character he is asking me sums as we go: 'Seven times nine, boy?' And again: 'Seven?' 'And four?' 'And eight?' 'And six?' 'And two?' 'And ten?' And I am hurrying along to escape the figures and the endless questions to which there are no answers. I am arriving at that house which is to stay in my imagination for the rest of my childhood and on into my adult life. It is a dismal place, with some of its windows bricked and others barred. Next to the house is an old disused brewery and from it smells of sourness spread across the courtyard. I stand at the gate with Mr Pumblechook, and by the time I am lying on my bed with the book, he has reached up and rung the bell. Then from high in the house a window is opened and a voice calls out, 'What name?'

This is where my imagination holds me. I am a long time in the instant of waiting before Estella comes with the keys. I am there to be rescued by her, to be rescued from numbers and work and brought inside another world. The air seems cool and still. I cannot hear any birds singing. As I see her for the first time and the keys jangle and then click loudly in the lock I am already in love with her. I go with her across the yard and think like Pip of how beautiful and self-possessed she is and then enter the amber dark inside the house where she has left a single candle burning. Then another long journey in my mind: up the dusty stairs of Satis House beside Estella, the stairs that seem to go on and on and continue through my dreams, even as that name *Satis* is to play and reverberate in the back of my consciousness. *Satis*, which Estella says means *Enough*, but is at first to me nothing but the first incomplete part of *Satisfaction*, which surely lies just ahead through one of the many doors of the house.

'Go in,' she says.

And then there is that hauntingly unbearable exchange when Pip says politely, 'After you, miss,' and Estella burns his face with the reply: 'Don't be ridiculous, boy, I am not going in,' and walks scornfully away with the candle plunging him into that dark.

I lie in my room and the words of *Great Expectations* capture my imagination more than any I have ever read. They have a fierce and powerful hold and within them I move forward into the large room lighted by many wax candles with the curtains drawn against the day. In that strange phantasmagoria where the smell of burning is thick and heavy and the air seems strung with twisted cords of dust there appears Miss Havisham, seated in her chair like a throne, resting her head forward on one hand to study me as I enter. It is not the satins nor the silks nor the lace, it is not the long white veil, nor the bridal flowers that hang from her neck that hold me, it is her eyes. For though they are sunken and ruined they look out at me with a harsh brightness, as if they were a hawk's and I the small bird caught in an air pocket far below. She moves her hands to her heart and asks if I know what she touches there and then announces it is broken. And it comes to me then, this marvellous flash of epiphany, that I am there to mend her, I am to be the agent of healing. And because I know this desire so profoundly from my own life I feel it as a thing not at all unusual but in fact entirely natural. So when Miss Havisham commands Pip to play, and amuse her, and when he fails, being unable to perform anything under this imperative, I am sorry for both of them, and want so to see him succeed. I hear her shrill voice call out, 'Play, play, play!' and see his hopeless standing, the kneading of his hands, the swift downrush of ideas tumbling over each other in his head and becoming nothing as he is transfixed there, like one whose parent has dragged him out to perform for aunts talc-powdered and terrible.

When Estella is called she comes bearing the candle, and though it is not said here I know her name is star and while the night falls into the fields of west Clare outside I follow that star and do not sleep. Only vaguely do I hear the noises of the house about me as my parents go to bed and shut off the lights. I have a torch beneath the blankets. When Estella is commanded to play the game of cards and scowls saying, 'With this boy!' I feel her scorn and my face flushes, familiar with the sense of shame for something I have not done. They play the game beggar-my-neighbour, which is one I know, and when Estella laughs at Pip for referring to the Knaves as Jacks, I pause on the page and realize I have never heard of the word Knave before. And when she looks at his hands and boots in contempt, I feel my own hands large and coarsened from working with the turf and know my boots downstairs are ones at which Estella would certainly laugh in derision. And still my eyes race forward. I look for her name on the page. I want to know what Estella thinks, what Estella will say. Hours pass. In the fields outside the cows stand for the brief time of summer dark, the birds do not sing. Foxes and badgers and things furtive travel across the dewy grass while in my room I lie, tangled in the secrecy and desire of the first real love of my life.

*

In September Matthew leaves for the university in Dublin. He comes down the stairs with a suitcase and it looks like he is going to some faraway country, which in a way he is. My mother stands beside my father in the hall and holds her two hands together in front of her. My father is in his navy suit waiting to drive the car to meet the train in Ennis. He might be a hired chauffeur so removed is he from the scene. But if you look closely you see his mouth is tightened, his chin risen as though above a helmet strap and his eyes fixed as if for battle. (And so in time I have come to realize it was for him, the battle to bring his children up, to get them across the thresholds of boyhood and youth.) Matthew is saved now, he thinks. He is a brilliant student on his way to success and happiness. My father has the quiet air not of victory but of relief at the absence of further losses. Yet, as ever he cannot bring himself to say so. He watches Matthew endure my mother's quick light embrace, a kind of flutter of touch that could not be called a hug. Everything about Matthew is uncomfortable in this moment. He wears the new round-necked red jumper and the blue pants that my mother has bought for him in Bourke's in Kilrush. He wears a blue shirt with the collars out. His shoes too are new, but something is awry in the combination of these things, and he looks as if in the skin of another. His white face is pimpled and his eyebrows are dark and lowered into a single line as he waits to be gone. When I come over to say goodbye there passes through me the desire to hug him, to tell him that he is a kind of hero for me and that in my heart I am cheering loudly his genius. But in the space of the few feet between us in the hall such feeling flies away, belongs in the world of another family, a family in books, and I do nothing. He picks up the suitcase.

'Goodbye, Matthew.'

'Goodbye.'

He is not looking at me. I think he is stricken with a terrible embarrassment and it is something he wears like a disease visible on his skin.

'Right so.' My father turns and opens the front door and leads the way outside through the garden to the car. And in that moment, as the morning light floods in through the doorway and they step into it, my mother turns around and her hands fly loose of each other and she shakes them twice as though releasing drops of water and hastens off into the sitting room. If this is a test, I fail it. If I am to run outside and lean in the car window and run alongside and tell Matthew I am proud of him, I do not; and neither do I go inside and console my mother. I stand in the doorway and do nothing once more, as the moment is taken and folded carefully and placed inside of me. Then I close the door and go up the stairs to my room to look for Estella.

And just so does my own life slip away from me. More and more after Matthew has gone I close the bedroom door and find my only real pleasure in reading books. I do not write stories now. I despise myself for the ones I wrote when I was younger and one afternoon when I come across them in a drawer I tear the thick wedge of pages – with some difficulty – and go downstairs to throw them in the range. Instead of writing now, I read. I read the two endings of *Great Expectations* and am glad of the one where Pip and Estella reconcile in that dreamlike sequence amidst the ruins of their earlier lives. I skip back and read again Chapter

Eight, where Pip comes for the first time to Miss Havisham's house. I come to know it better than anything else and cannot quite explain it to myself, except that within me is growing all the time a secret shame of my own family. I look sourly now at the village and the farmers of west Clare, with their old tractors, hay padding the seats, plastic bags covering the broken side windows. My mother and father are equally distorted and in my mind have become strangely like Joe Gargery and Biddy, hopelessly unable to understand. I leave them all and go to live in the pages of the novels of Charles Dickens. I read *David Copperfield* and find there the fabulous population of figures all more real, more comic, more alive than anyone I have ever met. I am a boy going by bicycle to school, past meadow and hedgerow, through wind and rain past the rumpled green of the hill fields of Clare, but all the time some part of me is away in the smoke and fog of London. There in the back alleys and laneways of imagination slip the shadowy figures of Steerforth, Chuzzlewit, Jaggers. Always somehow clothed in narrow suits of grey or black, they move hurriedly with long strides through the streets, charged with the high voltage of emotion. In all of them is something desperate; they are desperate for love or money and are driven to the edges of crime and into it too, and in this there is a powerful attraction for me that I cannot quite explain.

Matthew returns home from university infrequently. He has studies to do, he must stay on and work in the library. Though my father sits at the switchboard in the post office still, Matthew does not phone, but sometimes sends a short letter which, in sharp jagged penmanship, says little. He is gone. I work on at school waiting my turn to go.

One evening my father stands outside my bedroom door. It is closed and he does not open it without knocking.

'I am going to the library,' he says through the door.

'All right. In a minute.'

I hear his footsteps heavy on the stairs. He is a big slow man, weighted ever more with a loading of things unsaid. I no longer hurry down the stairs to chase the offer and be with him. Sometimes I lie on the bed and hear the car start outside and hear him wait a few moments to see if I am coming. I stay lying in the bed knowing he is waiting and then see in my mind the careful way he has of pulling away in the car, checking traffic in all directions and signalling, though the country road is deserted for miles around.

Tonight I finish a chapter of *The Mayor of Casterbridge* while he is downstairs in the hall in his hat and coat. When I come down he opens the front door.

'Get a coat,' he says. 'I am starting the car.'

He closes the door and then there is only the thrumming of my mother's sewing machine in the back room. I should hurry out and join him, I should put on a coat and woollen hat, but I go into the kitchen and pour myself a glass of water. Then, taking no coat or hat, I walk out into the wind and rain carrying the Hardy. When I get into the car my father does not remonstrate, does not mention the delay, or the lack of coat, or anything else. He switches on the car radio because there is a programme about the general election that is due. And as we drive eastward on the road to Ennis the reception comes and goes, the wipers slap, and the words filter through and fade and, in this way, seem to concern the government of a country far away.

We arrive at the yellow glow of the library, and at the desk I wait beside my father to return my books. The librarian is a woman of paper and powder. Her face is parchment wrinkled, there are mottled patches on her cheeks that she has dusted a rosy tint. She is thin as a sheaf in her off-white cardigan. Her lips are pressed together as she finds my name in the card-deck.

'Foley, Jim?'

'Yes.'

My father is stepping away into Non-Fiction, but stops when he hears the tone.

'Your books are overdue. And you have one not returned.'

I stand there, I say nothing. What is it to her what books I have? What does she know?

'Jim?' My father is at my shoulder.

'I don't,' I say suddenly.

'He returned the three,' my father points out.

'This is from before. It has never been returned. You must have received a notice in the post.'

'We didn't.' My father is quicker to respond than I am. He is pressing close up to the counter now. Upon the parchment face a hand scribes a creased line of astonishment at this facile denial. The woman's shoulders are sharp and straight as card. To her my father says, 'We didn't receive any notice.' His voice is too loud and seems to me to bruise the library air. Men and women look up from between the shelves. In front of us the librarian's face crumples and moves and rosedust falls upon the white hands holding the desk.

'I'm sorry but you did,' says the parchment. 'Or the post office lost it.'

'The post office didn't lose it.' There is a sudden burst of colour in my father's face, and all of him seems on that instant inflating with something like rage.

'Well, I'm sorry but he has the book.'

'What book is it?'

'*Great Expectations.*'

'Jim, do you have the book?'

'No.'

'There. He doesn't have the book.'

The rosy parchment stiffens, the strain tightening the mouth, raising the eyebrows. There are a thousand words written there, and among them is a kind of repugnance of this big country man standing there with his greasy-haired liar of a son, a distaste for these people with their rude manners and loudness in the county library. Lending books to people like these is not why she became a librarian. And as I cringe there I can read all of this on her expression, and am ashamed of us too. I want the scene to dissolve away into the quiet. But out of my father, released from a source secret and sealed for so long, comes now a torrent.

'Don't you look at us like that.'

'Excuse me, I am not looking at you in any–'

'I can see you don't believe him. He can see it. What do you think we are? You think we come here to steal books? I am a post-master. I am coming to this library for twenty years, do you know that? Twenty years. If my son says he hasn't the book then he hasn't. You've mislaid it somewhere, that's all. And you needn't go looking at us that way and–'

'The boy has the book, or has lost it. It has not been returned.'

'I'm after telling you he hasn't.'

'I'm sorry but this is a library and I'm going to have to ask you now to leave.'

I am looking at the floor. I am looking at the green linoleum with a marbled pattern and the place where two lengths of it have been joined and there is a thin dark line. I do not look up at my father. I do not need to look to see the flushed look of his face or the strange brightness of his eyes.

'Jim. Come on.' My father slaps a book he had been intending to borrow on the counter and turns toward the door. He swings it open for me and as I pass through, he speaks loudly back to the woman at the counter, 'We're going now and we won't ever set foot in your fecking library again.'

Then we are out in the cool dark rain and pacing quickly to the car as though pursued. We get in without a word. The engine coughs and the wipers jag up and back. There is a moment when the engine is running and we are ready to pull away but my father does not slip the car into gear. He sits there. Something is batter-ing about in the cage of his chest. He is a man with no war to go to and instead must sit and battle motionlessly, making mute the various and multitudinous enemies that only he knows. He moves his mouth, and when I think of it later I think I hear him sigh or groan. I think I hear the sound of pain swallowed up in the hum-ming of the engine. But I say nothing. What my father has done for me goes without the slightest acknowledgement and I sit slumped and then reach forward and turn on the radio and roll the knob to find a station with music. A scratchy wavering noise comes from the single speaker, a music that seems blown in waves on the weather. But that is good enough for me. It is better than the silence.

The car pulls away into the night. In the noise of the engine and the radio and the rain I do not hear the gasp and suck of my father's breathing, but I feel it. I feel him like a great valve struggling to open and close in the seat beside me. His rain-speckled coat is buttoned over his chest. Beneath it he wears his blue suit and his white shirt and a flattened tie of faded claret, all of which seem to imprison him as he drives. His chest's rise and collapse is sudden and short. Upon his white forehead beads of rain or sweat stand and run as he grasps the wheel. He needs a cigarette, and struggles with his coat to find one and then find the matches. I don't offer to light it for him. The car climbs the hill out of Ennis, the windscreen clouds and like a brief explosion my father jolts forward his right arm and sleeves a small arc.

For reasons I cannot explain to myself, I am filled just then with a bitter shame of him. I look away into the small triangular side window so that I will not have to look at him. What was he thinking? What was he doing banging down the book and announcing that he would not be looked at like that? Could he not see that made it worse? Could he not see how, when he stood before her like that, she thought worse of him not better? He might as well have announced: we are backward people, we're from the west, you won't mess with us. And now we cannot go back to the library again. What kind of idiot was he to announce that as we marched out the door? Did he think anyone there cared? The shame boils up and then settles sourly inside of me. I say nothing. I am the youth with white curdled face and low-cast eyes coming in the hall door and going to my room, where I throw myself on the bed without taking off my wet shoes or greeting my mother.

Rain comes against the window. The whole of the countryside is lashed. The dark shapes of the hill fields fold into one another beneath the black blotched sky. I stay in my room. I reach my hand down between the bed and the wall and draw the stolen copy of *Great Expectations* from its hiding place. I have finished it already twice, there are passages I can recite by heart, but I do not want to let the book go back. By means unclear and beyond my own understanding the book has come to seem *mine*. I know the life of Pip more closely than my own. I not only know his feelings but I have felt them and they are my own. And through the sharing experience of the growth of his soul so too has mine grown to the point where everything of the world I have known repulses me. I imagine myself an orphan, inhabiting a house with adults who have no understanding of my mind or character or any of the dreams foaming in my head. I am living with strangers, I tell myself. I picture the squalid damp little village of Dun, the crookedly parked cars and tractors, the muck-fields that cling and clamp on boots and are tramped about the street and into the shops, the heavy thick smell of earth and animals and rain that pervades all. All of these now rise, lurid and appalling, bubbling up inside me in a lumpish stew, and it comes to me more clearly than ever that I know why my brother could not wait to get away. He was quicker to see it than me, that's all. That's why he withdrew to his room. Getting to Dublin was for him like Pip going to London, I tell myself. And so it will be with me too. I will go to study literature, I will become a writer.

I lie in my bed and read again passages I already know well. I am lying there as the rain beats on against the dark windows. I am lying there still when I hear the sounds of my parents turning off the television and the lights downstairs. I hear my father go to check that the front door is locked. Then my mother, taking her time, her light step is on the lower trestles as my father waits a moment to follow her up to the bedroom. I hold *Great Expectations* in my hands. I should return it to its hiding place behind the bed and turn out the light. If the light is on my father will open the door and look in to see why I am not asleep. I lie there. I hear my parents' different steps as they approach, their pace one of such profound and careworn weariness that for a moment I imagine them as figures of dust, soft grey accumulations shifting and powdering away as they near the landing. My mother's slippered steps pass. The bedroom light is on. I hear my father's black shoes take half a stride past my door and then stop and turn, and then the handle of the door is moving.

I close my eyes. I lie there with the light on and *Great Expectations* open on my chest.

My father comes inside the room. He must think to do nothing more than shut off the light, the switch is near the door. But then he must see the book, and whether he knows yet which book it is or crosses the room simply to make easier my sleeping and discovers it then I cannot say. I feel him over the bed, and then feel the lightness on my chest as his great hand comes and lifts the hard-covered library book to look at it. Surprise or dismay or puzzlement must pass across his face, but I do not see it. I lie and listen to his breathing and pretend to be asleep. I do not know what I want to happen next. I do not know if I want him to lean down and shake me awake or cry out or curse or strike at the bedclothes. But I do know that what I do not want is what happens.

My father folds the book flap carefully inside the page where the book was splayed open. Then he bends down and puts it on the floor beside the bed. That's all. He crosses the room and turns out the light.

In the morning at breakfast he does not mention it. Neither does he seem to have told my mother. Not that day nor the day after nor the one after that is there the slightest suggestion that he knows that I have stolen the Ennis library edition of Charles Dickens's *Great Expectations*. Then, on the fourth day, while he sits in the little cage of the Switch and is lifting the cable to connect a call, *Putting you through now*, a sudden claw of pain comes and clutches his chest. He lets out a small moan and presses his head back so that it hits the shelf with the phonebooks behind him. His right hand holds the cable and his left comes to his shirt front. He makes another sound. The iron of the claw seizes into him again and he thinks he is being taken as if by a great and implacable eagle. But it is not so, and he is not taken upward. A thin grey-white cuckoo-spit of pain leaks from the corner of his lips and he moans again and falls sideways off his stool. And he is lying there, holding the cable of the unconnected call with the switchboard lighting and buzzing, when Mrs Dempsey comes in the post-office door and finds him.

'How is it going?' Hannah asks me. 'Are you going to the village soon?'

'Yes, soon.'

'All right. Only I'm ready, anyway. Whenever.'

'Yes, fine.'

She pauses a moment. She does not want me to ask her how she is feeling. She is a teenager but wants to be a woman. Yesterday when I sat on her bed and tried to begin to talk about you she stared away into the distance and then to that distance said, 'Dad, I'm fine, OK?' as if daring any disproof. Her tone was not harsh, it was soft and quiet and yet firm. She does not want to talk. She wants shampoo. She wants to be allowed to eat in her room while she's studying. She thinks we shouldn't all have to sit down together any more: That was one of your rules. She's a vegetarian, anyway, she has told me. She doesn't like what I cook.

She stands beside me a thousand miles away. 'What's this book about?'

I don't quite know what to say. I could say many things. I could say it's about the truth, say that it begins with my family, but is about love and whether love can endure in the pages of a book. I could tell her it's about how to carry on, about how if you are a storyteller you tell stories, you tell them to make some sense of all that is random and harsh and cruel in the world, but all this seems portentous and absurd. The old nausea twists in me again. What am I doing? A forty-four-year-old man sitting before a screen writing about his childhood. Christ. This is not what I want. What I want is to bring you here, for you to stand here beside my shoulder and tell me it will be all right.

'It's a short book about love,' I say.

'God.' Her face scowls like a critic's.

'I know,' I say, 'terrible, isn't it?'

'No, but . . . no, I'm sorry, I didn't mean, just . . . love, now?' The idea of it is still sour in her features.

I get up. I want to say something profound, something a father should say here. I want to say, here in this season of dying is a story of love. But I do not, and can think only of the dying now anyway.

'It's all right,' I tell her. 'It's just a story. Come on, let's go to the village.'

*

Rain, the endless rain. It rains more than it rains in the books I write. We stay in the house in our separate rooms. Hannah comes down with her plate of uneaten dinner. I hear her scraping it off but cannot bring myself to go and confront her. Jack sits before the cartoons on the digital channels and the bright colours play across his eyes.

I read back some of what I wrote last week. The real is always so much harder than the invented. And can seem so little, as though nothing at all is happening. So unlike a story. When it is a story we look for its hidden meanings where in life there is none. It happened so, that's all. All the implausibility of real life seems so contrived when it is written down. When Hannah came downstairs earlier in the evening I was sitting staring at the screen. I must have seemed especially puzzled or lost for she came and stood beside me and put her hand on my shoulder.

'Are you stuck?' she asked me. Her eyes seemed to have such kindness and understanding then, and I saw you there in her beside me.

'I'm not sure. I might be.'

'What makes you stuck?'

'What makes me?'

'Yes, how come you can write along for a while and then just stop? What makes that happen?'

'Faith,' I said. 'You lose faith. You read it back and you think it's not . . .' I raised my hands inches off the table and held a mute parcel of air in which lay the concept of truth. Hannah smiled at me.

'I'm sure it is,' she said, 'I'll make you a good cup of tea.'

She went out of the room and I heard her fill the kettle and get down the cup and the small rattling of the cutlery drawer as she fished for the spoon. And for a moment the simplicity of that, the ordinary little ceremony, seemed in some way extraordinary and I thought to myself, we might manage yet. We might.

Now, later, Jack and Hannah are sleeping. Beyond the window the night has fallen and drawn the valley and the trees within its darkness. I cannot see the lights of any house. Clouds have come for the stars. Some hours ago I lay down but couldn't sleep. For a time I stayed there in the bed beneath the black square of the skylight where the rain beat so, a dull language beyond understanding. I lay beneath the rain and suffered your absence until I could not be still. And at last I came down the steep stairs that we made to the loft room when Hannah was born. The fire was gone out, in the hearth a small bed of whitened turf ash. I went through the cottage, past all the paintings in the parlour, and was like a ghost of myself silently visiting the children. They were both sleeping, but neither lay straight in their beds or seemed to dream in ease. Hannah's head was twisted to one side and almost hung over the edge of the bed as if she had turned sharply away from looking at something or been struck and fallen so. Jack was tight and ball-like and had gathered the down quilt in about him so that none of it was free or hung loose and was instead like a bulging coat he wore for protection in the dark. I thought to move them, to rearrange their limbs in more peaceful poses, but I was afraid they would wake so I stood a while and did nothing and heard the rain. I told myself this too was some good, just being in their doorway watching over them, as though I was protector of their spirits, and bad dreams would not pass while I was there.

*

I cannot sleep. You are like a terrible ache everywhere in the house. You are in the smallest things: picture frames, cushion covers, the colour of the walls, the sponged yellow you painted, the wash of blue, the stencil of a gold star. Here you are in the books that are yours and that sit amongst mine: Why We Garden, Bonnard in Nice, One Hundred Years of Solitude, Traditional Home Remedies, Tender Is the Night, The Wild Flower Garden, The Wapshot Chronicle, *Antony De Mello's* Awareness, Birchwood, *Willem de Kooning*, The Complete Book of Self-sufficiency, *Hans Hoffman*, Van Gogh in Arles, Anatomy of an Illness.

I stand at the window and look out at where I know the valley and the farms of the Keanes and Dooleys to be, but the rain and the dark have taken everything and there is nothing but my own reflection. Above my head at the window hangs the mask we brought back from Venice. Its ribbon-ties dangle and to my sleepless eyes seems to sway slightly. The sorrowful jester; I look up at it and there we are in Venice in April. We are crossing the Accademia and going down to the Hotel San Stefano. The sharp wind is blowing and the canal waters slapping. You are looking for a place to paint and want and don't want to open your easel in Venice. How can I? you ask me. Your brother Gerard has told you that he has AIDS. We have fled to Venice for two weeks the way lovers do, when the world is too harsh. How can I paint? you ask me. How can I paint pretty pictures when there is all this pain? We wander through the university district and along by the Campo Santa Margarita and come upon the shop Commedia, where you see this mask. This is Venice, you say. This will be for our time here. Your wise eyes are beautiful as you look at me and your hair blows about. Can we see this one, please?

It twirls above me against the dark window. I think of the book I wrote afterward trying to recapture something of that time, and its characters and plots suddenly sicken me. I touch the mask. Then I turn quickly and put a coat over my shoulders and outside I duck and hop across the puddles to the cabins and open the door to let out the dog and bring him inside for company.

The night is moonless and falls in rain. The wind is in the naked branches of the sycamores and is like the sea caught there trying to escape. Loose corrugated panels of the hay barn flap and creak in chorus and in the darkness there is noise of rain spilling everywhere. No gutters have been cleaned this year and all are blocked and dripping and flooding. A long remnant of black plastic silage-wrap has travelled the wind and hangs darkly now in the top of the blackthorn, thrashing like the flag of the demented. When I open the door Huck looks at me a moment in puzzlement.

'It's all right. Come on, Huck, come on, boy.'

He stands and doesn't move, as if this is a test I have set and he will not fail it.

'Come on.'

Still he stays there. He knows he must stay in his cabin until the morning, and now, though the door is open, he won't budge in the dark.

'Huck! Now! Come on.' I walk a few steps. 'It's all right, come on, boy, come on.' And in the instant I give him when he still doesn't move it occurs to me to say your name, and in that rained-on darkness in the yard I call out, 'Katherine, Katherine, where's Katherine? Where's Katey? Come on! Find Kate.'

That is all it takes. He rushes forward then and like all retrievers is suddenly frantically on the search. He goes quickly nose-down across the puddles and moves in an S off through the night. I call after him but he does not come back and is gone through the blackness to find you.

I go back inside the cottage. It is two o'clock in the morning. I cannot sleep. Rain will fall all night now.

*

Today the visit of Mick Hehir. He passed around the front of the house to the back door, the slow tramp of his too-large wellingtons announcing him.

'Hello, the house. Hello, boy.'

Huck greeted him before I did, nosing into his thigh and nudging the great hand onto his head like a pleasurable crown.

'Hello, Jim.'

As Mick greeted me he kept his eyes on the dog, patting the heavy *flanks and telling him, 'You're a fine fellow, aren't you? Look, the size of you.'*

He has not called in for some weeks now. I have heard his old tractor passing along the road in front of the cottage every day, but I have not gone out to meet him. He patted the dog. He took off his cap and half rolled it and then offered it to Huck for its scent before pulling it back and smiling and telling the dog he was a terrible fellow. I put on the kettle – an automatic response – and stood by it, waiting then in the slow building of the boil.

'Well, Jim.' He looked over at me, but the dog wanted more of his hand and turned and jumped his forepaws onto Mick's lap. 'Lie down, lie down, ya . . .' He made a snap with his cap. 'That fellow's as friendly as ever.'

'He is.'

A pause, the noise of the kettle made the kitchen seem quieter than it has ever been.

'Any news?' Mick asked.

'No. Not really.'

'Bad weather always.'

'Yes.'

'Fields are muck. Bad time of year altogether.' He paused and felt for his cigarettes in inside pockets of his worn tweed coat. 'Children are well?'

'They are.'

'At school?'

'Yes.'

'Good. That's good.'

The kettle was singing. As he hunted again I brought him the fireside matches.

'Lovely,' he said, flaring the match and drawing the first smoke inside him. 'Muck is right.'

I made the tea and slopped out the bags. When I put them down on the table Mick leaned forward as though the tea he had seen me making was a great surprise.

'That's beautiful now, Jim, beautiful, thanks very much.'

I went and found a packet of biscuits and put them on the table. I had not thought to get him an ashtray and he had been flicking his ash into the cupped palm of his left hand. I brought him a saucer, his eyes turned to the kitchen window and he studied the movement of cloud or the flight of a bird, sucking loudly on the tea.

'Yes,' he said after a while although I had asked no question. He drew on the cigarette. Momentarily he noticed one stain among others on his trousers and he rubbed at it briefly and then gave a small uplift of his head as if to toss aside all such mysterious accumulations of life. 'Yes,' he said again. 'Muck, that's right.'

He leaned forward and, with some delicacy, fished out a biscuit with his broad fingers and with one hand halved it against the table.

'How is the writing going?' he asked. 'You writing any new book?'

'No, Mick. Not really. Not at the moment.'

'No, I suppose. No.' His face scowled as though it was a question he knew he shouldn't have asked. He reached and fingered the unshaven side of his face, his blue eyes turning again towards the window and the sky. And then he said, 'Do you know a fellow I used to read? Long time ago now. When I was I don't know maybe twenty-five. Not the kind of books now you might, but by God this fellow could write. Westerns, you know, they were. He wrote loads of them, I'd say.'

'Louis Lamour.'

'Lamour, that's him, that's the fellow.' His face lit. 'The way you knew that now. Jay, but they were good. I read four or five of them.' He smiled. 'Back when I was working on the lorries, before I came back to the farm. Louis Lamour, that's the lad. By God, yes. Four or five of them.'

He gave a little laugh then and for a few instants sat there in the contentment of remembering his own innocence. His cigarette burned. And though his face was peaceful and his manner at ease I was filled with a wave of compassion for him, my sixty-eight-year-old neighbour. I thought of his lifetime lived here in this parish, where he and I had both been born, where he had married Breda Casey and had no children and then had one day come home to find his wife dead in the kitchen. I thought of the rundown house over the road where now he lived alone in the grey gathering of loss, where his fireplace filled with plastic milk cartons and plastic bags as though he felt himself without justification or occasion for a fire. I wanted to say something to him, to ask him what he thought about the books now and why he had stopped reading. But I knew that in his eyes they were things for youth, they had no place in the world of men. I wanted to ask him about his loneliness and what he thought of in the tractor driving down to the fields and walking out to the cattle day after day. I wanted to ask him if he cared any more, if the days had any meaning. But such questions are beyond the nature of our relationship, and I asked him nothing. Just as he asked me nothing about you.

Some portion of the morning passed as we sat there, a kind of company to each other. Then he stood up and drank off the last cold mouthful of his tea in a short swallow.

'Well, work will wait no longer.'

Huck stood with him and raised his head and Michael bent and patted him once more.

'Thanks for calling in, Mick.'

He shrugged loose of my thanks. I thought for a moment he was going to say something, thought he was about to offer some words about the living and the dead, but he only mumbled something like, 'Should have called before.' And then he was out the door stamping his wellingtons and gone. His tractor roared and I followed its sound going down the meadow road between the Five-Acre and the Fort fields. Then, like dust, all my silence gathered inside the cottage once more.

*

This evening I sat with Jack at his homework in the kitchen. I unpacked the books and took out his pencil case and ruler and spread them out on the table. He sat in the chair beside me and frowned.

'Why do I have to do Irish?'

'It's important to do Irish, Jack.'

'Why?'

54

'Because it is our national language.'

'I hate it.'

'It is the language of our country.'

'No one speaks it.'

'Some do.'

He opened the pencil case and took out red and blue pens, and then opened the copybook and pressed flat the page and began the business of lining it. Neatness is important, the Master has taught him. He will have to do it again if it is not neat. Even though the homework is only the copying out of some phrases in Irish, the page must be lined in red and the handwriting steady and straight. Jack took on the task with the seriousness only an eight-year-old could know, bent so close to the page that his nose nearly touched it. The six-inch ruler was shorter than the page and when Jack came to slide it down the margin angled outward. He leaned back and, before I could speak, reached and tore off the page.

'Jack, it was all right.'

'It was crooked. It looked stupid.'

I knew enough to say no more, and I watched while he drew the line painstakingly again.

When he was ready he looked into the text as though it were a puzzle.

'What does the question mean?' I asked him.

He shrugged at me as if this was an absurd thing to ask. 'I don't know.'

'Well, then, how can you answer it?'

'I find the words.'

'You find the words?'

'Yes.'

'But, Jack, you don't know what they mean?'

'No. I never know. It doesn't matter.'

'It does.'

'I find the words that match the question and that's the answer.'

I lifted my head and looked at the back window where the night had fallen. Then I made my mistake.

'Stop, Jack, it's not right. You'll never get any better, you'll never understand it. At the end of the year you'll be as bad as you are at the start. You can't do it this way.'

'I'll get it right.'

'It doesn't matter.'

'It does.'

'You won't learn.'

'I don't care.'

'You will.'

'I don't want you to help me.'

'Well, I'm going to.'

'I don't want you to, go away.'

'No.'

'Mammy let me do it that way.'

'But—'

'She did. She did.'

'Mammy was American, she didn't know any Irish, she—'

'I got it right!' he screamed at me. 'With Mammy I got it right!' Then his face turned bright red and the tears balled and rolled from his eyes.

'Jack . . .'

'Go away. Go away!' He turned his shoulder over and down to the table and shut me out.

I stood up. My hands were trembling.

'All right,' I said, 'that's all right, Jack.' I reached and patted his head but as my fingers touched he pulled away.

He kept his head down and did not speak and I walked out of the kitchen. I went and stood by the fire and wrestled with failure. I listened to the small sobs of my son; the sniffles he sleeved, then the rip as he tore free the red-lined page pinked with the small wet blooms of his tears and began again.

To escape the feeling of defeat, I went through the cottage and up the stairs to Hannah. She was doing her homework with the television on, a splay of textbooks across the floor. She was working at her Irish, the sound low on Sky News. The War in Afghanistan *said the banner behind the newsreader, as maps and charts and images dark and infrared flashed and vanished. She watches no other channel now. And I realize that since September the precariousness of the world has entered her consciousness. On the television she has seen news coverage of anthrax and other terrors and feels at any time they might say, 'Stay tuned, the world is about to end now.' Her face is so much older and her skin seems drawn and pale with worries I cannot take away. I have thought to say that she should not watch Sky News, to even make the argument that we are safe here in Ireland and that such things should not be allowed to take the joy of youth. I have heard myself preparing a speech that no parent should make aloud. The speech that such things do not concern us, that what happens in Afghanistan or Palestine or Israel is someone else's trouble; ours is just what happens here in this small house in the west of County Clare. But I cannot say it.*

In her mind now are these images of war and terror, of the towers falling, of villages smoking in the mountains, the flash of night bombs, the still smoking crater in Manhattan, the firemen and the flags at half-mast. It is a condition of how we live now. We are shown everything, but given no time for feeling. We see the murdered and the maimed and the murderers too, their names running on a reel through our heads for a week, the brief celebrity of pain, before one melts into the next. There is nowhere to go to learn how to heal this, no instruction for those whose suffering is only to be bystanders watching from a place of safety. What is Hannah to do with these images of horror and loss that she finds so compelling? I cannot be sure. I want her not to watch. I want her to shut the news off and break down and cry for you, but that grief has transmuted, gone behind her eyes. She should be crossing into the country of love now, I thought, should be writing a boy's name on her schoolbooks, should be dreaming intangible dreams of happiness, not looking up at the television to see the end of the world. I stood at her bedroom door not quite crossing inside.

'How are you doing?'

She looked up, puzzled why I was there.

57

'Fine.'

'Good.'

The screen went to Afghan fighters, rifles raised in the air. Hannah glanced at it.

'Doing your Irish?' I said.

'Yeah.'

She turned her head down again to the text and picked up the dictionary. I didn't leave and so without looking up from beneath the fall of her hair she asked, 'Yes?'

She was still searching for a word.

'Jack is a bit upset,' I told her. 'I pushed him a bit with the homework and he started crying.' She looked up at me then.

'You shouldn't push him.'

'I know.'

Sky News took a break for the weather and showed sun faces over England sponsored by Ryanair. Rain beat against the skylight over our heads.

'He hates school,' Hannah said.

'He doesn't really hate it.'

'He does. You don't know.' She still didn't look up, but her tone was sharp and cut into me. *You don't know.* I leaned against the doorjamb and steadied. I wanted to make a defence, to assure her that I knew each of them perfectly and that nothing that happened in their lives escaped me, but knew that I could not. Perhaps she was right, perhaps Jack was in terror of school, perhaps nightmares rode rough his sleep, what did I really know?

'Tell me,' I said.

For the first time Hannah looked at me and I could see at once she regretted the place in the conversation she had entered.

'No, just he hates it, that's all.'

'Why? Do they bully him? What? Tell me.'

'Dad, no, stop. It's not like that. Why do adults always think it must be bullying? It's just . . .' She stopped herself.

'Hannah, please.'

'He feels a freak.'

I heard her say it and my heart fell. There was that moment of recognition when the truth comes and rises like a blade through you. You see the thing you did not want to see.

'Since Mam,' Hannah said quickly, then added, 'It's no one's fault. It's just he feels weird, that's all. They treat him differently.'

Since Mam. She could not bring herself to say more. Whole words are wounds now, Sick, Died, Death, Funeral, words for which there is no healing.

It was another age of slow, lumpish heartbeats before I asked her, 'What can we do for him?'

Hannah's blue eyes were full and softened and directed at me then with the kind of hopeless pity children reserve for their parents when the adults stand before them like figures less evolved.

'No, but he'll be all right. It's just a hard time for him now, that's all. There's nothing you can do. Only maybe tell him he doesn't have to do the homework, give him a note. Let him stay home with you some days.'

She paused and seemed an ageless rock of sense to me just then. 'OK.'

She turned her head to the television again. The top story of the war was being repeated, flashes of explosion blooming in the Afghan night.

'What about you, are you all right?' I asked her.

No,' she said, not looking up, 'I hate school too.' She waited a beat then she turned up her face and smiled at me. 'Yes, Dad, I'm all right.'

I went down the steep stairs and through the cottage, filled with a sudden hopefulness like a man carrying a cake with candles burning. I would sit down now with Jack and calm and reassure him. Although some part of me resisted the idea, and thought it might only make things worse, I would take Hannah's advice and tell him to take next day off school.

When I came into the kitchen Jack was no longer crying. He had finished the Irish homework and the sums and was drawing a square house on the back of one of the draft manuscript sheets that I give him. The house had four windows evenly placed and a path straight down the centre. He was bent over it with concentration, and perhaps because he did not look up at me, because some moment I had imagined failed to happen, or because the rain beat just then against the window, I did not say to him what I had come to say. I stood there, and in some strange inexplicable inversion, because he was almost happy I felt almost unbearably sad. I stood there and nearly wept and thought of you. Then I turned softly and slipped away to the sitting room where I sat a long time staring out at the dark. Until at last I came in here and turned on the screen once more.

My father does not die of his stroke. He is rescued by Mrs Dempsey and struggles some of the way back to us across trenches of paralysis and shock and ache. His left side seems wounded, his mouth downed at a slant as though he has been making oily inferences and arrested in that gesture. He cannot move his left side and his words are so buckled and warped he will not attempt to unroll any language.

For four days Matthew comes home from college. He seems almost another person to the one who left in the car with my father. Gone are the red jumper and wing-collared shirt. When he first comes off the bus my mother makes a soft involuntary gasp so changed does he appear. His hair has not been cut. He wears blue jeans and a beige corduroy jacket that seems much too large for him. He comes in to see my father where he lies in the bed. My father makes no sound, he does not move his head. He blinks once. Looking at him Matthew nods as if music plays. Then my mother, who is holding her hands together, says she has tea and some food ready. I know that she has been preparing for Matthew's arrival since the night before, that there is fresh brown bread and baked ham and the sort of lattice-pastry apple tart she makes and queen cakes. But Matthew tells her he is not hungry. He says he has brought books and has study to do. With that he goes out of the room and my mother seems to me then diminished in some way, to be as insubstantial as a fine shell that collapses in your fingers. She says nothing. She holds her hands. I want her to be angry and remonstrate, but she never does. She is become ever quieter, and it is as if from the Christmas morning when Louise died some part of my mother has been dying ever since. She is being erased from the centre out, and says nothing, and goes and sits by my father's bed.

Later I go to see Matthew in his room.

'Yes?' He is lying on the bed with his shoes on and a maths text in front of him.

'Hi.'

'Yeah.'

I do not come further into the room. His head has not turned from the book.

'How is college?'

'It's all right.'

'Is it hard?'

'No.'

I pause.

'I'll be there soon, I'm going to do English.'

He raises his head to look for a moment at my statement in the air. He seems to consider it so, as if the problem of my life and its possible solutions are drawn there on an invisible board.

'Good,' he says, and looks back down at the book.

'You think so?'

'Yeah.'

And that is enough for me. But I risk destroying the moment and ask him again.

'Yeah?'

He does not look at me.

'Yeah,' he says.

In a few days he is gone again. He takes a lift from one of the Johnstons to Ennis and tells me to let him know how Dad is doing. I stand in the street in the village and watch him inside the window of the car as he disappears from our life again.

Dr McHale visits. He is an affable old man who has found that the best care is to sit beside the patient and nod. He does this for an hour beside my father. He does not suggest physiotherapy or any course of recovery but rest and a small bottle of tablets that he says the chemist will make up in town. My mother looks at him, he nods at her. When Dr McHale asks my father if he would like to try sitting in a chair my father shakes his head and his crooked mouth ever so slightly. The doctor nods.

My father will not move now. The knowledge that he will not return to the switchboard has in turn unplugged his connection to life. He cannot be the quiet faceless hero of anyone now and prefers to lie inert in his room. He does not think of the heroism of facing what has happened to him and defeating it. I come to understand the word *stroke* means struck, for that is how he appears, struck down. I have no experience of anyone who has suffered this, and in my mind I turn the word over and over. Who has struck my father? What blow descended from above? I can think only of Saul on the road to Damascus and a primary school picture of him falling off his white horse in a blinding light. But in that there was a significance I cannot find here. My boyhood faith in God has been steadily eroded, and I am already confirmed in disbelief, so this is a difficult argument. Still, I do not want to think it was my own fault, that the shock and disappointment of seeing the stolen book arrested the steady clockwork of him. But blame and guilt are not far away. They come like unannounced visitors, fierce and familiar, and lodge without speech in the corners of my spirit. And it takes some effort to banish them. I lie on my bed in the night and bring the copy of *Great Expectations* up from its hiding place. Why did I steal it? I cannot understand myself. Why did I let my father see it? My face flushes. I put down the book and shut my eyes but in my mind see only a gallery of characters from Dickens. Here is Mr Sowerberry studying the boy Oliver, there Gradgrind with broad whiskery sideburns, and there, scuttling in half-shadow, Uriah Heep. Such figures. They traffic back and forth and pause to consider me: is that the fellow, is that the one wanted to kill his father? I shout out then, and the sound of my own voice brings me back into the real, and my mother is opening the bedroom door in her nightdress, small and frail-looking, her long hair all grey and combed out and the ghost of herself not far away.

'Jim?'

I sit up in fright.

'Jim, go to sleep now.'

She watches me a moment, and I want her to cross the room and put her hand upon my hot forehead, but I am too old to ask her this, and the way between us is already broken up and blocked with invisible obstacles that arrived, it seems, when neither of us was looking. After a moment she steps back and closes the door softly and is gone, and her footsteps are softer still.

In the days and weeks that follow it falls to her to bring to the bedroom the parade of mashed, pulped and juiced foods my father can take, to bend and aim his straws and to ferry to and fro his chamber pot. There are days I come home and am called into the room where the scent of lavender water is tangled with the bitter tang of urine, and my mother has my father propped, half-standing, half-hopping, with his dead arm dangling, his pyjama bottoms down, in some terrible dance of the dying. I hold my father's weight in my arms, and he seems a long thin crate shipped from a foreign country and made of lesser stuff than a human man. His shrunken purple penis pees wide of the pot. My father in my arms makes a strangled noise that may be shame or anger or both. There is a milky sourness on his breath. My fingers grasping his bare arm make his skin flake.

Afterward when he is lain back in the bed my mother thanks me and tells me to go out. She does not say that she is going to sponge bathe him now, but I hear her go and fill the basin with hot water and the sharp odour of the disinfectant will travel into all corners of the house. I close the door of my room and read Thomas Hardy's *The Return of the Native*. I have been drawn to the sense of fate in Hardy, the weird twists that keep tying things together in the plot. I lie there reading of Eustacia Vye and her longing to escape from what Hardy calls the 'furzy briary wilderness' of Egdon Heath. It is a world strange and timeless as in unsettling dreams, with bonfires blazing on the crests of hills and red-faced figures appearing and disappearing out of the dark. I am drawn into this embrowned world, but while my imagination tries to take refuge on the heaths of Wessex, the scents of sickness and disinfectant rise and cut off the way. I smell them inside my room, on my clothes. I tear off my jumper and throw it in a corner, but still all I can feel is the nearness of dying. I go out of the house into the cool damp air of the late February afternoon. I walk into the village where there is no one about. I pass the post office where Connie works the Switch now and where my father's mind sits still connecting the calls, unable to believe that they continue without him. I have no plan, I just need to be out of the house. But then I see the Crowleys outside Brady's shop getting into their car, and I ask if I can have a lift to town.

Within half an hour I am among the shelves in the only book-shop there is in Ennis. As soon as I walk in I feel at ease. There is something about the crisp clean edges of the books, the gathered congregation of authors, which opens a serenity inside of me. That late afternoon, with the dark already fallen and the streets outside wet and lit and moving with the homeward traffic, the bookshop provides a sense of escape into a world made of words. I go to the Fiction section, and look there at books I have already read, at the lined-up volumes of Dickens. I have read *Dombey and Son*, *Martin Chuzzlewit*, *David Copperfield*, *Hard Times*, *Little Dorrit*, but none has seized me the way *Great Expectations* has. With that novel I have come to understand the phrase 'to capture your imagination'. I take the Penguin edition from the shelf and part its pages to look at the opening words. I already know them by heart, but even take new pleasure reading them in a different typeface:

> My father's family name being Pirrip, and my Christian name Philip, my infant tongue could make of both names noth-ing longer or more explicit than Pip. So, I called myself Pip, and came to be called Pip.

I don't read any more than that. I flick the pages for the scent that rises from them and think of how Pip invented himself, inventing even his name as later he invents his entire identity as a gentleman. I replace the book on the shelf imagining who I might become when I have invented myself.

I have no money to buy any of the books I want. There are authors whose names I have heard only, but want with a kind of desperate hunger to read. My eye scans the names: Jane Austen, Emily Brontë, Joseph Conrad, Dostoevsky, Henry James, James Joyce, Franz Kafka, D. H. Lawrence, Edgar Allan Poe, Leo Tolstoy. I stand before them and take a book out from the shelf and read an opening line. It is getting late. The shop will be closing soon. The Crowleys will have finished buying the cabbage plants and hay-knife they came to town for and will be waiting for me at their car. Behind me in the shop there is a slim red-haired woman seated at the counter reading a book and from time to time she looks up to see if I need help. I am the only customer left. I do not want the shop to shut or to be asked to leave. I stand in my green anorak and jeans and for reasons then that lie deep and clouded and unformed in words, I know I am going to steal a book. The heat of the thought rises through me like a burner lit. Sweat beads in my hands and on my face. I turn and glance back at the counter. The red-haired woman smiles at me kindly and turns down the top edge of the page she has been reading before closing her book.

'Are you all right?'

'Yes, yes, I'll be just a minute.'

'Take your time,' she says, and opens her book again.

In an instant then I move along the shelf and am out of her line of sight and do not see myself in the mirror high in the ceiling. I am out of Classics and into Non-Fiction, my heart hammering in my chest. I should go, I should just leave now. I press the clamminess of my hands against the sides of my coat. My eye runs along the line of titles. Then I reach and take a fat paperback volume on Ireland in the thirties, and hold it inside my coat.

I feel it flat and cool against the heat of me and do not move. As though in crude pantomime of heart attack I have to clutch my hand at my chest to keep the book from slipping down.

'Find something?' the woman asks, closing over her book again.

'No.' I cannot look at her face, and go to the door as she rises from her chair and follows me. Figures in my head loom and rub their hands and press forward and say, *Stop! Stop, thief! You're caught now, fellow!*

But I am not.

'Goodnight,' the woman says, and locks the door behind me. I hurry up the wet dark path of O' Connell Street and across into the car park by the river, my mind fizzing with the strange effervescence of the crime and the beginning of rationalization. I have stolen the book for my father. I have stolen it for him. That's what I did. Yes. It is the balance owed for the library one, I reason, and sit into the Crowleys' car, making believe to myself that such accounts exist or matter or that redemption can be so easily stolen back.

Swift night clouds, obscured moon without her stars. Dark country-side spread out before me at the table by the window, the dog snuffling dreams at my feet. I read back a page, feel the old temptation. How easily I might change the truth into a story. How easy to write that moment as a turning point for the boy Jim. To say he returned to his father with the stolen book and sat by his bedside and read it to him. I might say he came to sit there every day after school in his final year and read in a quiet voice and that although the father did not speak to him there was perhaps on the last day before Jim left home some minor acknowledgement. Perhaps the old man raised his hand slightly from the bedclothes and Jim reached over and took the cold fingers in his. Some tidy moment of resolution and the sentiment of an imagined forgiveness.

But of course it is not like that. Forgiveness, like redemption, is not so easily won.

When I return with the book I go upstairs to my room. I lie on the bed and look at it and then put it down the side of the bed by the wall. I think I cannot bring the book to my father without admitting something. I have never given him a gift without occasion and the youth I am that night cannot bring himself to feel that largeness of spirit. Some heat of impulse that had risen in the bookshop has cooled now, and I think only of the sorry mess that is my family and my own longing to be away from it. In the years since I was a boy I have lost all sense of the beauty and wonder of the landscape in which I am living. I do not see the gently sloping fields and meadows of Clare as anything but a prison now, the towns to me backwaters and bogholes where ignorant lumpish men with thick ears and bad teeth discuss the price of bullocks. I am disgusted by it all now. Nothing noble or graceful or fine seems possible to me in such a place. I think of it all as Pip did of the forge where Joe Gargery worked, as a place so beneath the aspirations of my imagination that I cannot understand how my parents could have lived there for so long. That they did can only lessen them in my mind. Such is the monster I am become. I do not think then of considerations of money or work, or the many reasons that underlie the choices of a life. I do not see the great transitional skies of the west swept with wind or the dance of greens and greys and blues in each hour of the day. To the youth that lies on the bed there is only the dream of escaping to the capital city like his brother.

I sit my exams and do well in English and Latin. The university awaits at the end of summer.

And the summer that comes is another of those played like a trump card from the deck of the heavens. It is delivered with skies of such blueness that they seem from the very beginning to stack in memory. Here is the summer that will outlast ten others in your mind, here is the last summer of youth when I might be out in bog and field from the cuckoo's first singing until the bats flit in the twilight. I might be abroad in the parish in tractor or transport box, fork to shoulder, brown-armed and freckle-faced, hair crisped in sun and crinkle-dry with the dust of hay. I might swagger on the cusp of manhood then, out among the older farmers in the last year before I go away. Briefly I might glory in my own arrival at that point and take their glances filled with the bittersweet knowledge that here was another of all those who would leave the landscape on the very moment when they might have been most useful in it.

But I do not. That summer my father stays in bed and my mother attends him, and I grow long-haired and lazy and read books in my room. Because I cannot go to the library, cannot face the humiliation of being recognized, I take lifts to the town of Ennis and visit the bookshop and from there steal the poetry of Dylan Thomas, of Wallace Stevens, and Sylvia Plath. I steal *The Rainbow*, and *Sons and Lovers*, and *Tender Is the Night* and more. The woman with the red hair watches me sometimes and smiles and I think I am discovered. But she says nothing.

The summer passes slowly. In the village I am another of the postmaster's odd sons. I am aloof and snobbish, they say. When school ends I discover I have no friends. No one calls at our house, and there is none that might be expecting calls from me. On Sundays in the drowse of summer Mass I see some of the fellows and we make half-nods toward each other but say nothing, and are like escapees shamed and mute and in fear of discovery.

In the pew I stand and sit and kneel in automatic response, but I feel no sense of sacrament. I want Christ to come down from the cross. I want the flash of rapture, the dazzle and blinding light of faith, anything that will lift the scene out of the tedium in which it is mired. I cannot bring myself to go to Communion. *Only say the Word and I shall be healed*, the congregation murmurs. But I do not hear the Word. I sit while the Communion line forms and look among the aged and the weary and the bent for the girls in their summer clothes. Some are very beautiful. They parade up to receive God as if it is their right, as if they know that beauty is part of the divine. I sit in the pew and feel unworthy. And the burden of this feeling is such that when one turns to look at me I cast down my eyes, and when I pass by another in the entrance-way of the church, all language seems stolen from me and I lower my head and hurry away. I cannot understand the other fellows who can stand outside the gates and laugh with the girls. I walk out the country road as the cars pass me on the way home from Mass, birds in the hedgerows sing. I think I am in love with a girl called Helen. Her eyes are dark, her hair is fair. She has been away at the convent and has in her bearing something of the haughtiness and pride I have imagined in Estella. I walk and think of her and list poems I should send her anonymously. I say her name, Helen, and feel the word in my mouth as though it is something sensual and delicious. Before I get home I have begun to compose a first poem to her.

For a week then I do nothing else. I write phrases of a love poem to Helen. *Pity the one who Love takes and drowns in cold implacable lakes . . .* I write a line and try and count the beats and measure them evenly. Then I try the measure in syllables and without rhyme. *of loss and longing*, something *and* What? I say a phrase over and over to invite the next one to follow. When it doesn't, I sit there, rocking in my chair back and forth in the warm, dead air of my room. *Here beneath these waters beats . . .* When I have more than a couple of phrases I write them out in longhand in a copybook. But there is something about seeing the lines in my handwriting that makes them seem trivial and childish and embarrassing. They have none of the apparent permanence of printed poems, so, because I have no typewriter, I block print the lines instead and try to imagine myself a monk-like engraver of earlier centuries, working the words of love indelibly into time. *These your eyes will touch and touching so . . .*

Within a couple of weeks I write eight poems to Helen. I have still not spoken to her. *nor I who dare to speak . . .* I go into the village to get milk and tea and other messages for my mother and I linger in Brady's shop and outside in case I might see her. And sometimes I do. I see her coming down the path in a yellow dress and I cross quickly to the other side of the street, my heart racing and my hands like great lumps of hot flesh shaking by my sides. In a scene from science fiction I feel I am transformed on the spot into a misshapen creature, a Gollum, a Grendel of scales and foulness. The gross nature of myself, my lank flop of long hair, my absurd spattering of freckles, my squinting eyes and large lips, all rise to appal me then. I look away from her. I hurry down the path and wait at the end of the village, arguing with myself and the voices inside my head whether to return to catch the sight of her going home.

Later in my room I work on the poems. I am stricken by a sense that my body does not resemble my soul in any way. Only the poems do that. They are what I will offer her, and in the moment she reads them, I believe that she will recognize it is me, for I am convinced beauty is gifted that kind of insight.

In the progress of long hot days and short nights my mind is a fever of language and longing. I cannot think of Helen without thinking up sudden phrases of description, sequences of sounds. *In the grove of the honey-sucking bees . . .* I am given to bouts of assonance and sibilance, for the sounding of the words is itself a kind of contact. I am happiest while I sit at the table and work on a poem, though the struggle of composition is such that the letters and words might be metals gold and silver and my desire a hammer banging them into shapes. I have fallen under the spell of the Hopkins poems I have read, and cannot now write a clear straight line without tricks of inversion and plays of sound in rhythms sprung. *This my heart halved, unwholed, by holiness of yours.* In my showiness the feeling gets mangled. Sometimes I finish a poem and lie back on the bed with the sheet of it and feel it is perfect. I think when Helen reads it she will be so moved that she will walk out into the street and up to my house. But the rapture is short-lived. And within an hour, and sometimes even less, I can detect something rotten in the poem. I pull at a phrase that seems untidy, *eyes and sighs and silence soon,* and quickly the whole thing unravels and I am filled with disgust that I could have offered her such a mess. I am an idiot, my poem as ugly and unworthy as myself.

After several attempts I have eight poems cleanly printed on separate sheets. I do not sign any of them. I wait one night until my mother has gone to bed then I place the poems in an envelope and put a stamp on it and go out into the mild night. The sky is thick cloth of blue. It hangs so low there seems no air. I walk down into the village where the streets are empty. The heaviness of the summer sky has trapped the smells of stale stout and diesel and dung and turf and cigarette smoke. There is a beer bottle left standing on the window sill of Duggan's and inside it three-quarters of a pint of pee. Close by is the sweetsour breathing of the animals standing in the fields that ring the village. I walk with my poems down through the single crooked street and feel what I think of then as a deep and sweet melancholy that seems fallen there. I take out the envelope and read where I have written her name and address. On that instant I decide that I cannot do it, I cannot send the pages to her.

Then I slip them inside the post box and they are gone.

And strangely in that moment I am like a prisoner released. A white balloon of joy inflates beneath my heart. I walk out into the centre of the street. In the film of myself I might be dancing. The poems are gone. Some threshold has been crossed, I believe, and now my life will never be the same again. All I have to do is wait.

And I do, and come to know that waiting is sometimes the greater part of suffering. At first I do not leave the house. I am expecting a knock on the door, the phone to ring. A hundred times I imagine the hands that open the envelope and lift out the poems. I stand somewhere in the corner of her room and watch as Helen turns the pages over searching for the name of the sender. And then she reads them. I see the scene as out of a nineteenth-century novel. Net curtains blow on summer breeze, trembling fingers hold the pages, birdsong, summer morning a haze beyond the window. Perhaps there is a piano nearby. Helen reading. She finishes the first poem. Roses in her cheeks. Begins the next. All that is missing is the horse and carriage outside to take her to me.

A day passes. And then another. I decide that it is shyness that is stopping her. She will not come to the house; I must go out. By means of irrational reasoning I believe that if she sees me on the path in the village she will know they are my poems and she will stop and speak with me. So I rise early in the mornings and go out. I tell my mother I want to spend time in the parish before I leave for university. I walk down into the village and beyond and back again. The sun is shining. Tractors come and go, drawing milk tanks to the creamery. Delivery vans arrive and unload. I pass three hours waiting for a sign of her, and silently negotiate with myself all manner of deals. When at last Helen comes she walks down the street with another girl and they are laughing. I pass the two of them going the other way and she does not look at me.

The following day I am there again. I am to be a martyr to Love, I will wait until she recognizes me. I have never spoken a single word to her, but I think I am more deeply in love than Keats or Yeats ever were. In the dead hour in the middle of the morning when the farmers have been and gone and the village falls into an empty dream, Mrs Brady comes and stands at the door of her shop and asks me what I am doing.

'Nothing. Just walking.'

She is a large woman whose husband kept pigs until his heart exploded. In her blue-patterned housecoat she folds her great arms across herself and seems to rest her upper body on them as though upon a short wall.

'You're up and down that street all morning. Did you lose something or what is it?'

'Yes,' I say.

'Well, what?'

'What?'

'What did you lose?'

'It's all right, I'll find it myself,' I tell her and turn to head back down the village.

'Please yourself,' she mutters after me.

It is hours later when at last Helen comes again. I see her go into the shop and I hurry up the street to be at the door when she is coming out. But when she does, Mrs Brady comes out with her and suddenly they are both standing in front of me.

'Well?' says Mrs Brady. She folds three chins at me, and makes white bristles stand out at odd angles.

I say nothing, so she explains me to Helen:

'Young Foley here lost something, won't say what it is, and has been walking up and down looking for it all day.'

They turn to study me.

'Well?' she says.

'What is it?' Helen asks, looking directly at me. I look away. There is nothing I can say. I have said all that is in me in the poems and am awaiting only her word.

Mrs Brady fills the absence with words of her own. I hear her say, 'Odd fellow, our Jim, aren't you? Always writing stuff, I hear. Doodling away, isn't that right?'

I stand there for several years saying nothing, inside me a gurgling stew of shame and loathing. I need no one to tell me the absurdity of my character or the vanity of my hopes. I am locked there. I say nothing.

I think I hear Helen say, 'Oh, do you write poems?' But it is as though my ears are not connected to my mind, or the words that enter them are written on sheets balled up and thrown, and some part of me is sent scrambling after them. What did she say? Did she say she liked my poems? I am the idiot in the village standing before the beauty. My lips may open and close, my eyelids bat. There may be a moment when my hopes have not bled from my eyes and drained into a pool about my feet, when I might seem to be in any way worthy. But if so, it is only a moment. Cold curdled lumps rise in my throat. My face is a ridiculous gawp, my pale paws of hands absurdly dangling; look at my clothes, look at the big flat shoes with the toes bruised out of them. Some fissure opens in my brain then between the real and the imagined. *It is not to be like this*, I think, and then make the leap to go one step further: *It is not like this.* And so, because I cannot reconcile the fictional and the actual, I turn quickly there on the path to rush back into imagination. For a second I see the crowd of Dickensians block my way; I see the buildings spin to the side like things made of paper; I reach to lean on what is not there and there are stars fizzing in my eyes and the thump of blood in my ears and Helen is saying, 'Did you write me some poems?' and turning to Mrs Brady and telling her, 'I think he wrote me poems,' but I do not hear her reply, only the chuckle that precedes it because I am fainting then and falling falling into the street.

Hard to write some things without cringing. So much easier to make a story. What did that insufferable fellow know about love? That idiot who is hidden somewhere inside my skin? Make a poem of this: once there was a man who loved a woman, and she reached out a hand and took him into the real world. But one day there was a blackbird standing in the garden and it would not fly away. That night the woman could not sleep. Then she could not sleep the next night, or the one after. I have a pain, she told the man. And soon she became ill and brought her illness to a dozen wise doctors all across the country. And in a moment then she died.

Where is the poem for that love? What did that young boy before know about sacrifice and selflessness and what happens when you give yourself to another person so that they are inseparable from you? So you cannot imagine how the day will dawn and the light burn until night without her? So that

Shit.

*

'He's crying.'

'What?'

I turn and see Hannah standing in her nightdress.

'Jack is crying, Dad. I went in to him and tried to get him to stop, but he's sort of sleeping and crying.'

'It's all right, it'll be all right, Hannah.' I get up quickly from the screen. 'Thanks for trying. I should have been listening for him, I didn't hear a thing.'

But now I do. Before I even follow her back through the kitchen I hear the low wailing like a hinge loosened in the wind.

'I'll go in to him. It's just a dream. You go back asleep.'

She is stopped there on the landing outside the bedroom doors, her eyes narrow and her hair mussed. I think she wants to say something, and may be about to but the crying is too intense or pitiful and she presses her lips together.

'Are you all right?' I ask her. 'It's a dream, probably. He won't even remember it tomorrow. It's . . . it may have nothing to do with anything, just normal, just part of growing up. All right?'

She does not look convinced.

'Go in to him, Dad.'

'Yes. Goodnight, Hannah.'

'Night.'

In his covers Jack is turned and curved so that his forehead is pressed down on the pillow, his back arched and his knees propping him up. In this position he is rocking back and forth and crying. I am not sure if he is awake or at least not fully so, and I sit down on the edge of the bed carefully. I am afraid of things I do not know, afraid there may be a way you are supposed to proceed here, a whole methodology framed for parents encountering children in nightmares. And that this procedure is critical if you are not to cause further grief or damage. Do I wake him? Do I shake his shoulder and startle him out of it? Turn on the light and dazzle him back to the reality of his room? I know you would know what to do. I know at some point I did too. But for now I am lost and afraid. It is as if I have forgotten a language I had once learned and now find myself in the country where everyone is native but me.

I sit there. Jack cries on.

Hannah appears at the door.

'Dad?'

'All right, all right. I'm sorry, Hannah. He'll stop now, go back to sleep.'

She goes again. I raise my left hand and gently, so gently, place it on the back of my son. The heat of him rushes through his pyjamas into my palm. Still he rocks over and back. I move my hand in a small circle and bend down to whisper into his dream.

'Shush shush shush.'

I am the sea-sounding father in the dark bedroom then, believing or not quite believing but having no other instinct than to make soft waves of sound over and over. I add his name. I keep my hand on Jack's back and the crying changes pitch and is lower now, and then broken with gasps of breath. Still his eyes are closed. The rocking slows and slows and is then like a wheeled cart or a pram, that rolled free down a dangerous hill but now arrives at a stop.

'Good boy, Jack, good boy, lie down now. Lie down.'

The words may be meaningless or not, may soothe him or not, I cannot say. Perhaps it is only the sound of a voice that counts, any voice, perhaps the nightmare would let go of him anyway.

He lies flat now and still, his forehead damp. What terrors he had seen or felt will remain a mystery. I do not know if I am supposed to ask him about them or not, but know that I will take the easier course, fearing what he might say.

I know. I know in this I am a weak father. But I think I could not bear what he might say. What might shatter in me. Already there are pieces of you like glass everywhere.

To compensate for my weakness, I take the extra blanket from the corner of the room and the Disney cushion from the chair, and with these make myself a place to lie down on the floor beside Jack's bed. I will be there for him if the nightmare returns. I will make the sounds of the sea.

By the time I get to university in Dublin, my brother Matthew is just finishing his degree. In the time since he left home a greater distance than that of geography has grown between us. He has come home to visit occasionally, but his air of secrecy only unsettles my mother. He sleeps long hours. It may be as my mother says that he is catching up, that the life he lives among the calculations in college does not allow his brain to rest, and now back in Clare he can find the off switch and collapse. She does not mind. In fact she prefers him to be sleeping. When he is awake and moving through the house he somehow seems to have grown too big for the dimensions of the building. He is tall and rangy and his hair is long. He has a scruff of beard and wears the same jeans and sweater every day. When he goes in to visit our father he does not sit but stands perfectly still. Illness to him is something of an error. It is a miscalculation and should be righted. He doesn't stay long with our father. Later, he asks Mother what exactly is wrong with him and meanwhile studies the growing decline in her, sees the increased nervousness of her manner, the itchiness, the trembling, the sense there is all the time when she is not sewing that the world is about to split apart in her hands. Matthew listens to my mother's answers without comment. He sits at the table and nods or says, 'I see,' and it is as though he is gathering all the information needed for a final calculation, and that this will yield a solution.

One day he goes into the bedroom and calmly asks my father why he does not try and get up. There is a gurgle and a flattened phrase of response which serves only to puzzle Matthew more and he shakes his head and says, 'It makes no sense. Why do you not want to get better?'

Again my father cannot answer him in more than swallow-sounds and some movement of his eyebrows.

'Well,' Matthew says, his voice firm and a little louder, 'you must get up, you have to bloody try.'

I hear this from the door where I am waiting for Matthew to come out and I cannot believe this is my brother.

'You can't lie there the rest of your life,' he says. 'You'll kill Mam. You will. People have strokes, they recover. You have to fight it.' The words and their tone are a violence that crackles and runs live in the room, a current seeking earth.

'Come on,' he says, 'I'm going to get you up.' He reaches then and puts his arm around the back of my father. I hear the noise and I come into the room not sure of what is happening.

'Jim, come here and help,' he says.

My father's eyes are frightened and fly to my face, beseeching.

'Wait, Matthew, he—'

'He has to get up. You'll be all right, come on, we can hold him, let him get his balance, let him feel what it's like to be standing again, we'll support him.'

My father is propped forward like a man of rags, his chin slumping onto his chest. Matthew's arm passes around his back beneath his arms. He must feel the thinness of the old man or the flaking and sores of his skin, for he turns his head half to the side and says, 'Jesus.' I am standing beside him. 'Come on, Jim, come on, take back the blankets, get his legs out. He'll be all right. You'll be all right,' he tells my father whose face is suddenly blanched and whose crooked mouth drools as his words cannot come. There are groans escaping him, and slow soft moans that may be pain or effort, I do not know. I turn back the bedclothes and release a pungent smell. I find my father's feet and they seem so small and pale that I cannot imagine them ever bearing him through the world. They are cold to my touch. I lift and place them to the edge of the bed.

'Matthew,' I say, 'maybe we shouldn't.'

But Matthew is already further on in the solving of the equation and every part of him is focused on it. He cannot go back through the problem now; there is only the inevitable pressing forward, the pure mathematical linkage of step after step that in his mind will result in his father standing, his mother recovering peace and the beginning of the return to ordinary life. It is his way. To watch him as he struggles to draw my father's body forward on the bed is to watch a scene apparently devoid of compassion or sympathy. He seems to proceed merely upon logic and reason; the certainty that the action he is taking is the one required to solve the problem, nothing more. But I know there is more to it than that, although then I cannot quite formulate it. I am swept on by my brother, by the force of command he suddenly has there in the rising dust and dead scent of the bedroom.

'Turn his legs out, come on, I'll help him forward, guide his feet down to the floor.'

I think my father rears backward then or stiffens or shows more resistance although I cannot be sure. He is brought forward on Matthew's arms to be perched on the edge of the bed. A bottle of 7Up is knocked over on the bedstand and falls and loses its lid and spills with smells of lemon and sugar on the floor at our feet. Matthew kicks the bottle back.

'Shit.' He holds my father balanced there. 'Does he have slippers?'

'I don't know. He had. He hasn't worn them in . . .'

'Doesn't matter, doesn't matter. He can stand without them. Just to stand will be good. Come on, get ready. You guide his feet.'

I am kneeling on the floor and holding my father's feet inches off the ground. Matthew was prepared to do this without me, but now that I am here he thinks the resolution of the problem is all the more certain. My father will stand, he will begin his recovery here.

But my father groans louder and there is something fierce and frightened in the sound now and it opens in me a wound I will feel still years later. He moans and uses all his energy to rock himself back and forth on the edge of the bed as though this will save him. Crossed over in front of himself his arms shake stiffly.

'Now,' Matthew says and lifts him with a jolt. I guide the cold feet to the floor and hold them there, as though some reverse gravity operates and if I let go my father will float upward off the ground. He is a sagging figure held in place. His head has fallen forward so that when I look up I see his crown lowered as if he bows. The long wings of silvered hair over his ears are awry. Just then his eye catches mine, and again seems to ask me to save him, to make this stop. But I cannot. I think I partly believe Matthew is right, that it is rational, that perhaps he will stand. Perhaps it will be like those moments in films when the shattered glass is returned to itself as the sequence runs backward. I want to believe it, that some such rewind can happen, and we can be as we were once in a simpler time long ago.

'You are right now, you are standing, get your breath,' Matthew tells my father. He stands beside him with his arms hooped around him. The old man's chest is working in short sharp gasps, each one an effort, and it occurs to me then that he is about to have a heart attack.

'Matthew, he wants to lie down, let him back on the bed again.'

'No, no, give him a minute to feel right, he hasn't stood up in so long that he'll be dizzy, he'll have forgotten what it's like.'

So we speak across my father about him. He tries to say something to Matthew but Matthew is not listening. I kneel and hold my father's feet. I look down so as not to risk catching his eye again and study details of the wooden floor, places chipped and scored, fragments of dirt, crumbs of biscuit, the pool of 7Up.

'Now take a few steps,' I hear Matthew say. 'Help him, Jim. Ready?'

And it is a scene nightmarish and grim and endlessly haunting, the scene in the cluttered little bedroom at the end of summer. The father knows he cannot walk and does not want to. But his sons make him.

It is not quite walking. Matthew pulls our father forward in a great lurch and I move his feet. And then again. There is no sense at all of any participation on the old man's part, but in fact the opposite. Anger is thrashing and beating around inside of him but finds no release. I know this. There must be rage, but it burns only along the fuses of his mind and behind his eyes, for his body as an instrument of expression is useless to him now. We are in control of it and move him a step and then another. Our father shakes his head and keeps on shaking it.

'Stop,' Matthew tells him, 'stop it, concentrate on walking.' His tone is harsh and snaps like a belt in the air and I wish I had never come into the room or could get him to stop now. But I already know that scenes and chapters end with their own inevitability and that I move my father's feet toward it as if it is already written, fated. My father's moans become continuous, but Matthew is not listening. My brother has a surety and faith that seem not human, that match action and reaction in a modus of mechanical precision. I look up to see his face, the fixed focus of his eyes and extraordinary composure.

'Now, you see,' he is saying, 'you can get up, you can move about, you can stand. You can, look.'

And with that he removes his arms from around my father, and it is a gesture out of travelling theatre, the magician standing back to reveal the miracle. There should be a clarion of trumpets, a flash of light and puff of smoke and a burst of applause.

I move my hands an inch away from my father's feet.

And he comes crashing down on top of me. His head hits the floor and there is a terrible crack.

'Jesus,' Matthew says.

I am knocked sideways and turn and see the lump of my father and the blood on his head.

'Feck's sake,' Matthew says.

The door opens and my mother cries out. Her hands fly to her face. Briefly she cannot move, but stands assembling the sharp pieces of what she sees. Matthew is furious now. His calculation had not been wrong, the logic and reasoning were true, but have been ruined by the stubbornness of our father. He reaches down and holds the old man's shoulder.

'You didn't even try,' he says.

'Matthew!' my mother shouts at him. 'Stop it!'

'He did try,' I say. 'Dad, are you all right?'

My father's eyes are blinking rapidly. There is a cut on the top of his head and blood and saliva leaking from his mouth.

'He didn't try and stand. There is no reason why he shouldn't,' Matthew is telling my mother as she swiftly kneels and lifts my father's head in her hands and cradles him.

'Leave,' she says.

Matthew doesn't.

'Leave, Matthew,' she says again.

He makes a move to bend down and help her lift my father back to the bed, but she turns to him and says loud and sharp. 'No! Go! Now!' And there is a sudden fierceness in her leaning across my father's body as though protecting him from us. And in that moment I think I see something of how she loves him. I think I come to understand that she does not resent at all caring for him, or the fact that she has become his servant. Because in some way she is relieved, that here at last has come a means whereby she can demonstrate her gratitude and love for his rescuing her all those years before. She believes that there is redemption here, is certain that God has provided this fallen man so that she might atone by giving the rest of her days to him.

'Leave, get out,' she says.

I go to the door. Matthew does not move. He looks down at the heap that is my father and slowly shakes his head in disgust.

'Feck's sake,' he mutters and turns and walks out of the room.

And he goes further than that too, although perhaps we do not realize it yet. For the two days he remains at home there is a bitter sharpness in the air, as though we have swallowed leaves of holly. Matthew says nothing. I come into his bedroom and stand and ask him what time he is going back to Dublin.

'Six.'

'Are you not staying until the morning?'

'No.' He reaches in his pocket and takes out a packet of cigarettes and lights one.

And just that, because I do not know he smokes and because of the casual careless way he does it, lets me know more than anything that my brother is gone somewhere. And I am paused half in fear and half wanting to follow.

'Dad's OK,' I say. 'He has a cut, but he's OK.'

'He could stand. Doesn't want to, that's all. He's going to kill her.'

'I don't think . . . I think maybe . . . maybe she . . . Well, I don't know.'

The smoke rises. Matthew has more to say but will not say it now. There are words tight and loaded like bullets on a belt inside him.

'I will be in Dublin in two weeks,' I tell him, 'I can't believe it.'

'Yeah.'

I am waiting for him to say something to me, to offer me something the way an older brother might, reaching back across the difference in age to draw the younger one across. I am thinking of brothers in books I have read, but mine is not like them. I want to tell him things. I want to say as I have to no one yet what happened with Helen. I want to say her name out loud and give the whole story: how after I fainted in the street I was brought home and put to bed and had McHale come and nod at me. How one day my mother brought me an opened envelope that had been delivered to the door by Helen, and in it were my poems with no letter or note. How she studied my face so briefly and then went to open the window and let in the air. How one week later I saw Helen at Mass and stood outside the church gates where she passed me by without word or gesture, leaving the town two days later to go and study hotel management in London because that was where her boyfriend was. I want to tell Matthew all of this. Twisted inside the cabling of my motives is the desire to let him know that I am no longer a small boy, that he should think of me as an equal, a friend.

On the bed he smokes his cigarette. I watch him study the smoke, as if it unreels like a film, complex and intricate and almost beyond interpretation.

That evening Matthew walks out of the house and takes the bus to Dublin. He does not say goodbye to my mother or father or me.

*

When I see him again it is my first week of university. I have left home for the first time. There has been a little scene in which I tried to speak to my mother in Matthew's defence. 'I know it was not your idea,' she said, holding her own hands. 'You are gentle.' And I thought she would cry then, but she just shook her head a couple of times and went to work the sewing machine. I entered my father's bedroom when he was sleeping. I watched his face in repose and thought I saw there a look of complete resignation and surrender, as if he knew we were all lost to him now, there was none of us left to rescue, no cable to connect. I thought then to go and get some of the books I had stolen and that were hidden behind my bed. But I didn't. I walked away and did not wake him.

Now I am in Dublin, come to study English and French literature and begin properly my journey to become a writer. I am taking French because of my grades, because I love the sound of it, the delicacy and beauty that seem to underlie even the simplest phrases, because I have heard of Rimbaud from the songs of Van Morrison and Bob Dylan, and because it is foreign. I love to say words in French and make connections within their music, *visage*, *paysage*. I have enormous dreams like fabulous creatures made of silk inside of me. They rise and billow and at times in those first days I feel my feet hardly touch the ground. *I am here, I am away.* I am away from the endless lonely fields and the brown bogs and the smells of cattle and tractor fumes. I am in the city of James Joyce. And even as I say that to myself, so the squalid dirty grey face of Dublin is hidden from me and I do not notice the grim wan look of the crowds passing over O' Connell Bridge or little swirls of rubbish, paper bags, bottle tops, cigarette wrappers, that fly around my feet on the wind. I walk across St Stephen's Green. I go straightaway to the bookshops, to Greene's and Hodges & Figgis, and I stand inside the doors and look at the shelves. In a kind of quiet rapture then I pick up books and hold them and smell the smell of words unread. I believe, I think, in some undiscovered law of proximity, that there is an element of alchemical magic, and that simply being there in the places of writing and writers is the first step in my own transformation.

I am staying in a room in a house in Rathmines belonging to Mrs Emily Haddington. She has buried her husband and lost what she calls her boys to America. She does not say how long ago this is, but she herself is over sixty, and might be seventy. She is a frail construct of decorum and old gentility. She does not appear in the mornings until her face is made. She wears dresses of printed flowers and a looped string of pearls and chooses her shoes to match. Only the whiff of gin betrays her. Some mornings she does not arrive in the kitchen at all and the four of us that live in her house, two Galway engineers, a Wicklow student of commerce and myself, sit around the family table and then one by one go and rummage for food. The two engineers do not hesitate. They pull open drawers and presses and leave a scrambled mess behind them. When we see Mrs Haddington again, she nonetheless offers apologies to each of us like so many folded linen napkins. Her eyes are lost in puffy purses she has painted blue.

'So sorry, dear, you see, I suffer dreadfully with migraines.'

Mee-Grains, she sounds them, and at first I do not know what this is, and imagine some kind of indigestible grit of self.

Me-Grains. Standing in front of her I play with the word and my mind is taken with it and not with sympathy.

'You all managed, did you, dear?'

She does not really wait for a reply but moves gently away through the house, her two hands slightly out at either side as if expectant of a fall.

The halls and corridors and each of the rooms of 44 Penworth Ave., Rathmines, have the same air of slow but inexorable decay as their owner. Mr Haddington was a solicitor of some importance, we have been told, a man who loved his hunting and fishing in Oughterard. But throughout his house now wallpapers of ducks and ponds, of salmon leaping, of red squirrels and idyllic woodlands are all peeling. In the wardrobes there is the smell of mothballs and from the old wooden coat hangers that have been left by the Haddington sons, the ghost scent of waxed jackets and fishing gear. At the end of the corridor behind a woodwormed door Mr Haddington's bath is footed, its enamel cracked in a lightning fork.

My own room is painted a deep green and is high-ceilinged with a window to the tree-lined avenue. There is a small table whose Formica top has been chipped away at the two corners out from the wall, and the soft timber beneath is scored from a thousand idle hours with criss-crossings of blue ink. The bed's springs play a doleful music of struggle and ache as I lie there and read from my reading list on the first days before starting university. There is a fat tome of poetry that covers almost a millennium and in this I pass the afternoons, falling in and out of brief sleeps to the composed cadences. I skip the poets I do not like. I dismiss Pope and Dryden and much of the eighteenth century. I like Shakespeare, Wyatt, Marvell. Above all I like Donne. I believe I find the ring of truth in his poems, even when it seems he is being merely clever. I read everything by him in the book, even some verses that are tedious and obscure, and study the portrait of him with dark eyes and sensuous mouth and a wide-brimmed hat. As the first autumn afternoons fold softly into evenings outside, I read the love poems first, 'Lovers' Infiniteness', 'Love's Alchemy', 'Love's Deity', 'Love's Diet', 'Love's Exchange', 'Love's Growth', 'Love's Usury', among others, and afterward his religious sonnets. And here is God again. It has been many years since I was that boy speaking to God in my own language, many years since I dismissed Him as a figure either deaf or uninterested. But in the religious sonnets of John Donne I discover again a sense of a personal God, one who can be addressed and beseeched and chastised as anyone else, who *exists*. There is such confidence in the tone of the poems that even though Donne decries his own weakness of belief or depth of despair, I still feel he has faith he is being heard. The poems are a revelation to me. I am a week in Dublin and waiting to meet my brother. I know no one, have no friends and cannot seem to mix with the other students in the house. So I go into the city and browse in the bookshops and come home and lie on the bed and read, and in that way enter a kind of other world outside of time and place, where there are only the poets and God and me.

There is a knock on the door. It is evening and I have fallen asleep reading 'The Lamentations of Jeremy'. Rain is running down the dark rectangle of the window.

'Are you there? Someone here for you, dear.'

Matthew is waiting downstairs in the sitting room. He is standing by the fireplace and lifting one of the china dogs when I walk in.

'Matthew.'

'Well.'

He seems again entirely different to me. He seems older. His hair is cut short now and he wears a thick overcoat like a man of forty. He looks at the fireplace, at the pictures on the wall.

'Here you are,' he says.

'Yes.'

'No so bad.'

'No, no it's fine.'

'Bit stuffy.'

'It's all right. I have a good room, do you want to see it?'

'Let's go out.'

I get my coat. We go out the front door and down the steps like gentlemen. Matthew has an umbrella and we stand sheltered a moment as he decides the way. I am in a deep fold of contentment then. I am not thinking of the scene with my father or the manner in which Matthew last left home. I am not going to speak of it. Instead I am thinking of Pip and Herbert Pocket and scenes in London when fellows walk out beneath the street lamps on their way to sit and talk in clubs, fellows with hats and gloves and all the time in the world.

'Down here,' Matthew says.

The leaves on the chestnut trees are falling and fallen. The rain pulls them down and the path is already smoothly plastered with their dead shapes, dark and pointed like black stars. Few cars come along the avenue. We walk without talking and arrive at Keogh's pub on the corner of the Sandford Road. Entering it is like moving inside some uncle's comfortable old coat where the smells of beer and smoke and living swirl around you at once and hold you closely. There is a brownish fog in the air and an out-of-time chorus of voices. Fifty men have their backs to us.

'What will you have?' Matthew asks loudly.

'Nothing really, I'm fine.'

'What? Go on, what do you want?' And after a beat, the withering moment: 'I don't care, I'm not going to tell anyone.'

'Just a Coke, be fine, thanks.'

'Coke?'

'Yes, thanks.'

'Sit over there. Be back in a minute.'

I watch him go up to the counter, and feel a mixture of awe and revelation at his ease as he commands a Jameson whiskey for himself and a Coke for his brother, and returns bearing them before him through the crowd.

'Here. One Coke.'

I try not to watch him drink the whiskey, but there is a kind of compulsion in me and I notice everything about him: the way he takes it inside his mouth with a kind of delicious desperation, how it seems a sort of sour medicine to him.

He takes another swallow and holding the glass leans forward and says, 'Jim, how are you fixed for cash?'

I am so surprised by the question, it takes me an instant. I am touched that Matthew should be so concerned for me. I lean toward him. 'I'm all right. I'm fine, thanks.'

'No. That's great. But that's not what I mean. I mean, you've got plenty, right?'

'I haven't spent a thing, only on the books.'

'Good.' He turns the glass with its last golden remnant and studies it. 'You know I'm going to be finished soon now?'

'Yes. You'll have your degree.'

'Degree's not worth a feck.' He sees my surprise at his tone, and as if he has misstepped he softens his voice. 'It's a piece of paper,' he says. 'Nothing. But listen, soon I'll be out of here and I'll have plenty of cash myself, right?'

'Right.'

'Yes. Only right now you see I have this opportunity.'

Matthew has dropped his voice and I cannot quite hear him over the noise. I have felt the tone of secrecy and revelation in his voice and do not want him to repeat what he is saying out loud. I nod and press my face further forward.

'I won't go into it,' he is saying. 'You wouldn't understand it. Hardly anyone would. It's complicated. Only it's a great opportunity to make a good bit of money. And quickly. You know?'

'OK.'

'Yes, so, I'm kind of caught, you see. I've used up the last of what funds I have.'

'What about the college, wouldn't they maybe . . .'

'No.'

'Maybe you could give classes . . .'

'Look. The fecking college won't give you anything. They don't care if you've passed every fecking exam they've set, they don't care if you know more than half the bloody professors and all the textbooks put together, they'll give you nothing but a piece of paper at the end of it. None of them know anything about the real world, anyway. You know?'

He looks up at me quickly. I have never heard him speak like this before, but take it as evidence of my arrival in the adult world now. I hold my Coke and say, 'Sure. Yes.'

He drinks the last of the whiskey.

'The real world, Jim, is a lot fecking harder than the one you make up in your head. Let me tell you that. The real world doesn't give the steam off a cow's piss whether you can pass exams or not. That whole business is just a game, a way for some old feckers to make money, you know?'

I am not sure if he stops to hear my response or not, whether it is a test to see if I am an ally or not. I don't know and so I don't answer, and he stands abruptly and, muttering some word I do not catch, goes up to the bar. I watch him slice through the crowd and then I turn and study my half-glass of Coke, trying to assemble the pieces of this new vision of the world and of my brother in it. What does he want the money for? How much can I give him? I am flushed in the heat of a hundred concerns. I am the fellow who spent the afternoon lying on his bed reading the religious poetry of John Donne. I am not prepared for this. But I want more than anything to be an equal with my brother and by the time Matthew returns with another whiskey and another Coke I have decided I can spare him fifty pounds.

He sits down.

'Here. Coke.'

'Thanks.'

Neither of us speaks for a little while. When I glance at Matthew's face I see the look of abstraction he sometimes gets when he seems to be studying whole strata of calculations and their permutations, one beyond the next, and each reducing toward some final absolute. He seems to see the world in such formulae, to believe that for every problem there is a true and perfect solution, and that life is only that, a series of such problems. He takes a swallow of his drink.

'What are you going to do, Matthew, when you . . .'

'What?' He turns to me and seems to come unwillingly back from a distance. 'I'll be gone. This is a hole, Dublin. I used to think back home, you know, can't wait to get up here, all that. God, when you think of it, but it's just as fecking backward, as small-minded and cheap and . . .'

He shakes his head then and smiles a sour smile. He looks away again and lifts the whiskey to his mouth.

'I can give you a hundred,' I say.

'Can you?'

'Yes. Definitely. No problem.'

'That's a start.'

I had thought there would be a feeling of celebration, of triumph, and of closeness then between us. But there is almost a grimace as Matthew says thanks, and it is as though the offer itself is a kind of defeat. He says nothing more after that. He sits, the life gone out of him, and the noise of the bar comes over us and there is nothing left but to wait and finish our drinks and then to walk back to my flat where I go upstairs and get the money and give it to him as we stand inside the hallway at the front door. Matthew takes it, does not look at or count it. He makes a kind of shrug, and then turns and is gone beneath the street lights and the rain.

*

From the distance of my bedroom in the village in County Clare I had imagined university to be that hushed reverential place it was in the novels I had read. Not quite domes and spires, but a kind of island of the intellect, a cathedral where those of pure and passionate mind came to further their education before going to change the world. I had read the list of faculties and subjects of which I knew nothing, and been in awe. Here were professors of all things, experts who had devoted their lives to singular subjects and were in a way priests of their realm. I imagined when I entered university I would enter a world separate from the squalid and mundane one that featured on the evening news. I would pass through the doors into a pure domain of ideas, of debate and discourse, of finely focused considerations and points of dispute. Studying English literature I expected to meet those like me for whom the poems and novels they had read had lit a fire in their heads, I imagined those that came from all over the country to sit in lecture halls and hear about Shakespeare or Blake or Eliot or Donne would be ones already inspired in some way, and come to feed a restless hunger for more.

On the first morning of lectures I leave Mrs Haddington's and cycle to the university. The campus is new then and lies sprawled like a child's awkwardly joined construction. The faculties are in separate buildings and signal their own importance with large signs, suggesting that each is its own kingdom, that Engineers will have nothing to do with Scientists and they in turn will shun those dilettantes who study Arts.

The initial lectures are held in large tiered theatres. When I stand for the first time inside the doorway and look down and see the hundred and so students and hear the excited encircling buzz of talk in the moments before the lecturer appears, I feel a kind of exultation. I have never in my life felt part of any group, other than the gathering of writers' ghosts that linger in bookshops. But there that morning I feel I belong. Some students are busy in conversation with those next to them, others, sitting alone and looking expectantly to the empty podium, wait with pens in hands for the professor to come and the doors of knowledge to open.

It takes a few weeks, maybe a month, for the brightness of my innocence to dim. By the cold mornings of November I am already skipping lectures. I only have to attend two each day, but still manage to miss more than half of them. In English there are few professors or lecturers who come to the theatre with any passion or fire. There is Jim O'Malley, and Michael Paul Gallagher and Declan Kiberd and few others. But more common are those dry figures of toneless voice who enter from the side and draw out their notes and proceed to dull the eyes and minds of those looking down at them. They progress like wallpaperers, covering everything with a grey paste of critical analysis and reducing the achievements of writers to aspects of Form and Style. They do not care if the students talk or walk out or lay down their heads to sleep. They take no heed of the evidence of their own tedium but pass on through the pages of their lecture, creating layers of dead words that bury any interest or enthusiasm that might exist.

I attend a class on Dickens and the Nineteenth-Century Novel. I have been looking forward to it and cycle across the Saturday-morning rain as though travelling to meet a favourite relation that has been a long time away. I know my Dickens well. He has been the long-time companion of my boyhood and youth, and books like *Great Expectations* and *David Copperfield* have *mattered* to me in a way I cannot explain to anyone. But I believe that if anyone understands and shares this love, they will be found in the university. I come into Theatre L. There is a scattering of students there. Some, strategists of education, have already studied the previous exam papers and decided that it is not necessary to answer on the nineteenth century. All that reading can be avoided, and the time better spent intensively covering more narrow topics where marks will be easily garnered. I do not care. In a way it is better that the theatre is not filled. I sit in an empty row and soon a grey-haired man with a grey moustache comes through the side door to the podium. He seems not to notice that we are there and rummages in his bag until he finds his notes. When he has these he taps the sides of the pages twice and then without looking up begins to read in monotone.

'Dickens,' he says 'is, we might say, the great conman of the nineteenth-century novel, the crowd-pleaser, the entertainer, the sentimentalist. While the modern sensibility shudders at some of the indulgences of his work and the unrelieved sentimentality of novels such as *Oliver Twist, Little Nell,* the Christmas stories, and so on, the phenomenon of his mass success is nonetheless important to consider in the light of the development of the English novel. Our interest here is less in the works themselves and their clever manipulation of the hearts and minds of the English public and more on the episodic form, the impact of serialization, and the role of the novelist as social reformer. A novel like *Great Expectations* is less significant to us for the study in the development of those nineteenth-century pillars of character and plot, which, after all, are quite mechanical here – the orphan, the inheritance, the progress from the country to the city, the reversal, and so forth – but rather for the way Dickens treats money and class and what he seems to be manipulating his characters into trying to say to what was by that time a captive audience.'

And so on the lecturer drones. Almost at once I abandon taking any notes and a kind of fury builds out of the hurt in me. I sit flush-faced and look around at the students taking down each word he says. What is the matter with them? I am hot and angry. Another might stand up and shout down at the lecturer, another might argue or heckle or make noise, but in me all words go unsaid and twist and whirl behind my eyes like sparks rising up from a blaze. I say nothing, I sit and burn until the lecture ends when I rise quickly and hurry up the steps.

Outside the corridors and halls are empty. Those not taking lectures are gone across the clear perspex tunnel to the library. I am the white-faced long-haired student in a worn green coat. I am the silent down-looking youth inside whose mind boils that strange brew of pure arrogance and terrible shyness. I walk through the corridors and then turn up one of the stairwells. I go to the third floor and pass the closed offices of the English professors. I walk on through Linguistics and Arabic and Music and mount a final stairway to the small quiet wing where older students take classes for masters'. There is no one around; I sink down onto the floor. Words, sounds, a kind of rhythm, beat in my temples. I nod my head slightly. And some doorway of release opens in the front of my mind and I hear myself mutely say the phrase, '*What are you that here beget the death of dreams?*'

The words are in my head. It is as if they have a pre-existence and that there are others just beyond my consciousness. To reach them I say the phrase over and over, running it to its end to invite the next one across the rim.

> *What are you that here beget the death of dreams,*
> *And take from love the air of . . .*

The phrase comes in part and then ruptures. I say it over. I am finding a kind of pulse and in the place of the missing words I make soft noises that fit the beat, as though the frequency is slightly tuned out and soon I will be able to modulate it. I work at it, making sounds in gaps where the words should be. And, although I could not explain why to anyone, it is to me then the most central, most important thing in the world. It is almost as though if I can get the words right, if I can get the thing said, in the sounds that are right for it, I will in some way be . . . what? becalmed? repaired? redeemed?

I work at it through the afternoon. The light falls away. I make progress through eight lines by the time the lights come on below.

When I cycle back through the rain to the house Matthew is waiting. Mrs Haddington is standing in the hallway in a pink dressing gown with a string of pearls around her neck. Matthew is smoking a cigarette, something she does not allow in her sitting room, but she does not like to say so to the gentleman, she tells me. She is perched outside the room like a nervous bird.

'He is my brother, Mrs Haddington.'

'Oh, I know.'

'Yes. I'll take him out now. I'll tell him about the smoking.'

'If you wouldn't mind.'

'No, I will.'

'Thank you so much. It's just you see that Mr Hadding–'

'It's all right, Mrs Haddington.'

'You are such a gentleman, and you're soaked through, poor boy. Go on. Up to your room and change.' Her eyes blink. She smiles at me kindly.

'Good boy, Alexander, I'll put on the kettle,' she says and turns and moves away down the hall to make tea for her returned son.

I go in to Matthew who gets up at once and in haste looks about for somewhere to stab out the cigarette and at the same time takes my arm and is leading me back out the door.

'Come on,' he says, 'let's get out of here before the old bat comes back.'

We go out again into the rain. Matthew raises his umbrella and when I stoop in beneath it I can smell the whiskey. We bump awkwardly along down the path, not quite in step, splitting apart in places where trees and hedges reach out, coming half together again. Matthew is agitated more than I have ever seen him. There seems a whirring clockwork racing inside him. He lifts the umbrella high to look for the pub.

'Where is this fecking place? Down here. I thought it was right here.' An overhead branch forks the umbrella. 'Shite.' He wrestles it free but the fabric is holed and two of the rods are broken loose.

'It is,' I tell him, 'it's just over there.'

'We're wet anyway,' Matthew says and pitches the umbrella into a garden.

We get into the pub and the scene from before replays itself. There is the same brown crowd, the same fug of smoke and beer and noise, the same pause as I sit at the table and wait while Matthew shoulders to the bar. I still have the half-poem inside my pocket. I plan to tell my brother about it.

Matthew comes to the table with a double round of drinks cradled against his chest and at once my plan disappears. He puts the Cokes in front of me and sits and taps his right hand against his chest for the cigarettes. He stiffens the length of himself and angles slightly to fish the lighter from his trouser pocket. Even in the way he snap-lights the flame I read his impatience. The world is too slow for him. Everything labours in such an elephantine manner. We are all so many steps behind. He sucks and blows the smoke. He runs his tongue on the inside of his teeth. His eyes are studying the room, and when this is done he looks at an array of fast-changing ideas that are chalked and erased and chalked and erased on a board just to his right. He studies them, he smokes, he comes forward and drinks the whiskey.

'Listen, Jim,' he says. He looks around anxiously, as though there are eavesdroppers. 'You know that money?'

'It doesn't matter, Matthew, I'm fine.'

'No, but . . . Shite. It's . . . Well that's great, no that's great. It's not that. No. I mean you will get it back, and thanks but . . .' He pauses, he considers me for a minute, considers if I am capable of understanding what he knows to be the truth about the world. He takes another drink. His left hand comes up and scratches the side of his face as though something burns there. 'Feck. People are so thick, do you know?'

'Yes.'

'Do you know the laws of probability?'

'Not really.'

He pauses a minute. He will say no more to me. He will leave it go, but then whatever clicks and turns wildly inside him requires release, and he shakes his head as though in response to the argument of an invisible other. He is hearing or saying something in his mind and for a moment it is as though I am not there. Then suddenly he sees me again and makes a bitter smile. 'People fecking think the world is like this,' he says and holds up his right hand with the cigarette, 'and that if it turns it will turn like this nine times out of ten, and then end up like this.' He moves his hand through the air in an arc and turn. 'And in fact, they're wrong. It's not. It's not at all. Imagine. Imagine the whole idea a fecking mistake. But they're too small-minded to see it. It's like this.' He raises his left hand. 'You know?'

I have not the slightest idea what he means.

'Yes,' I say. I am looking at his eyes. I am seeing there something I had not seen before, the glimmer of a kind of madness.

He leans forward to tell me more, he might enlighten me, he might save me now.

'You know the whole fecking idea.'

'What?'

'The whole game. You know, you grow up, get some bloody job, work for a miserable pittance, slave away in a fecking concrete box, head down eyes down, never mind days weeks months passing, do some menial bloody stupid nonsense for hours, finish, go out, sit in traffic, go home, some crappy little cheap thin-walled fecking dump estate, pay the mortgage, pay the pension, pay every fecking penny to something or other, fall knackered asleep, and then what?' He drops his voice to a whisper, he takes a last draw on the cigarette. 'You wake up, you do the same thing over again.'

He leans back and shakes his head scornfully. His lips are drawn tightly together as if he holds there a mouthful of thorns.

'That,' he says. 'That's the world of our father. And look where it got him. I'm not going to do that.'

'You won't have to,' I tell him, and hear myself sound like his older brother. 'You have your degree, you can work in–'

'Do you know the kind of idiot work they have mathematicians do? Do you know the bloody waste people make of their lives, people with brilliant . . . people who could solve any fecking equation, formula, code there is? Shite jobs, that's what they have them do. They don't want people to be brilliant, they don't. People hate brilliance, hate it, makes them uneasy and inadequate, they feel all awkward. What they want are the smart boys all right, but not too smart, someone dependable, you know?'

He leans forward and begins the second whiskey.

'No thanks,' he says, 'no thanks very much. I'm not going to do that.'

I do not know what to say to him. We sit there either side of a gulf. When he speaks again his voice and manner have lost their edge as the whiskey turns inside him.

'Listen, don't worry about any of that,' he says. 'Don't worry.'

'I won't.'

'You're good, right?'

'Yes.'

'Good.' He pauses. 'You'll be fine, Jim.'

'Thanks.'

Another pause.

'You don't want anything, you're OK with the Coke?'

'Yes, no, I'm fine, thanks, Matthew.'

'Good. That's good.'

He swallows a few times with difficulty as if something inside him keeps rising against his wishes.

'Anyway, Jim,' he says. 'I wanted to see you.'

'I'm glad.'

'Yes.' He stops and is looking at me the way you look back from the growing distance of a ship pulling away into deeper waters.

'I'm going away for a while.'

'Where?'

'England.'

I sit there, astonished. I say nothing.

'Soon. I'm going soon. You can let the folks know.' He is not looking at me now. He is studying the empty glasses on the table.

'Have you something got? I mean . . .'

'Jim. Jim jim jim,' he says softly, gently rowing away. His eyes come to mine and they are glassy and full. 'It's all right, little brother. It's all right.' He smiles. 'Come on, I'll walk back with you.'

And we go out into the night then where the rain has stopped falling and the hedgerows and bare trees drip drops of after-rain and the cars move in slow doleful parade. We walk without speaking and are sometimes side by side and sometimes not. My brother moves now with less haste, his urgency slowed in the alcohol in his bloodstream and the things he wants to say softly muted. The dark above us is without stars. We are shadows turning into shadows. When we reach the steps of the house Matthew stops and looks down at his shoes and gives a small laugh.

'Don't mind what I was saying,' he says. 'Just blowing off steam, you know.' He looks at me and then cannot seem to hold my eyes and turns and his teeth catch his bottom lip. 'Listen, by the way, you don't happen to have . . .?'

I do not let him suffer the full question for I know what is coming.

'Sure. Hold on.' And I go up the stairs to my room and take all the money I have and bring it back to him.

Like a cavalier he takes it without looking to see if it is ten pounds or twenty or a hundred and pushes it inside his coat pocket.

'You're sure?' he asks.

'Yes. No problem.'

'Thanks.'

We stand there for what seems a long long time, but is only instants.

'You'll be fine,' he tells me.

'Yeah. Thanks.'

'You will.'

'So will you,' I say. 'You'll call me?'

And he makes again the small down-looking laugh and turns his shoe on the fallen leaves that floor the ground. And then he is gone.

*

He is not there at Christmas when I go home. I come with baggage of revelations and epiphanies, as though from a Russian circus with white doves fluttering inside my bag. I have so much I could release, but on the bus journey westward across the country I feel my spirit close up and lock. As the towns slide past in grey splashes, Portlaoise, Borris-in-Ossory, Roscrea, Nenagh, Limerick, I seem to be returning to a prison behind the bars of the rain. How can I tell what has happened to me, of days spent missing all lectures and lost in the drift of imagery and rhythm, of the poetry of Yeats, Donne, Thomas, Wyatt, Spenser, Stevens,

Eliot? To my parents, and I imagine to all who lived in the village, the listing of such names would be no different than place-names recounted by someone who had returned from a foreign holiday. They would be listened to and indulged, but with the sense that they were without bearing in the real world. And perhaps thinking this, thinking this is no country for poetry or magic, by the time the bus arrives in the village I have decided to reveal nothing at all.

My father is in the bed where I left him. He shows no signs of any improvement. He has some words but will not say them, for they come wobbling like bent bicycle wheels. He hears himself and is disgusted and halfway through the sound tries to spit or snap shut his mouth to catch the word before it rolls away. He is a work of spasms and reflexes, of lowering eyebrows, flickering eyelashes, an orchestrated twitching of his mouth as whole volumes of things he wishes to say pass up from their source and arrive in his face. None of them reach the air. Instead, as his saying of them fails, the silent words play in the muscles of his face and in the pale blue of his eyes until they settle again and he lies there in a resigned peace once more.

My mother comes and goes from him, with quiet attentiveness. Sometimes her arms possess a wild jerkiness and she reaches and holds herself, or her shoulder rises on one side as if she is about to dance off into some imaginary wings and she lifts the side of her face with a pained expression and tightens her lips until the instant passes and she is herself once more. On the day before Christmas I am sitting in the chair beside my father's bed. My mother comes in and apologizes for disturbing me though I have not being speaking.

'I'm sorry, Jim, I must tidy up your father.'

I go to stand up.

'You don't have to leave if you don't want to.'

She has a basin of hot water and some cloths and there is the strong smell of eucalyptus.

'Now, love,' she says.

I can discern no reaction from my father.

She dips the cloth in the hot water and I watch the steam rise up her arms.

'Hot,' she says, and then, adds, 'he likes it hot. If it isn't hot, it won't do.'

Then she lifts the cloth and squeezes and brings it to my father's face. When she takes it away again his skin is pinked and his eyes wide. I think she has revived him. And it comes to me that this is to be a little operation of resurrection, that here I will watch my mother inch my father back from death. She lathers the brush in the shaving bowl and brings it to him, bending down and leaning forward as though her eyes are untrustworthy. The first stroke she makes is across his upper lip. She dips and lathers, dips and lathers and paints. She works the white foamed cream over his face and is careful not to get it on the lobes of his ears or the tip of his nose. When he is perfectly bearded in white she stands upright and her right hand goes to the small of her back and she says, 'Now.'

Just that. Nothing more. *Now*.

For an instant I do not know if she is speaking to me or summoning the miracle. She looks at him. And the moment translates itself into me and becomes an expression of love in a language I do not yet fully understand. I watch her take his cut-throat razor and see the window flash upon it as she brings it across to the bed. Then she leans forward and, because there is a trembling in her hand, she begins to shave him with absolute concentration and care.

And it does not escape me, the pity and love and mercy of this scene, this unmaking of Santa Claus as the white beard of foam vanishes and from beneath it the face of a younger man seems to appear. Nor does it escape me that it is the day before Christmas and another of our family is gone, that down on the kitchen window sill is the card from Matthew sending best wishes. I think I feel the presence of the ghost of my dead sister, Louise, and the one of myself as a boy, and perhaps even that of my father as the face of himself years earlier seems to be revealed like a painting beneath my mother's loving hand. All such enter me that day and lodge in that part of my heart where regret and grief and yearning lie waiting for a salve. I sit there. I do not say anything. I do not offer to help my mother shave my father, for I think it would seem an intrusion on this most delicate of dances between them. I sit in the small bedroom. I absorb the details, the grey light of the afternoon, the quiet in the country outside, the sense there is of all being in preparation for Christmas. And with one knee raised to lean on the bed, my mother follows with the blade the lines of my father's face.

*

I return to university three days before I need to. There is something in me that cannot bear to remain at home. I know that I could stay and take a job in the post office, that I do not need to get a university degree, and that then I would be on hand to help with my father. My mother would not ask me this. I think she would not want me to do it, but if I insisted she would be glad. These things have run through my head over Christmas, but I cannot stay. I tell my mother I have to return early to get back to my studies, I forgot to bring home some books I need and should go back now and get working. She nods at me. She makes brown bread and scones and wraps them in the inside bag from the cornflakes box. She gives them to me as I am going out the door and I take them but am embarrassed and leave them under the seat on the bus when I arrive in Dublin.

In Mrs Haddington's house there is only her and myself. She had thought her boys might be home, but business, she says. *Business, dear, you know.* She comes and sits across the table from me in the big kitchen. The wound clock ticks loudly three hours the wrong time. She does not eat anything but only drinks tea in a china cup. Her hair is thinned and grey, the colour washed out of it and not replaced. In places her scalp appears through it. Over Christmas I do not think she has been out of her dressing gown.

Her face is made up and her pearls are at the thin cords of her neck, but her pink slippers are blackened and threadbare. There is no food in any of the cupboards. She does not care to eat. *Thank you, dear, for asking. You are a gentle soul.* We sit in the great emptiness of the house. Winds of gale force come across the Irish Sea and for a day it seems we are in a ship creaking in every timber. Windows whistle, sashes rattle. It seems a season of penitence and scourge and not celebration. The knocker on the hall door is lifted and dropped and a hundred times taps with ghosts. Above us, slates are picked off the roof and fly in mad twists down into the garden.

While the storm continues I go to my room and read. I read all the hours of the day. I read Yeats. I pay little attention if any to what is happening in the country. I do not seem to notice the great social change I will read later is happening then in Irish society. I know nothing of debates about Europe and neutrality. I hear the news of Northern Ireland and the protest marches and the bombs and sometimes glimpse the faces talking on the television, but somehow I am adrift of them all. I am in another country, one inhabited by Lady Gregory and Maud Gonne and William Butler Yeats. I read him until his rhythms enter my head and beat and declaim there. It is a kind of delirium. Reading poetry for hours on end, falling into half-sleeps, blurring moments when the divide between waking and dreaming does not exist and I cannot say if the line in my head is one I have read or invented. While Dublin is huddled beneath the whips of the January wind, I do not go outside. I live in the house with Mrs Haddington. I stand at the window and look out on the morning traffic crawling into the city in the rain and I think of what my brother said about what people are doing with their lives. All that is dull and grey and wrapped in drear nauseates me; the mealy-mouthed, the brown-coated, the fag-smoking, sniffling, phlegm-raking, shuffling, slouching. This is not the world where I belong, I think. I will not be a part of it. I lie on the bed and read the poems.

One evening I come down to the kitchen and bring the *Selected Poetry* of Yeats with me. I am alone at the table reading with a mug of tea and a buttered slice of stale bread when Mrs Haddington comes in. She sees me reading and walks around to the sink where she runs the water in the kettle. She puts it on the hot plate where the drips soon hiss and crackle.

'Will you be a poet, Jim?' she asks me. Her voice is very frail and thin. It seems she has been sleeping and only half woken.

I look up from the poems.

'Maybe,' I tell her.

'You have to be in love to be a poet,' she says.

I make no reply. I do not know what to say, for I am not living in a world where love seems possible. I meet and know no one but the characters in books. The kettle makes a sharp bang as it heats on the reddened plate. Mrs Haddington is looking across at me, but I have the sense that what she is seeing is herself years earlier. In a dreamlike voice she tells me, 'I knew a poet.'

'Did you?'

There is a pause, the clock still relentlessly ticking the wrong time.

'Oh, long time ago now, dear,' she says. She is still looking at herself and at him too and at the verses he must have written for her.

The kettle gathers heat and begins to noise.

'Yes,' she says, after a time, 'a poet.'

And I turn my eyes from her face and say nothing while the water steadily boils.

*

If I am in love at all, it is with words and books still, where I enter as closely as seems possible to me the world of another. It doesn't seem to matter then that these are ghosts, or that my days spin past in this unreal world. And the experience is not unlike that of being a child sick in bed and all day reading an adventure story, and sleeping and waking with the covers of the book sticky in your hands or splayed open upon your sleeping chest. Real people and real things do not matter at all, but exist through a kind of distant muffle downstairs. Just so then, in this self-centred world of the imagination, in a drowse of words I pass the days.

And a year passes me.

And then another.

I come and go from lectures sometimes. I sit exams and somehow pass them and survive in the unreal world that is become mine. I go home rarely now. I invent excuses to my mother, who asks me in a slight voice on the phone if I have heard from Matthew. I lie to her about that too. Twice he has called me, from phone booths in England, each time with a kind of hurried desperation.

'Jim?'

'Yes? Matthew? Matthew, where are you?'

'I only have a minute.'

'When are you coming home?'

A buzz of traffic, cars or planes or trains I can't tell.

'Where are you?'

'Have you been home?' His voice has a note of timidity and even shame.

'Yes, they want you to come. Call them.'

I pause, my brother says nothing.

'Matthew, are you all right?'

'If something happens, call this number, leave a message.' He says the number and I stand in the hallway writing it on the front page of the phone book.

'All right?'

'Yes, yes, I have it, but—'

'I have to go.'

And the phone clicks before I can ask him anything else.

When my mother asks I tell her he has called me several times, that he has a powerful job that involves him being away in foreign countries for long periods. It is secret, I tell her one evening on a scratchy line when I am weary and all but at the end of invention.

And from that, she somehow takes it to mean that he works for the British government and that his genius has found a home in work that is too important for even his own mother to be told. She invents all of this herself, from the fragment I tell her, solely from the word *secret*. I watch it happen, and see it give her some peace, and do nothing then to expose the lie. I hear no more from Matthew.

At Christmas of course I go home. I go like Pip going back to the forge where he was made, where the flaws in the workings of his character are most cruelly exposed. I sit on the train and the journey westward in the rain is a sour one back into myself. I take the bus that meets the train, and sways and bumps back along the dark road west. Darragh, Lissycasey, places I have passed a thousand times, are knots on the rope of descent fathoms down into myself. Houses let their lights burn. Out across the boglands are single candles in farmhouse windows. Quietly they announce a presence in the blanket dark. The few of us, passengers for the end of the line, know that the candles burn not for us but for God coming, and we sit in our separate seats, weary witnesses, softly rocking and nodding and saying nothing.

I walk from the bus up along the street of the village and the rain falls. All is held in a kind of damp melancholy, with no sense of celebration. I pass out the end of the village and head into the greater dark of the country road. I am at home and yet more ill at ease than anywhere I can imagine. When I come in the front door, my mother opens the kitchen door and looks at me. She has been sitting there waiting for I don't know how long and now that I appear she has the look of someone wakened and frightened by a dream. I go to her. I say her name and embrace her, but even as I feel the thinness of her body and the shape of her bones I am thinking there is some part of her not within my arms. Some further part of her is away, is gone. When she steps back out of my embrace she looks anxious and frightened still.

'Are you all right, Mam?'

She turns to the kitchen. 'I have something good here for you.'

'Mam?'

'Come, sit down. Sit down, Jim.'

She turns away to get a plate she has prepared, more at ease when she is busy than in standing in front of me.

'Is Dad . . . how is he?'

'He is asleep.' She stops and turns, and speaks hesitantly as if I will refuse her. 'Would you go see him, first? If you like, and come back to eat.'

I go to the bedroom, walking through some element heavier than air, wherein movement and progress are inordinately difficult, wherein time and distance are compounded and loaded with echoes. Here are my steps across the carpet, and here too are those I took one Christmas many years earlier to go and open the door and find death waiting. It is easier not to see my father. It is easier if I can pretend he is recovering, or, if not that, then to move him far into the future when he is already dead and buried and now returned to live in my memory as the big quiet man at the switchboard. Either father in my imagination is better than the one I have to face when I open the bedroom door. He is lying on his side, a mound in the bedclothes smaller than I imagined. Where is that big man from my childhood gone? In the dark of the room, low lit from the doorway behind me, I see the shape of him and want to cry. I move up along the bed, and then I see that in fact his eyes are open.

'Dad.'

His eyes are still and I do not know if he sees me or not. I listen for his breath and when it comes it is a whisper of thinnest air moving through cracked lips.

'Dad. It's Jim. Can you hear me?'

Nothing. Not the slightest change or movement. I crouch down so that my face is next to his and I can smell something like old smoke on his body in the bedclothes and the soft damp autumnal scent of his fading away.

'I'm home,' I say, and then add, 'for Christmas.'

Nothing. He lies there, his eyes open in the dark.

'Dad?'

Nothing. His breath a slow labour that continues.

I wait a time and my father does not seem to see me and then I go downstairs to my mother and eat the bread and the scones she has prepared for me. Both are pasty and lumpish and seem to have been cooked without some of the ingredients. The raisins are hard as stones.

'He's worse, Mam,' I begin to say, but she turns away to the sink and I know that she does not need me to tell her anything and even that I have forfeited the right to any role but distant witness. She works at the sink though there is nothing to wash but the sink itself and the plughole down which the water gurgles like a drowning. Her legs are so thin in her stockings they might be brush-handles. Only her ankles stand out and seem sore and stiff to flex. Sometimes her shoulders shrug involuntarily. Her hand wavers and she catches it. I do not know if these are signs of an illness in her. I do not ask. After a long moment when she has settled herself she turns and dries her hands.

'I will be in with your father. I will see you in the morning, Jim.'

Later in my room I lie on the bed and feel the guilt that comes from failing to love. I seem to have lost the means of being human, of reaching out to my mother and father and making any healing happen. I lie there in the dark and the half-dark. After some hours I hear the noise of my mother at her sewing machine making dresses for Africa.

I lie there. I think my father will be dead in the morning. Christmas will come and he will die. That's the way it is in our family, the perverse combination of death and love, God coming and taking him away. I lie there and want to weep, but I cannot.

My father is not dead in the morning. My mother props him up in the bedclothes and he has some time when he is lucid and his eyes watch me as I enter the bedroom. I have brought him a gift of a book for Christmas. I place it on the bed and stand there.

'Well,' I say, 'Happy Christmas, Dad.' And after a bit, 'It's not a bad day out.' And later still, 'There'll be rain, they say.' And after another few beats, 'No sign of it at the minute.' Each phrase is like a false turn in a maze.

I sit down on the chair and the quiet falls over us. And in that quiet of Christmas morning I find myself listening to my father's breathing again. Though I do not know that it will be the last time I will hear it, I feel some strange connection to it, as if it is my life and not his that depends on each weak pull. I do not want him to die now. I want the breaths to keep on. I want there to be further chances, further possibilities when things might turn out differently, when I might script a twist in the plot and introduce miracles.

There are long pauses sometimes, and I think he has died, but then the breath comes again, steadily, as though he is rowing through still waters, away, and away. Father Dolan calls to visit with the Communion host around midday. He is a big-faced elderly man who puffs as he comes up the stairs and stands and mutters the words of the Communion rite matter-of-factly. Because my father cannot reply, Father Dolan says the words for him, very quickly: 'Lord-I-am-not-worthy-to-receive-you-only-say-the-Word-and-I-shall-be-healed.' He raises the host and pauses an instant, as though waiting for the Word, and then he bends to push it on my father's half-hidden tongue. 'Happy Christmas, Tom,' he says. He leaves soon afterward, ten calls to make before Mrs Crowley has his dinner cooked.

I sit again and some time later, maybe an hour, my father turns his head slightly in my direction and opens his mouth and I see the white circle of the host sitting there undissolved. I don't know what to say. I don't know what message is being sent or how to receive it. I don't know if I am to reach in and take the host from his mouth, if my father is rejecting it or simply unable to eat it. His face turned toward me, tears well in his eyes and fall sideways down his face.

The host hangs there, then it falls out silently onto the pillow. I stand up.

'Christ,' I say. 'Dad.'

My father's eyes look at me. He makes a sound, maybe three sounds or the same one repeated. I do not understand and he makes them again, words pushed together into nonsense, a message garbled. He watches my eyes, and I feel it is as though he is trying to link a cable to me, to make some connection happen. Again the three words.

'What is it? Do you want this?' I ask him, lifting the host.

He shuts his eyes.

'Do you?' I say again. And he opens his eyes and closes them again and in that I interpret that he cannot swallow the undissolved Communion.

I wait there holding it.

'What'll I do with it?'

The wet host is in my hands. I think to throw it in the bedside bin where used tissues are piled. But I cannot. My father's eyes look at me. They look at me and at the host in my hand and he mumbles three sounds that I translate to be 'You take it.'

And so I do. I place the host that fell from his mouth in mine, and stand there while it melts with his taste on my tongue. My father's eyes do not leave me. He makes a single sound that I tell myself is thanks or good or perhaps is my name. And then I sit leaned forward in the chair beside him, in a kind of serenity, as though in the presence of grace.

Three days into the New Year I say goodbye to my mother, whose arms shake unless she holds them together, and I go back to my flat in the house of Mrs Haddington. I go when I know I should not. I go because I cannot bear not to. I read. I wait for the phone call to come, telling me my father is dead. I read the poetry of Gerard Manley Hopkins: 'Felix Randal, is he dead then?' I read the religious sonnets: 'Pitched past pitch of grief.' I read lying on the bed in the clothes I have slept or not slept in, and the rain falls on Dublin and the weak light of January briefly crosses the window and dies again. A hundred poems take an afternoon. I lose myself and lose my brother and mother and father and fall within the mesmeric rhythm of the phrases. A scratch of beard climbs from my neck. My eyes bulge and run blood vessels like things boiled. For a week I do not go outside into the air. I hear Mrs Haddington shuffle in slippers in the hall. I hear her stop outside my door and listen. From the top of the stairs I hear the clink of a bottle on a glass. And so it is we live on, grimly wintering, each expectant of a death. Sometimes I meet her in the corridor in her dressing gown and she touches her pearls and moves them around the soft sag of her neck.

'What is it you are reading, dear?' she asks me.

I hold up the paperback book for her. 'Dylan Thomas.'

'Oh, yes,' she says. 'Very nice.' And then after a beat: 'Strange isn't it, dear, so much humanity in the writing, but not in the writers.' She turns away. 'No, not in the writers.' And she is gone.

One day I find energy or feel the wedge of guilt press me into some resolve and return to the university. I sit in the back of a lecture by Professor Denis Donohue and hear about the great Americans. He praises *Moby Dick* and I go and get a copy, spending four days reading it until my spirit is awash in spermaceti and oil and brine and I feel I am the familiar of the desperate, of all Ahabs, endlessly scanning an empty horizon for some beast to vanquish. I read Hawthorne after that, *The Scarlet Letter*, and then Whitman, in one week the thump and march of hundreds of his poems opening in me the idea of America.

The winter lifts. In March I am reading Scott Fitzgerald and Hemingway as a timid spring arrives and then disappears behind veils of light snow. I am thin and cycle my bicycle on the slippery streets of Ranelagh and acknowledge the nods of a few students. But I have no friends. I fall in love with many girls with whom I never speak. I live only it seems in my mind, but tell myself that the rewards of such life are not inconsequential and sometimes I finish reading a passage of a book or a verse of a poem and feel I am on fire. I want to walk out in the street and burn there and believe that a corona of white incandescence might frame my head. I believe that any who might see me would stop there and be able to tell, for the rapture and inspiration would be such that it would be akin to announcing myself like an apostle in a moving crowd.

Only of course I don't. I don't go outside. I stay in the room. I read on.

I forget the world.

And then one day there is the call. It is Father Dolan. My mother is dead.

Mother.

What can I write? You slip away from me again, as have the many
mothers I have written since in so many stories, seeking but failing to
find you. The sewing I never asked you about. It remained like a
broken bridge that I tried to repair after, inventing plausible expla-
nations, giving it one time to a Mrs Drake on the South Circular
Road in Dublin. She sewed the threads like some long ravelling to
bring her back her sister who left one morning after an argument to
save the souls of Africa. I let myself away with such facile nonsense
once. Yes. That other story I wrote, telling of the brother who did not
return for his mother's funeral. A man addicted to gambling, a fellow
moving among the suntanned and the cuff-linked in London hotels.
Losing the fortunes of others. Sometimes winning. This Mick, this
geek, brain; the Catholic, they called him, mocking: everything num-
bered in heaven, eh, Mick? Patterns he found in all things, this Mick
Genius, and could not lay down his head to sleep until he had more
discovered: sequence of lights flashing outside, number of street lamps
between corners, cracks in the path, white cars to black, red to both.
Who gambled and lost four hundred thousand pounds belonging to
a gold-chained Cypriot and was hunted then by two men in a white
car and was hiding alone in a cheap hotel room turning cards on a
table when his mother was buried.

Stories.

I return home at once. I phone Matthew and leave a message on the machine that answers. It is not his voice. He does not call. I leave a second message and a third. I think he may be in another country and be given the message there. I tell him to call at any time of the day or night. When I return to the village big Martin Crowley the undertaker meets me off the bus and shakes my hand. He is wearing a black suit, has the arrangements made. I am not to worry about anything. In the house I relieve his wife who has been sitting beside my father.

'I think he knows,' she whispers.

'Oh, he does,' says Martin from the doorway, 'he knows.'

Then they slip out and leave me at his bedside, his eyes closed and his body perfectly still, as his breathing comes and goes.

'Mum's dead, Dad,' I tell him, and watch in vain for even the slightest response.

The neighbours have been waiting for me. Now that there is someone to console they come in hordes to stand in the kitchen and shake my hand. There are bottles of whiskey and stout on the kitchen table and sandwiches, but how any of them got there I do not know. Women come and go with plates and pots of tea. They have brought some of their own ware. Father Dolan sits by the fireplace with Dr McHale nodding at him. Is there any news of Matthew coming? I am asked time and again. He is away and out of touch, I say, he can't be reached.

'We can wait two more days for him,' Martin Crowley draws me aside to tell me. 'After that . . .' He doesn't finish.

I go upstairs and sit by my father while the rosary runs around downstairs. There are a hundred people there, none of whom visited the house or saw my mother in the past two years. The murmur of the prayers is intense, the words themselves blurred into a wave of sound that I do not believe will reach God's ears.

My mother is buried in the rain. Surrounded by so many, I am alone in the old cemetery, but cannot remember how to cry.

Martin Crowley tells me my father would have wanted something after, and that he has arranged for people to come back to Considine's pub. I thank him and leave them filing in there out of the rain. I come back to the house. The Crowleys' teenage daughter, Una, has been sitting in the kitchen on duty for my father. I give her some money and she leaves, and I go upstairs and find that he is dead. He has not moved from when I last saw him. There is no sign of any struggle. And I sit down with the realization that he had been waiting all this time for my mother to die so that she would not be alone and he could be the one going after to find her again.

It all occurs then as in a dream. The phone calls to Matthew, the messages left. The waiting, the handshakes, the line of cars bumped up on the ditch in the wheel tracks they left before, the tea and the stout and the rosary rumbling downstairs again while I excuse myself and hide upstairs with my hands over my ears.

I wait in the house after for Matthew for a week, knowing that he will not come. And in the dead gathered silence of the rooms I feel the exultant victory of sorrow. The dust falls mote upon mote with soft surrender and soon all is sheeted with a mouse-grey grief that chokes everything. The air itself is thick and bitter with implacable remorse for all that was and should not have been and for which there seems no remedy or relief.

I wait that week, and then can bear it no longer. I step outside the house into the garden. A dull rain is falling steadily and the sky seems a grey lid without edge. I lock the door and hold the key in my hand. Then I leave it under the stone for whoever might come there again.

Two

'Dad!'

My eyes pop open and Hannah is standing there, the grey square of the morning's sky in the roof window behind her. I am lying on the floor of Jack's bedroom on a makeshift bed of blanket and cushion where she has already discovered me once before. She is dressed in her school uniform, her left arm with her watch held in front of her.

'Do you know what time it is? I thought you were awake. I thought I heard you downstairs. Is he going to school? I have ten minutes, Dad. Ten. He isn't even . . .' She doesn't finish. She sighs and turns and is gone loudly down the stairs. Through this Jack sleeps. There is no sign now of the nightmares or ghouls I had come upstairs to battle. His face is in such perfect repose it seems a shame to wake him.

'You can go in late,' I whisper, but he sleeps on.

At the back door of the kitchen Hannah is feeding Huckleberry. She goes to the sink and rinses the can and puts it in the recycling box by the fridge.

'Are you putting all the cans in here?' she asks.

'Yes. Of course I am.'

'It's important.'

'I know.'

She picks up her bag, looks at me. 'Well?'

'Would you like to go in late today?'

'Dad.'

'I know. We're late. I'm late. But it's not the end of the world, Hannah.'

'Dad, no. No. I have to. I have maths first. I can't even do half of them when I'm there. I'll call for a lift.'

'No, don't. I'll get Jack. I'll bring you.'

But she is already dialling the phone faster than I can say the words. And within a moment it seems there is a lift on the way. She will walk down to the end of the road to meet it.

'You shouldn't sleep up there,' she says. 'I don't think it's right.'

'I know, Hannah.'

'It's not really going to help him.'

'I have to get him to stop crying.'

'But then you should go. You shouldn't stay there on the floor.'

She looks at me with your eyes and I know she is right.

'You're right. I will.'

'Bye.'

'Have a good day.' Her kiss brushes my cheek. 'Maybe I could help you with the maths sometime.'

She is out the door and only gives me a glance, back over her shoulder, but I can interpret it. Maths, you? it says.

*

Down in the village today the cars were lined on both sides of the street, which means only one thing here: death. I do not go to funerals. In my childhood my father seemed to attend every funeral in the five parishes. He sometimes included a funeral in Ennis or Kilrush, but mostly it was to those whose names he knew from the switchboard. None of them would be his friends, to none of them would he be particularly close, but still he would go, in black suit and white shirt, to file into the funeral parlour and shake hands, before coming directly home. He never went to the pub or the house afterwards, only the funeral parlour or sometimes the church. As long as he gave his handshake he was happy. In feckless youthful arrogance of course it was a trait I despised. I thought it hypocritical of him, of all of them. There were a thousand people who shook my hand when my father died. If I have since spoken to ten of them I would be surprised.

Still it is part of the life here. There may be some unwritten law:

if I come to a funeral of yours, you must come to one of mine. And in this way the tally is kept and in despair we will all have the consolation of company, or what appears to be so.

But it is not for me. I have let my side of the tally down, I am sure. I have missed funerals I should have attended and in time drifted further and further from the life of the parish as my father knew it. I am sure there are some who have missed me: Did Jim Foley not come? He's a proud old bastard, isn't he? Strange distant family, the lot of them.

And some for whom perhaps I am already dead.

I hear nothing of what goes on now, who is married or pregnant or separated, who crashed a car, who was brought in the ambulance, and truly I do not really mind. But today, driving down the village with a funeral Mass on and the village utterly stilled, I had a feeling of such immense loneliness I cannot quite find words for it. It sat on my heart. I looked for somewhere to pull over, but the street was filled with parked cars. Even in the entranceway of the church there were two angled in behind the hearse. So I stopped there in the middle of the street and opened the window for air. Nothing came behind me. Nothing came up from the cross. There was no man or woman or child on the footpath. Not even a dog trailing through the emptiness of the morning.

I opened the window and on the air could hear the softened singing of the choir inside the church. And the aloneness, the feeling of being cut off from some central element of living, was such that I seemed an outcast. There flew into my mind the image from Donne of the trumpets calling at the round earth's imagined corners, and from the ends of the parishes everyone living coming to gather inside the doors of the church. But not me; I had heard no trumpets calling.

I sat in the car in the centre of the village that was stopped in prayer and felt more alone than I think I have ever felt.

'Say a prayer,' I said to myself. 'Say one anyway. Go on.'

And perhaps I would have. Perhaps I would have said one just to feel some sense of the communal, of the congregation of humanity, part of that warm assembly of yearning and aspiration. Because perhaps just in saying a prayer I could have imagined God listening. But whether I waited too long or a sign was being sent to me, there came up the street then the large eighteen-wheeled delivery truck from Limerick that knew nothing of funerals or the ways of this parish. It drove up until the driver took the phone from his cheek and gestured down to me that he had nowhere to pull over. I waited a moment – but said no prayer – then reversed back out of the village and came home.

*

Peas and potatoes and lamb chops. The dull meal I serve to Jack and me this evening. Hannah of course makes her own. Something Asian, I think. Across the table I begin a preamble to the subject of my sleeping in Jack's room.

'Jack, you know sometimes you have bad dreams?'

'Uh-huh.'

'And that's all right. That's normal. Everybody has them sometimes. And when you do your dad will come up and be there for you. And, well, you know . . .'

'Uh-huh.'

Hannah stops turning the spoon in her yogurt and watches me.

'But, em, then you're OK. You're able to go back asleep, and the dream, because it was only a dream and not really something, you know, real, is gone. It's, it seems real, I know that, but—'

'God, Dad, just say it.' Hannah shakes her head at me. 'Jack, Dad is not going to sleep on your floor any more when you wake up. He'll go back to his own room. OK?'

There is an instant while Jack thinks, as if the news is delivered in slight satellite delay.

'OK,' he says and nods and carries on eating.

'See? Simple,' Hannah mouths over to me.

'I never asked him to sleep in my room,' Jack says.

Later, he sits a long time at the kitchen table working with pencil and crayons at his homework. He has asked me not to watch and when I come into the room he crouches down over the page and curves his arm up around it.

'I'm not looking,' I tell him.

I sit by the fireplace and put on the music of Martin Hayes. Sweet melancholic fiddle-playing, notes bending around in the air.

Jack comes in at last carrying the page.

'Can I see now?'

'Uh-huh.'

He hands it over and watches me. On the page is the carefully block-printed heading FAMILY TREE underlined in red crayon. Then, beneath it, is Jack's version of a large tree crayoned brown. There are a few leaves of pale green and upon these names are written, beginning on the right-hand side with Great-Granda Foley. My eye scans down over them, my grandparents, parents, and on down to Hannah and Jack himself. On the other side of the tree however, there is only a single leaf filled in. On it is written MAM, KATE. Nothing more.

'Is it good, Dad?' His face is so earnest it might crack.

'Yes, it's very good, Jack, very good.' He smiles then.

There are other names you could put in, I think to tell him. There is another whole side of the tree leafless. People whose names he should know but will not now because the one who would have told him is dead. I think to offer to write them in, but there is something in the pride and happiness in his face that forbids it.

'You can look at it for a bit, if you want,' he tells me, and goes to watch the television.

I hold it there on my lap, this lopsided tree, as the music plays on. I know the missing only through fragments I have been told, partial anecdotes of characters that emerge out of the fog of time and vanish again, others whom I imagine, some I met. There is a whole history of them, the indomitable Kellys and Lynches, that the longer I sit there the more I think of, and think that all of them too can be recovered, brought back out of the dust of oblivion and given their part. Why should all perish and the tree be so ravaged and crooked?

I get up from the armchair and cross to the table here where I turn on the screen. I put the family tree down alongside me. Here, then, I think, let me trace them all. Let imagination fill the gaps of knowl-

edge. Let words like sap run, and figures reappear like so many leaves in spring.

Or something like that.

Need and hurt and the habit of a couple of inflated metaphors making believe resurrection is that simple.

I write for an hour, then two, then lose all sense of time while I click out the words. I write onto the page one Conleth Kelly, brown-eyed and barrel-chested. In the summer of 1860, at age nineteen, he sails from Cork for New Brunswick aboard the MaryAnn. *I tell how he joins the army and during the Civil War becomes a captain, losing his right arm. Afterward his retiring general secures for him a position in a savings bank in New York; he remains a bachelor until late middle age when he marries Miss Margaret Henshawe, schoolmistress. They have a son, Paul, your grandfather. I paint the scene of his going away to within the ivied walls of St Christopher's College, his last sight of his father. I blur my own experience into his, but then invent good friends for him, Woodham and Griegson and Rochester. He becomes a gifted golfer, plays left-handed, wins tournaments up and down the east coast. He resists for a long time joining the bank. Then, on a weekend visit to New York, he reads of Miss Eileen Farrell, the child prodigy now giving a recital to mark the occasion of her eighteenth birthday. Three months later they are secretly engaged and he has taken a job at a branch of the bank in New Jersey. Your mother, Kathleen, the eldest of four sisters, is born one year later.*

And here are the Lynches, Joseph, John and Padraig, growing up in a farmhouse in Tarbert, north Kerry. Here in 1906 comes Joseph Lynch to Queens. After five years working for a haulier's, Brophy, he joins the police force. At an Irish dance in St Catherine's Hall he meets Bridget – called Bridey — McCarthy from Kilfinane parish in Kerry. Their first son they call Michael.

He has left the army and is studying law by the time he meets your mother. I write a little scene at some place off 31st Street and Eighth Avenue where Kathleen has come with her sisters Eileen and Maureen to celebrate a birthday. I have her fall in love with him on an instant.

128

When he holds her he squeezes the breath out of her. She rises on her toes in his arms.

Their first home is in Queens. Kathleen is pregnant and busies herself, I imagine, tidying the apartment, keeping everything just so. The order and stillness of the rooms masks the anxiety of her mind. She smokes. In the late afternoon, while she is awaiting his return, she pours herself a drink from the decanter on the sideboard.

I sit before the screen and at last write, 'In April of nineteen fifty-four you are born.'

But then I stop. I look at the screen and press the backspace and watch the cursor take back the words one by one, erasing them into snow space again. Does writing make nothing happen? What does it matter? What does it matter what words I write. I stop and get up and walk away through the night house. In the kitchen are the unwashed dishes from dinner, pots with remains, milk and juice cartons, the untopped container of spreadable butter. We grow less and less tidy, less and less we care about such things. The house teeters on the edge of becoming a dump. I should insist to the children more, but can't. Some cog in the works of living has fallen out, and though the wheel of our days still turns, it does so with a buckled warp, all the time losing ground. In a week, I think, ten days at most, the rubbish and the leftovers, the souring and the spoiled, will overwhelm us. The rats will come and brazen it, summoned by the stench of decay.

Tonight, then, in that most peculiar of feelings, disgust at the evidence of our own living, I begin a midnight washing, dishes, pots, tables, countertops, window sills, the outside of the kettle, the inside of the kettle. I am a lemon-zest man, spraying and rubbing for all I am worth until I stand at the sink and look over about the kitchen and feel the brief moment of its cleanliness as a kind of grace almost. Or at least a pause, an immaculate moment of balance, between the floating and fall of another speck of dust, the ceaseless gathering of waste.

Opals of rain on the window, I stand by the kettle, its slow boil the only noise in the house, but one for which I am grateful. There is something consoling in it. I drown the teabag and it floats to the top.

I spoon in the sugar, two, and then another guilty bit. I open the fridge for the milk and lifting the carton feel the lightness of it. Empty. Not a drop left. Neither is there another carton. I am caught between anger at why one of the children would put an empty carton back in the fridge and what that says, what message is there, and the knowledge of the morning crisis ahead. No milk for breakfast and nowhere to go now and get some. The easy symbolism of it is not lost on me either. Milk, mother, sustenance. Nor the irony, here in this townland where not so long ago every house had its milking cow. Those days too are gone. Forests of spruce grow all around us. Soon even the valley will be planted, the houses screened in until people can endure no longer and must move to the towns.

With my mug of tea I go and sit by the dead ashes.

In the loneliness that is everywhere then I think, you are going further away from me with every moment. I look at my hand and want to recall holding yours inside it. I want some sense of the feeling of you. I raise my left hand off my lap and clasp it with my right and shut my eyes and try to imagine it is you.

But it's not.

I cannot feel you.

I remember: 'You have a headache? Here, sit here. I'll give you a rub.'

I bring my hands to my temples, let my fingers touch as soft as memory remembers against the contour of my forehead, my closed eyelids.

But there is only myself, in the empty room, with the night rain falling.

The touch of you is soonest gone. Your face retreats now to reside in photographs. In scenes I recall the image of you breaks up, as if a stone has fallen into your reflection in a lake. And with eyes shut I wait and wait for the stillness to repair it, but it trembles and shimmers more, as though I am rowing across it, or the stone on the bottom is my heart beating.

Angry with myself, I go to the dresser and take down a picture of you smiling and beautiful on the lawn in front of the Old Ground

Hotel in Ennis following Hannah's Communion. I hold it to my chest. But soon, too soon, feel the pressing reality of the cold silver frame and glass, the cool impersonal mockery of photographs.

I go back to the keyboard because there is nowhere else to go. Nowhere else to look where I might find you.

*

The Saturday before Christmas I made the announcement. For once we were briefly all sitting around the one table. Hannah had made a first-attempt pudding and wanted us to try it before she made the real thing. While she plucked the lid off the steamer and dropped it in the sink, Jack and I sat and made faces of anxious hope, raised eyebrows and wide letterbox lips.

'Do you want any help, Hannah?'

'No.'

'Be careful, you can burn yourself with the steam.'

'Dad.'

'All right.'

'Crap.'

'What?'

'I think it's stuck. It's not supposed to get stuck. I greased it. I did everything they said in the book.'

'Here, let me—'

'No, Dad.' A strand of hair falling across her face, she blew aside. 'I can manage. Sit down.'

Test of life, of love too perhaps. She wanted more than anything to pass it, for the upended pudding bowl to be lifted off and the brown rich flat-topped dome to be revealed. As proof. Proof of our enduring, of the continuance of the ordinary, that despite fears and doubts Christmas could still be.

Her back to us, she groaned.

'That's not fair.'

'What?' I stood.

'Oh nothing, nothing, sit down, it's coming.'

Jack grinned, showed me his gritted teeth.

131

Hannah skipped along the counter, switched on the whippers for last-minute beating of the cream. On too powerfully, it splattered ('Crap'), then switched to a soothed hum.

A moment, then she carried the bowls over to us.

'Voilà.' She smiled apologetically. 'It's probably not any good, but it's just a first attempt and I'll be making another one. I don't know why it stuck. It shouldn't have, I did everything they said.'

'Sit down, Hannah, it looks wonderful.'

'I like it,' Jack said, before he had even tasted a mouthful.

'It is good, Hannah, it's delicious.'

'It's not awful, anyway.'

And so, in the little victory of that, with the three of us sitting there, I thought I saw my chance.

'Now, listen. I want to ask you both something.' Pause. 'I want to ask you to come to Mass with me on Christmas Day.'

Hannah's spoon stopped mid-air. She scowled.

'We never go to Mass.'

'I know.'

'We haven't gone since . . .'

'I know, Hannah. And that is probably, well, no, definitely, is definitely my fault.'

'It's nobody's fault. We just don't want to go, that's all.'

'But I just thought, it's Christmas and—'

'Dad, I'm not going.'

'Me too,' Jack said. 'I don't want to.'

'And what if I say you have to?'

Silence. Hannah got up from the table, half a bowl of Christmas pudding in front of her.

'You can't make us,' she said, and left the room.

*

Today the shopping, the crush for gifts. I prefer Easter to Christmas, not only because of the memory of my sister, but because there is none of the expectation, no sense of something that must be achieved, unless perhaps an inner thing. Maybe grace. But in Christmas grace is more difficult to find. Today I moved among the raincoated down Parnell Street, the bag-bearing, the puddle-jumping throng. So few faces smiling. Instead a set-jawed look of resolve, of mission, of things on a list still to be found. I had made no list of my own. I had a vain vague notion that once I stood in a shop I would know by father's instinct what my children wanted. Firstly, books, of course. And afterwards, music. But in the pulsing throb of what we used to call the record shop I became quickly overwhelmed. I was the only man over forty among the rows of discs, and besides the reissues of albums I once owned on vinyl I recognized nothing. How do you choose music for your daughter? How can you tell from names or photographs in a plastic case if this is something she will like? A girl no more than eighteen arrived at my elbow to help me. A look of pity in green mascaraed eyes. She led me to the Top Twenty, ten per cent off.

'She'll love this one,' she said, 'it's brill.'

I bought it, and four more, at the till holding the clutch of them like foreign passports of countries I have never seen. Any confidence in my selection vanished when Mascara said, 'If she hates them, tell her bring them in and change them, no hassle. All right? Happy Christmas.'

'Happy Christmas.'

Leaving, I read the hours of reopening for returns and those with gift certificates, for a moment thinking of that easier option, and the now more commonplace envelope with money: Here, I couldn't think what to get you.

Not me, I thought. I would always get presents for them.

But I would keep the receipts.

For Jack it was still relatively easy. The bicycle from Harry's, Lego from Toymaster, coloured pencils and a metal watercolour box in the art shop, and then, passing Custy's with the music spilling out, a flash of inspiration: a fiddle.

Afterward, through the rained-on crowds on the way back to the car, black fiddle-case in hand, I turned a corner into melancholy. I was passing one of the new boutiques for teenage girls they have in the town now, and in an instant knew that these were the clothes

Hannah wanted. And that if you were here you would be buying them for her. I paused outside the window with the shadow of you and felt the lump of grief in my throat. I couldn't go in, I didn't even know her size.

I carried on up O'Connell Street in the kind of utter loneliness peculiar to Christmas. Stopped at Eircom, bought her a mobile phone, fifty euros credit.

Later this evening, when I visited Hannah in her room to say goodnight, she asked me, 'Dad, why do you want to go?'

'What?'

'On Christmas. We don't any other time. You don't. It's just because it's Christmas, isn't it?'

'Maybe.'

'I don't think it's right. It's hypocritical. You don't believe.'

'Well.'

'What?'

'I'm not sure. Maybe I do.'

'Well, I don't. Not any more. Especially now. I mean, religion has just caused so much hurt. I mean, look.' She pointed at the television screen, a Sky News report on reprisal attacks against Muslims in America. 'That's the world, Dad, that's religion.'

For the hundredth time, I didn't know what to say. For my daughter I felt the failures of myself, and the world, and God.

'Well, will you still think about it? Will you just not say no? Maybe think about it for Jack. Or as a Christmas thing for me.'

News broke for ads.

'Hm, cheap present,' she said, considering.

'Yes, just think about it. OK?'

'OK.'

*

To tell the truth I am not entirely sure of my motives, or why I wanted the Mass. Whether I imagined it part of a sentimental postcard scene or some weightier instrument of healing or redemption. Tonight, at the end of Christmas Day, I sit here in an armchair of contentment, glad that we went. Hannah told me with a wink she had persuaded Jack to go. Only not to the church in the village, to the Midnight Mass in the cathedral in Ennis where we stood and knelt anonymously in the pews with the hymns rising like white flocks of birds overhead. Though we knew and spoke to no one, briefly I felt something communal, but lost it again during the sermon and the jingle of coins at the collection. Still, I think the word is heartened. Then this morning, Jack's face seeing the gifts on the couch in front of the fire.

'Hannah, you got . . . you got a phone, cool!'

'Yeah, cool.'

'I got a . . .'

'What is it, Jack? Open it.'

'It's a fiddle.'

'A fiddle, wow!'

'Wow!' To the chimney, a shout: 'Thank you, Santa!'

'Look at these cool CDs.' Hannah grinned.

'What did you get?' I peered over. 'I wonder are they any good?'

'Excellent,' she said. 'Here, something for you.'

I opened a recording of Dylan Thomas's A Child's Christmas in Wales.

'You can return it if you don't like it,' Hannah said. 'I have the receipt.'

Afterward, the slightly frantic preparation of dinner, pots steaming and bubbling, oven cooking some dubious beige thing called Vegetarian Roast. Not that any of us were particularly hungry. Countless cups of tea and a box of USA assorted biscuits had punctuated the morning. Nonetheless, Christmas dinner it was, followed by the second-attempt pudding which came smooth and unsticking from the bowl with a rich aroma that staggered me a moment with memories. As if we were our own guests we left the dishes there. And soon Jack was watching a programme on Disney Channel and playing scratchy un-notes on the fiddle at the same time. Hannah went upstairs. Now that the phone was charged, she wanted to text, she told me.

'Do you know how?' I asked.

'Of course.' Eyebrows raised, she shook her head at me smiling indulgence. 'Dad.'

I went out in the garden, where for once it was not raining. There was a perfect stillness laid along the broad back of the valley. Ragged lines of thorn trees held small herds waiting feed. The sky was empty, without birds. I walked through the damp grass, past beds that had overgrown and died back in the frost, ridges of the vegetable garden where this year only couch grass grew. Beneath the crooked ash that rose out of the wall I stood awhile and in the quietness there felt a wave of gratitude. Just that. Who or what I was grateful to I did not voice. But living itself, continuance, seemed on Christmas afternoon a victory. I studied the faded kind of beauty there was in the winter garden, the tranquillity of ruin, soft wet rot of leaf mulch, twisted blackened stalks of potatoes I never dug, hard compacted ground in the dream of spring. For a long time I felt the utter stillness of the place, and nothing came, and nothing went.

Later I came back inside the kitchen to make tea and have more pudding. I think in the sitting room I heard Jack say to Hannah he hadn't hoped for a PlayStation, he never wanted one, and wise sister she is told him he was right, a fiddle was much better. I took the gift I had bought for myself, a copy of John Cheever's Oh, What a Paradise It Seems, and sat by the fire reading it to intermittent fiddle sounds.

And after a time, I put it aside and returned to the table here. To text.

To send a message. So that one might be sent back to me? I considered it in those terms awhile, this business in which I am engaged. What message am I hoping for?

I thought to write down that first day I met you in Dublin.

'Here, you dropped this book,' I said.

And your face, and your eyes and the fall of your hair. That flat in Sandymount and my going there through the night-slick streets, fallen wet moons of street light, one-armed cycling, a clutch of books I wanted you to read. The train rattling by outside. Above the bed the mice in the ceiling that turned out to be pigeons. Days and afternoons and nights of books and talking and walking all the seaward streets from Sydney Parade to Sandycove. Pulling flowers out of gardens to give them to you.

The feel of your body in my arms.

I thought to write the sweetness of those moments when you changed my life, but cannot. If I was still a poet, perhaps. If I could write lyric. The parts of our lives when we write them down seem to belong in different books, by different writers even. What all these bits and pieces make up I don't know. There is no plot. Perhaps meaning is something we invent afterward, putting it all together, like imagined God. Christmas night, children in bed, rectangle of stars in the skylight above. I switch on the screen.

The swimmer rises from the pool and emerges from the pale blue water-light into the falling dark and the man comes forward and holds out the towel to wrap about her. She smiles and shakes her head thrice to each side to release any water trapped there.

'You should have come in,' she says.

It is the year 1980. That summer Jim Foley is twenty-one years old. He is tall and thin and freckled from the sun of his first week in America. He cannot swim. The style of swimming he learned in Ireland was on school trips to what were then called the baths whereby his feet touched off the ground as his arms made the strokes. Besides, he is too embarrassed by himself to get into the water with her. She knows this but does not care. She has seen in him a quality that outshines this. She is four years older than he and has loved and been hurt and was two years before to be married to a law student in Boston. That love failed and burned away and with the ashes of it still in her mouth she had gone to Ireland to study literature. He was one of those there in the wet and grey city of Dublin searching in books for things not found elsewhere.

Now, wrapped in a towel, she walks up the long lawn beside him in the evening. The grass is dried out and burnt from the July sun and underfoot feels like the cooled crisp aftermath of fire. They go up toward the house without speaking. The crickets are loud in the dark. The house ahead of them is large and painted blue and has a long timber deck with chairs. There are mixed woods on either side of it and he has been told that in the winter deer come from the bare trees and cross the snow to eat the hemlocks and even the rose bushes. It is a thing he imagines, having never seen a deer in the wild. When he imagines it he links the image with those that remain in his mind from Fenimore Cooper's *The Deer Slayer*, and in that way imbues setting and landscape with a kind of colonial poetic. The house is larger and lovelier than the one she told him of in Dublin. It is the dream-place her father made, and impossible to look at now without sensing the failure of that dream and the residue of broken love. Here there is a gravel driveway up from the dirt road and dog-wood trees and azaleas in bloom. The house stands atop a rise, its perspective on the landscape speaking of confidence, a gentled pastoral air, a sense of domain here in the woods – and nearby hidden in among the trees are other splendid houses with names like Stoneybrook and Oakridge and Avalon. They are the houses of people who have become wealthy, who have moved in pro-gressive stages further and further out of the city like a great migratory herd of black suits in search of pastureland. They are the houses of groomed men in pristine tailoring and coiffed scented women who carry heeled shoes in paper bags as they leave in the dawn, gathering at train stations along the Harlem and Hudson railway line with styrofoam coffee cups and the *New York Times*. They are the houses of the bankers and merchants of New York, brokers of power, who on weekends take off their suits and wear bright polo shirts and khaki shorts and penny loafers and go and play in country clubs whose membership is prized and exclusive. They take tennis lessons with the pro, they play in tournaments among themselves, and in the evenings stand on their decks with martinis and look at the woods and all that arboreal splendour as if that itself were another trophy, as if in that place beauty and nature belonged to the wealthy.

Jim and Kate walk up the lawn. Here, as night falls, the house shines from many windows.

'Well, how was it?'

Kate's mother is standing by the screen door as they come inside. She is a woman in her fifties, elegantly dressed, with square-framed glasses that make her eyes large. 'Oh, you should have gone in, Jim. You must be so hot after the day. I know you're not used to it.'

'No, I'm fine,' he says.

'I will be back down in a minute. I'm going to get changed,' Kate looks to him and smiles and goes.

'I would have gone in myself,' Mrs Lynch tells him, 'but I had to go to my meeting. Will you have something to drink, Jim?' She is already going to the kitchen as she asks, and fills some ice into a tumbler and pours cranberry juice across it so it clicks and knocks softly. 'Here.'

'Thank you.'

Kathleen Lynch watches him drink. She has met him only a few days before and studies him as if for flaws, as if his character is a crystal ball and she, who has known how the glittered can deceive, will soon tell if he is the real thing or not. If Kate is wrong in her choice, her mother will tell her. It is not too late. It is what a mother must do. He drinks beneath her scrutiny, the juice of cranberries bitter in his throat.

'Sit down, Jim.'

She is across from him on the couch. A thin fit woman, she jogs the road in the mornings. Although she doesn't go to the club any more, she is a fine tennis player. She plays against her son Gerard on the court beyond the pool. Even in the daytime she wears fine clothes and perfume. She cares for decorum and manners, perhaps because of a genteel notion or gene passed in her heritage, perhaps because she grew up covering for her mother's alcoholism and learned the importance of maintaining appearance, perhaps because these things keep chaos at bay. In any case she is a gentlewoman, and in the house all is as it should be.

'I can't imagine what this must be like for you. It must be overwhelming.'

He is not sure of the question or what to answer. With close-lipped deferential politeness he nods. He is wearing the clothes she has bought for him as a gift. They are lightweight, the pants sky-blue seersucker such as he has never seen, never mind worn, before. She has also bought him a blue blazer and button-down shirt and brown loafers that he wears like a uniform.

Mrs Lynch smiles. Jim looks into the cranberry juice as though to see its bitterness. He taps a block of ice with his finger. Mrs Lynch smokes thin white cigarettes only halfway through and leaves upon the remnants ruby stains of lipstick.

'How was your meeting?' he asks her. He asks because he does not know what else to say, and because of all the questions that are pressing in upon him now this seems the simplest one to ask. He does not think this elegant woman can belong to an organization called Alcoholics Anonymous. There is something in the alignment of his preconception and this reality that jars, makes him realize the country he is in now is more deceptive and complex than the one he has left behind. *I am lost here*, he thinks. *Lost*.

'Oh, it was fine. Last week was my tenth anniversary so I'm leading the meetings this week.'

'I see,' he says, though he does not, and knows nothing yet of such meetings, or what they involve or how so many come in shining cars to gather in brightly painted schoolrooms to spill the acid of their lives.

He sips the cranberry juice and the ice knocks. Through the screen he can hear the noise of the crickets, their racket more insistent now. Far down the lawn the lights on the pool are still on and it gleams like a blue jewel fallen from above.

'Jim?'

'Yes.'

'Can I say something to you?' Mrs Lynch turns on the couch toward him and holds her cigarette back as if out of the conversation. 'You know I like you very much. I think you're terrific. And I know you know that Kate has had her troubles and that it hasn't been easy for her. Well,' she leans back and draws on the cigarette and there is a moment in which she seems a diver considering the depth of the water and whether she will enter it now

141

or later or not at all. It is a long moment. Jim sits there in his new trousers on the edge of a world. *Lost.*

'I will make her happy,' he says.

The smoke comes out quickly at an angle. She smiles.

'That's a dear thing to say. It's very sweet of you. And I'm sure you will.' Mrs Lynch holds him steadily in her eyes. She looks at him as if trying to see through that moment into all the ones that will follow. She looks not particularly impressed by his declaration or its veracity or chance of becoming actual in the real world; what she sees is its innocence. She does not know whether to protect it or knock it down.

'I know you know that Kate has had a difficult time, Jim. Well, it's not been easy, her father and I . . .' She stops herself and stabs the cigarette and twists it there in the ashtray as though it might catch fire. 'Of course it's wrong of me to say. You can make up your own mind, but you have to protect Kate. She's . . . delicate.'

'Yes.'

'Over this wedding, I don't know how much she's told you but there's been hell.'

'I'm sorry.'

'Oh, it's not your fault, Jim. I don't mean to suggest any of it is you. It's . . . you see, nothing is more important to me than my children, Jim. Their happiness. But there's been so much hurt. So much anger, you see. So much.' She sighs and looks out at the pool and allows the moment to translate as a twist of despair.

She pauses again and turns and looks at his eyes and reaches then and takes another cigarette and lights it. The crickets are too loud and the room hot and the air thick and dead. Jim looks down at the new shoes on his feet that are too large for him and shinier than any shoes he has ever owned.

'I am not sure how much you know about alcohol, Jim. Kate told me you don't drink, and I think that's so admirable and so important. It's a disease. That's the fundamental thing. My mother was an alcoholic and my father probably was too, and well you come to understand things growing up like that, and . . .' She shakes her head slightly and draws on the cigarette and sends the smoke ascending from a fire where memories burn. 'I was never that bad. I drank when the kids were gone to school, but I always managed to keep myself together enough to have the dinners on the table. That's the thing about alcohol, you get so good at masking it, you can mask it to everyone who loves you for a long time, and when they get to see past it in the end you can still mask it to yourself.'

She pauses to let him consider this and consider what she is saying behind the smoke.

'Kate's fine,' he tells her.

Mrs Lynch shakes her head, 'Oh, I know, I'm not saying that. You don't understand, I'm just, well, I've seen so much of it, I suppose.' She looks directly at him, her eyes large and sorrowful.

Jim sits. *Lost.* Car headlights play in a sweep past the side of the house. Through the screen he hears the crunch of gravel, and a car door shut. Then Gerard comes swift and purposeful into the room.

'Hey. Jim, the old boy wants to have a word.'

There is an instant without pulse or motion, as if in tableau, plume of cigarette smoke perfectly perpendicular. Then Mrs Lynch stands up and walks a few paces on the white carpet and turns about, her tone sharpened, her eyes wide.

'You don't have to go out to him, Jim. You are not obliged to if you don't want to. What does he want, Gerard? What did he say?'

'He just said, send out the Irishman, I'll have a word with him. It's nothing, it's fine, Jim,' Gerard says, watching his mother move up and down the living room as if she is a bird caught within a glass. 'He's waiting.'

'I don't mind, I'll go out.' Jim stands.

'Go with him, Gerard.'

'He doesn't need an escort.'

'I'm fine.'

'Gerard.'

A moment later, the two of them step out the front doorway of the house into the warm night.

'Jesus. I don't know why she's so uptight,' Gerard says.

'Nervous, I suppose, the planning, the wedding hasn't . . .'

The car in the driveway is a red sports car and its engine is running and its headlights play broad beams out into the woods. Michael Lynch in an open-necked white shirt is sitting behind the wheel, tanned and handsome.

'Hey!' He switches off the engine, lifts his legs out of the small car and stands tall, extending his handshake, grasping Jim's shoulder with his left hand. 'Hey, lad.'

'Hello, Mr Lynch.'

'Lean as a greyhound,' Michael Lynch tells Gerard and grins. 'So, you're the one.'

'Yes.'

'Well, well. And how is the bride-to-be?'

'She's fine, she's changing. She was just swimming in the pool.'

'Isn't that grand? And how do you like it?'

'The pool? Oh, I . . .'

'The pool, the house, the whole thing, America.'

'It's . . .'

'Not like the old country.'

'No.'

'I went back three years ago, with my mother, to see it.'

From the corner of his eye Jim thinks he sees something move in the woods, a shade deeper in the darkness. Deer or demon.

'And you write poems? A grand thing, a grand thing altogether.'

'Well, I haven't really written anything in a long . . .'

'You'll say one at the wedding, will you?'

Michael Lynch grins at Gerard, and Jim cannot tell if he is the joke or not. He glances back toward the house where the figure of Kate's mother is standing in silhouette against the library light, and he is aware of himself amidst the drawn lines of a battlefield between the two of them. The heat of the night makes sweat blister on his forehead.

'Go on, Gerard,' says Mr Lynch, 'go on in. I have to give a word of advice to the groom.'

Gerard hesitates, long aware of the same battlefield, its trenches, its flags, its brief, bitter victories. He looks to Jim as if to one that has relieved him of the guard.

'All right.'

The shadow moves in the woods again. The crickets still pulse the dark, and Jim is assailed by the feeling of foreignness in that country and how far and away and alone he is right then. He tries to think of Kate and of love and has in this the simple and intense faith of a disciple, as though what anyone thinks or does or has experienced before in the world does not matter or apply to them.

'So, lad.'

'Yes.'

'Advice of the father-in-law,' Mr Lynch says. 'Well, the critical thing is this . . .' He pauses for effect and tightens his lips and looks high into the stars at the argument written there. He grins as he reads it, the timeless case for Love and Fate, the Promising Youth, the Maiden, the impossible burgeoning Hope. 'How is it that so much that is so good can go so bad?' he asks, as if to a gallery or jury assembled on the edge of the woods. 'Here –' he lifts his hand to gesture the place – 'I built this house thinking only of happiness.' He nods his head at the memory of himself and grimace-grins. 'And I have regrets. I do. But the thing is this, lad.' He puts his hand on Jim's shoulder and holds him in his gaze. 'The critical thing is this: never,' he says, 'never say the three unforgivable words.'

Jim looks at him.

'You understand?'

'Yes,' he says, although he doesn't and already his mind is in pursuit of what they could be. *Three unforgivable words. Hate? Disgust? Horror? What?* He is suddenly stricken by the thought of them, as if they are a secret spell, a fragment of language that turns love to rust. As if in fairytale he might say them without intending and everything would corrode instantly.

'Never.'

Jim nods.

The two of them stand there. Michael Lynch's mouth is shut tight, he has no more to say. They hear the front door of the house open but for a moment do not turn back to the yellow light that falls out the door as Kate comes. Then her father says her name loudly and opens his arms to embrace her.

'Hi, Dad.'

'He's a fine lad, your poet.'

'Thanks.'

'Lean as a greyhound.'

Kate steps back beside Jim and takes his hand in hers. They seem figures at the beginning of an epic tale, a journey that starts in night woods.

'Well, goodnight, then,' the old man says, and lowers himself back into the red car and turns the ignition. 'See you in the church.'

The tyres crush and spin some gravel. He hits the horn twice with the flat of his fist and the noise flies out through the still dark trees where shadows move.

'Well,' Kate says, 'now you know the whole family.'

*

The following morning, in warm sunshine, Jim Foley and Kate Lynch are married in the church of St Mary in the town in Wapaqua, New York. The church is a white-painted wooden building and moments before the ceremony the pews are one side crowded and one side empty. There is no one from the family of the groom. His best man is Gerard. As some of the guests arrive and see this, they move into the middle pews of the groom's side but leave the front five or so vacant as though for ghosts. The priest is a Father Murrihy, a stout red-faced man in his sixties, who has told Jim in the sacristy that he golfs in Ireland every summer.

'Rosses Point, Lahinch, Ballybunion,' he says, and presses his face forward and watches for some approval that does not come. 'You play yourself?'

'I don't,' Jim answers, and remembering adds, 'Father.'

'That's a terrible shame, a terrible shame. Wonderful country for golf. You'll take it up here anyway and be going back to play. They have great trips now, you can play five or six courses in a week. Wonderful. I'm going myself August twenty-third.'

The church is hot and close and the air inside weighted with scent. While Jim stands at the altar before the bride arrives, he feels sweat run cold between his shoulder blades. There is a clamp of dampness along his hairline, when he glances down the palms of his hands glisten, and he unsticks them from the pose of prayer and holds them behind his back. He looks at the tall arrangements of the lilies but their perfume is too thick and clotted and he raises a hand and touches his brow.

'You all right?'

Gerard smiles to him and asks the question through the smile so that none watching them might suspect trouble. But Jim does not answer. He looks up past the lilies at the golden tabernacle upon whose burnished surface is reflected a broken image of the congregation below. There, in ghostlike form, he sees his mother and father enter the church and come slowly up the aisle to sit in the empty front pew. He sees the image though it is hazed and unclear as if wavered with heat. Gently Gerard nudges his arm against him and whispers his name. But Jim neither moves nor answers nor turns back to look at the pews. He keeps his eyes fixed on the tabernacle (and by those studying his long back he is variously interpreted. He is a man in the grip of fear. Oh, I can see that. He is full of doubt, you can tell. Look at him. He is not sure he should marry at all. Poor Kate, fell for him in Ireland. Ireland? Yes. And he only arrived in America a week ago. No? Yes. Imagine. He doesn't look very Irish? No, and he doesn't have a brogue. No job, either. Oh dear. A degree in Literature from some college in Dublin. Writes poems. Really? But what . . .? Exactly. They're going to live with the mother until he finds something).

Jim watches the tabernacle where the ghosts of his mother and father sit in the golden scene.

'Jim? Hey, hey, Jim, steady there. You all right?'

He says he is. He says it's hot. And it is hot and getting hotter, and the July sun is coming down through the roofbeams of that old church and people are starting to fan themselves and half turn toward the open door as if they can breathe some air with their eyes. Dust motes travel the light. Coughs soft and polite are pillowed in palms. The congregation, a splay of pink and peach and lavender, grows restless. A murmuring gathers like a weather front. (Where is she? Is she going to stand him up? It's the father. Really? Oh, yes. Michael Lynch will want to make a grand entrance. You wait and see. But it's *so* hot. I know. Can we go outside? No. Are you going straight to the club after for the reception? If it gets any hotter I'll have to go home and change. Honestly, it's twenty past. Al, what are you doing? I have to go outside, I can't stand it.)

There is a rustle behind him, and on the creased reflection Jim sees first one and then another stand up and sidle out into the aisle and to the door. Then another, then a half-dozen. Gerard turns a quick glance around and back again, whispers, 'It's all right. They're just getting some air. How you doing? You all right?'

'Yes.'

'God, it's hot.'

'Yes.'

'I suppose we can't go back into the sacristy?'

'No.'

'She'll be here in a minute. I know she will.'

If he was another he might look back then and smile or make some easeful expression to relieve the tension building there, but he is not that fellow. He thinks that on the absolute aloneness of this moment is balanced a gamble. And that within an hour or less his life will have changed forever. She will come. She will. And he will place his hand – and his life – upon her own, believing like his own religion in the enduring of love, believing it an end and a purpose and even a destiny, and that the ordinariness and tedium of life, of finding a job and making a living, will be transformed by this. And as he waits there he is aware that nothing about this is usual, and that he is in a time and place where love is written with a small *l* and that such faith is a kind of freakish extreme. He does not care. He will be priest of passion, of devotion. Kate Lynch is the first woman he has loved. She is the woman he believes love will cure of all pain, not yet understanding that it is himself he wishes to heal by loving so.

'I think she's coming,' Gerard says at last.

And indeed there is then a softly fluttering wave of motion through the congregation, figures return to their seats, women turn about fanning themselves with Mass pamphlets. The organ starts. The first notes squeeze out flat and thin and doleful, but then Mrs Conway, who is on hire for the occasion (but unofficially, eighty-five dollars in an envelope later), finds her courage and presses down the keys with force. The music is thumped on its back and has no option then but to rise up and over the pews loud and triumphant. Mrs Conway puts her elbows into it. She leans up momentarily to glance down the aisle over winged spectacles, and then, because Kate is not yet in sight, she plonks back and goes at the keys even more forcefully. It is as though she believes the volume alone will draw in the bride, as though the music is a kind of enchantment and every week when she plays it there, look, a bride walks in the door.

And just so then does Kate. She comes through the sunlit door on the arm of her father and the men and women rise.

'Good luck,' Gerard whispers and turns and smiles to his sister.

Jim does not turn around. He stands a moment longer with his back to the aisle looking up at the tabernacle. (Father Murrihy is there and has decided in this moment when no one is looking to work a little stiffness out of his jaw. He opens and rolls his mouth, forefingers back the black bridge of his glasses.) But all of this – Mrs Conway, the priest, the press of heat in the wooden church – seems wrong to Jim Foley. It is as if he is watching a production and not within it, as if it is a play stiff and unreal and absent of something in its heart. This is not what he wanted. This is not what he imagined when he knelt on one knee in April by the train tracks in Sandymount and asked Kate to marry him. There is a chasm here between the thing imagined and the real, a gap unbridgeable in that moment. What Jim Foley longs for then is a sense of sacrament, for the nearness of the divine, for something like rapture. But in the place he finds himself such notions seem outmoded, embarrassing and sentimental. To find the holiness he seeks he turns then and meets Kate's eyes. She looks at him from beneath her veil and sees him like a candle burning, and hesitates a moment before the altar rails. Then, as if in slow-motion dance, she steps free of her father's arm and comes to stand beside him.

*

They have no money to live on and so at first that summer they stay in the big blue house in Westchester with Kate's mother. For interviews in the city, Mrs Lynch buys Jim a grey suit and black tasselled loafers and two button-down Oxford shirts. He thanks her and lays the clothes on the bed upstairs, looking at the flat figure shaped there, imagining the life to come. He makes a résumé of his life for the first time and finds little to put on it. He has never worked. He has only the qualifications of his education and the thousand books he has read. He cannot drive a car. He cannot type. Kate takes a job in a garden nursery in Mount Kisco, and is gone during the day while he looks over the wanted ads in the *New York Times* and searches for anything that requires knowledge of Dickens, Shakespeare, Joyce. He wants to read the life of Tolstoy that he has upstairs in their room, but feels such reading is not appropriate in America during the day, and instead he sits in the darkened library and circles jobs for which he has no qualification. He looks for anything with 'writer' or 'writing' in the title or description. He sees 18K and 25K, and other figures, but has no real concept of salaries or taxes or the cost of a life there. Mrs Lynch walks about the house with coffee and cigarettes. She sometimes looks in at the door and tells him she has a fresh pot brewed and he comes out into the brightness and sits with her. They sit on the deck. The summer sun is still burning hot and everything is crisped. The long lawn is brown from drought.

Mrs Lynch pours the coffee.

'You know, Jim, I wanted to tell you that I think you are adjusting extraordinarily well. It can't be easy.'

He watches a small bird cross the yellow light and hide in the thickness of a cypress tree. Mrs Lynch lights a cigarette.

'I think of all the challenges you face when you are first starting out in married life and I know it can be bewildering. It must be. For me, Kate's father had a job, there was never any question about that, so I never had to deal with what you are facing now. Well, what you and Kate are. And she is doing great, I think, don't you?'

'Yes.'

'Because of course she wouldn't be used to it either, going off to work and . . . not that she's not used to working. I don't mean that, not at all. She's a very hard worker, very hard. But I do think at the nursery there's too much heavy work, lifting things, and that can't be good for her, can it? Because she will do it, you see, she will go right ahead and do things she shouldn't because it's her job. Because that's the way she was brought up, to get on with her chores without complaint. Partly out of fear of her father, of course.' She draws on the cigarette and tastes the smoke and taps the ash.

'But, Jim, work like that, the nursery business. It's not really what she should be doing, is it? It's not what you'd want for her, I'm sure. And I'd be a little afraid of it, I guess, is what I want to say.'

'I see.'

The bird flies out from the tree and ascends on the sunlight. Mrs Lynch lifts the pot and tops his cup with bitter coffee.

'Of course, I know Katie's good with plants,' she says, 'and when you have your own house she'll make sure you have a wonderful garden. I can see that. But that's not the point. No. The point is. Well, what do you think, Jim? That's what I'd like to hear from you.'

'She likes it.'

'Well, she'd say she did anyway, because she wouldn't want you to feel badly, because she has that tendency, you see, to carry the burden of other people's feelings. To be a hero for them, I suppose. So there's no disappointment. That's the thing.'

'You think she's disappointed in me.'

'No, no. I didn't say that. It's just that in the first months of marriage it's such a challenging time. You are forming the patterns, aren't you? As to how you can live together, who does what, how it all works.'

There is a pause. She watches him studying his coffee.

'I love Kate,' he says.

'I know you do.'

'I've been hesitating going into the city.'

'Because it's been so overwhelming. I can only imagine, Jim.'

'But I will. I'll go tomorrow. I'll bring the résumés in myself.'

He says it as if it is a gesture heroic or valiant or a proof of something that only he knows to be true. He says it to tell her that he will make a life for Kate and himself there in America, and he will wear the suit and ride the commuter train and that into that world he will make himself fit. Inside him are all manner of declarations, stiffened words he might then proclaim to Mrs Lynch about love and about his faith in it and how she need not worry about him and Kate and how this love – unlike the ones she has known – will endure. He might tell her he had lost belief in God until he met her daughter, and might say such things because he feels in her the loss of the religion to which he is a convert. But he does not. He turns and stares down the lawn, and Mrs Lynch lights a cigarette and across the smoke studies the empty afternoon.

'My greatest worry always is my children, Jim,' she says absently. 'You'll see one day.'

That evening when Kate gets home she and Jim go down to the pool after dinner. She is tanned and her hair is made fair by the summer sun. He tells her he has five places in New York City to bring his résumé tomorrow. I will get a job and we will find an apartment and I will make a life for us here and love you, his simple gospel runs in his head. She takes his hand. What she sees in his eyes makes her want to kiss him and she does then, and they stand there, shadows against the blue-lit water of the pool.

The following day Jim wears the grey suit and the black loafers and takes the Harlem and Hudson line train into Manhattan. He takes the 9.23 when the serious commuters are long gone and the train is sparsely filled with those peripheral to the life of the city. He has a thin new briefcase in which he has his résumés and the life of Tolstoy. He buys a copy of the *Wall Street Journal* at the station and when Mrs Lynch pulls away in the Chevrolet he is standing on the platform with it under his arm. The train is hot, the windows begrimed. Some there in fine suits and shined shoes he thinks are out of work and on their way to interviews. There is the vaguest air of embarrassment or shame that is all but hidden in their demeanour. There is something about that late morning train that seems to state failure, an element of thinly masked desperation that is then unmasked later on the 3.38 return out of Grand Central. Jim tries not to look at the other passengers. He tries not to seem the imposter he feels.

The train arrives in Grand Central and the passengers hurry to lose themselves in the crowds. Jim bounds up the stairs and into the great airy concourse. The swirl of people moving in all directions is such that he feels as if he is thrust into a race but unsure of its start or finish, only that he should move quickly. He goes up the escalator into the Pan Am building. He has found the name of a Gabriel Conroy in personnel and because it is the name of a character in Joyce's *Dubliners* he thinks to begin there. He comes in through the glass doors to the receptionist. She is a woman not much older than he, but wears a make-up so flawless that her age is unreadable and her eyes like beautiful glass.

'Excuse me.'

'Yes?'

'I wonder if I could leave this for Mr Conroy.'

'Is Mr Conroy expecting it?'

'No.'

There is a moment. She moves a thin hand with perfectly crimsoned fingernails to touch the coffee mug on her desk. Her phone rings and she presses the lit button and Jim stands there while she takes the call and checks through the extension and then waits to know if she should send it through. He stands there and watches the workings of the Switch and feels passing the memory of his father at the big switchboard in the post office and it seems a thing from another life and long ago.

'I'm sorry, Mr Conroy won't accept unsolicited mail.'

'I see.'

'I'm sorry. Thank you.' The glass eyes are looking at him. If she feels sympathy, if she remembers that she was ever on the other side of the desk and in the world in which he is standing, she does not show it.

'Actually it's not unsolicited,' Jim says.

'I asked you if he was expecting it.'

The door behind him opens and a man with impossibly white teeth and a dark suit stands there.

She leans wide of Jim and asks, 'Yes, may I help you?'

'I have an appointment with Mr Bernstein,' he says.

'Mr Laurence Bernstein or Mr Leonard?'

'Mr Laurence.'

'Your name?'

'Silver, Jonathan.'

'Thank you, Mr Silver, please take a seat. I'll let him know.'

Exchange of politeness like polished glass. Silver withdraws and from a dispenser takes a paper cone of water.

In his grey suit Jim Foley waits, air conditioning catching the sweat-line at his collar, holding the manila envelope which is smudged with fingerstains from *Wall Street Journal* newsprint.

'His secretary will be out to you in just a moment.' Glass eyes sparkle across at Silver, shimmer crimson lipgloss.

'Thank you.'

'You're very welcome.'

A mouth of marvellous flexible plastic shuts tight as she turns to Jim.

'What is it?'

'What?'

'In the envelope? What's in it?'

He feels Silver watching him. He drops his voice to tell her. 'It's my résumé.'

'He won't look at it.'

'Can I just leave it for him?'

'He won't look at it. He only sees people sent by an agency.'

'Here. Will you give it to him?' Jim reaches in and puts the envelope on her desk and she shakes her styled hair very slowly from side to side and touches the glossed lips together and he feels he is a barbarian crashing against the gates.

'Thank you,' he says, but the embarrassment is rising up through him now and his face is flushed and he turns as he says it and is walking out the door when Mr Laurence Bernstein's secretary comes and collects Silver and his impossibly white smile inside.

Jim goes out into the noise and fumes of traffic and construction. He blinks in the sunlight of 42nd Street and feels ashes in his mouth. His shirt and suit feel somehow used now, things of a worn-out performance, and when he sees himself in the long windows he sees only the pretence. He has no destination, he moves to be moving, to be not standing there in that city where everything seems in constant motion and where stillness is the condition of the lost. He moves up Park Avenue as if he is out of the office on his way to a meeting. He hammers the footpath brusquely in the black loafers and goes up as far as 52nd Street and then turns west onto it when the light is against him. He taps along quickly as if pursued, but the dead heat is like a thick cloth hanging between the buildings and he feels no matter how hurriedly he moves he cannot get away fast enough. He rushes through the burnt smells of pretzels, the tang of salt, the acrid odours of garbage, the hot soiled scent of human effort, the twists of steam rising from underground. On Sixth Avenue he turns north and then west again on 54th Street, racing on and looking straight ahead of him. On Broadway he turns toward the park. He goes up two streets and then sees the Coliseum Bookstore and turns in there.

At once the air is cooler, and in the quiet of mid-morning when there are few customers the bookshop is a kind of haven. The very shelving of the books, the worn hue of the timber flooring, the stacks, the headed sections, Fiction, Poetry, Drama, the vertical spines, the smell that is the smell of words printed on paper, all make Jim Foley feel at ease. He goes past Bestsellers and Bargains and down to Literature. There he stands before books so many of which are familiar to him and which he has owned and read and from some of which he can recite passages. His eye goes along the names, Austen, Brontë, Collins, Dickens, Hardy, Joyce, the ABC of literature, and the silent saying of the names is like a murmured greeting as he comes within an assembled company of friends. He draws out a copy of *Great Expectations* in an unfamiliar edition and looks at it for a time. He reads a section from Chapter Nineteen where Pip excitedly gets ready to leave for London. And while he reads it he forgets for a time the failure of the morning and escapes from New York City and the disappointment of his first months in the real world. He puts the book back and takes out another.

An hour passes. He is the man in a new grey suit reading fiction. He stands there long enough for the white-faced youth filling the stock to notice him. He reads there with the briefcase on the floor leaning against his leg, and it seems he must be engaged in research or matters of serious import so still and absorbed and concentrated is his demeanour. He is there reading while a woman comes and hunts along the shelves with a book-list for her son and picks out a novel by Hawthorne and says something about the price of it and looks to him for agreement. Jim half nods and returns what he was reading and looks further along the shelves and then is suddenly nostalgic for his own youth and for what seems vanished now. He misses Ireland. Or at least so it seems to him, missing a place he does not realize he is just then inventing. He makes it up from fragments of the real Ireland, a country in the rain. He takes down a copy of *A Portrait of the Artist* and reads the opening. He knows it well. He reads it for the comfort there is in the familiar and in an Irish voice. He has not the money to buy it, and so for a time he stands there holding it and then he reaches down as if to check the contents of his briefcase and he slips the book inside.

'Hey.'

The man's voice catches him at the back of his neck, and before he turns he thinks – almost comically – to run. Except it is not Jim but the woman with the Hawthorne who is being hailed by a friend. He breathes a sigh, and moves along the shelf. He might return the book still, he might pay for it at the counter from the twenty dollars Kate gave him out of the cash she gets paid at the nursery. In his grey suit he might pretend he was on his way back to work with Gabriel Conroy in the Pan Am building.

But none of these are possibilities. He wants the book in an obscure way he cannot explain and he cannot spend Kate's money on it.

Soon he is back in Grand Central Station, sitting on an age-smoothed bench and eating the peanut-butter sandwich Mrs Lynch made for him. He lets two trains go. He waits for the 3.38. When his sandwich is done he sits there in the great cavernous concourse and watches the scattered figures crossing the floor back and forth before vanishing forever. He opens his briefcase to see the stolen copy of *A Portrait*. In his haste to hide the book inside his case he has accordianed creases into the four other copies of his résumé that he was to deliver that day. Feeling soiled and crushed and worn, he takes them out now, stands up and, while a man in three coats with a maul of plastic bags watches him, he crosses to the waste bin and one by one posts the summaries of his life into it.

A form letter comes from the school. There has been an outbreak of head lice in the parish. All parents are advised to thoroughly check their children's hair, and then to douse them with one of a number of powerful chemicals.

'Well, we won't be doing that,' I say out loud. Jack is anxiously waiting while I finish reading.

'Is it bad, Dad? What does the letter say?'

'It's about head lice.'

'Are they bad? Do I have them?'

'No. They're not bad, they're itchy.'

'I'm itchy.' He scratches his head furiously.

Later, scene out of another century, I lay out a sheet of brown book-covering paper on the table and have Jack sit with head bent over it. I arrange the lamp so a corona of light rings him.

'Close your eyes now.'

Then I stoop and peer and comb each rib of hair carefully aside. And I find them, the grey secret creatures, his head alive with them. Passing the kitchen Hannah comes brusquely over to see.

'Oh my God,' she says, 'that's so gross,' and rushes off to shampoo her hair again.

'What? What is?' Jack turns his head to look up, as though there may be animals I am taking out of his skull.

'Turn back, close your eyes, it's nothing.'

But in fact it is. There are many minute eggs clinging to the hair and they do not comb free and must be one by one pulled along and off. While I do this, Jack sits patiently bowed. He says nothing. He *suffers the situation so well I feel a great wave of compassion for him wash through me, and think that in relieving him of the eggs and this secret parasitical life, I am doing the kind of good that fathers should. As if the lice were imagined monsters or the fearsome figures in his dreams.*

After, I fold the brown paper onto itself carefully.

'Am I done, Dad?'

'Yes, you are.'

'Were there any?'

'There are none now.'

I lay the paper on the fire. Jack stands beside me to watch. The blaze climbs and thinly crackles. He reaches and takes my hand.

*

Victory followed swiftly by defeat. After two hours in the bathroom this Saturday morning Hannah emerges, her hair dyed the deepest shade of black. There has been no discussion, no warning. When she steps out my mouth drops open, and at once she reacts sharply.

'What?'

'I didn't say anything.'

'You don't have to.'

She walks quickly out of the room.

'Wait! Hannah!'

She keeps on going. I am at the foot of the stairs as she closes her bedroom door. When I get there I knock.

'Can I come in?'

'I don't care.'

I open the door. On her bed she is apparently deep in concentration on a book. On the TV Sky News is telling us the world economy is crashing.

'Hannah, I didn't say I didn't like it.'

'Well, do you?' Instant of pause. I am too slow to lie. 'I know you don't. You hate it; well, fine, I don't.'

'You're not giving me a chance.'

'Dad?'

'*What?*'

'*I don't care. OK? You like it, you don't like it. No big deal. I really don't care. Now, I'd like to just read, all right?*'

Weather sponsored by Ryanair shows clouds over Ireland.

I say nothing. I walk out.

Twice a week for the month of August, while Kate goes to work at Jimmy's Garden Nursery in Mount Kisco earning $3.75 an hour, Jim Foley takes the mid-morning train on the Harlem and Hudson line from Wapaqu into Grand Central station. Mrs Lynch drops him at the station. He has a sandwich in a brown-paper bag in his case and a clutch of newly printed résumés. He arrives in the city and walks up Park Avenue in the airless heat and then goes across town to the Coliseum Bookstore. He passes in through the doors as though they are the entranceway to his office, and once inside he has a similar command of his sur-roundings. He knows where everything is now, knows how to get straightaway to sections of Literature, Poetry and Drama, and whether the titles have been disturbed or misplaced since his last visit. Intently he stands before a row of books as if he is engaged in a survey of book spines or publishers' typography or the sizing of authors' names. He takes down a book and reads from it. He reads the first act of Tennessee Williams's *The Night of the Iguana* and no one comes and questions or disturbs him. After they have noticed him coming for several days the staff supposes he must belong to a publishing company or wholesaler's, and be research-ing something. They do not think that he can be there simply for the books themselves. He reads for an hour and sometimes goes out and has a coffee in Sherri's Diner on Eighth Avenue and comes back again. Some days he heads for another of the city's great bookshops. He goes to Scribner's on Fifth Avenue. He loves that name, *Scribner's*, and thinks of the sound and its associations, of the nib he can hear scratching on hard paper, scrib, scrib, of scribes and scribing, of scribbling too. And of the Irish word to write, *scriobh*, with its final harsher consonants, its V of sound, as though the parchment of monks in stone towers was rougher and the nibs sharp as knives.

It is a wonderful bookshop. The shelving is dark-stained, the books upon them ordered like a democratic republic, without judgement of merit or saleability, each one honoured. When he peruses the fiction section in the lower end of the alphabet he comes up beside the broad window that looks out on the street. There is only the glass between the literature and the hurrying figures and the noise and the August heat outside. Jim knows he should be out there. He should be delivering his résumé to offices about the city. Mrs Lynch has told him not to despair over the slow response. 'So many people are away in August, things pick up in September, after Labor Day, you'll see.' *Labor Day*, he thought, apt and ironic. For him things will not pick up then. He cannot bear to think of it, nor that he is failing Kate. He looks along the titled rows for help, for courage, for company. He takes a copy of Dostoevsky's *Crime and Punishment* and hides it inside his jacket.

He goes to Brentano's, to the Doubleday Bookstore, or sometimes to the dark splendour and promise of Rizzoli's, and reads there. After a time he can read his way around the city, and so pass the day going from place to place as though on a series of interviews with great writers. By mid-afternoon Jim Foley has finished his rounds and heads back to Grand Central. There in the main concourse he eats his guilt sandwich and posts copies of his résumé in the bin.

When he gets off the train out in Wapaqua he is to call Mrs Lynch to come and collect him. But the distance is less than two miles and he rarely phones, preferring instead to walk through that pretty town past Gristede's and Healy's and onto the dusty roads where the big houses are hidden in the trees. Often when he comes up the driveway to the house, the Chevrolet is not there;

Mrs Lynch is with her sponsor or someone she is sponsoring in the programme. Jim comes around the back of the house then, and he walks down the long slope of summer grass and he is hot from the walk from the station and weary with the knowledge of his own deception and failure in America. He comes down toward the tennis court to the end of the pool where the diving board is rigid and still over the blue waters. And he puts down the brief-case and takes off his shoes and his socks and the grey suit and the white shirt and burgundy tie and stacks all of these neatly along the near end of the board. He moves up alongside the pool to within his depth and stands on the edge. The afternoon sun is still warm and beyond the woods the humming noise of the highway is gathering rhythm now with the white-faced rush of the home-ward bound. He stands there. His thoughts are too many and too entwined in a hot ball for him to know them clearly. He cannot say he is thinking of failure or loss or the uncertainty of love or the sour taste of vanquished dreams. He cannot say he is think-ing of his dead father or sister or his lost brother or the hope that love will erase all of these. He stands there. Then he opens out his arms and falls face first into the water.

There is in those instants a kind of clean erasure when he crashes through the surface of the pool water and his body absorbs the shock of the cold. For a few moments there is nothing but the startling chill of it as Jim plunges down through the bubbles of himself. His eyes are wide and he opens his mouth in a gasp and his mind is briefly freed of thinking. He is a body cold sinking in blue water and the cold is like a skin.

He stands to his neck and shakes back his head in a brief glit-ter and brings his hands to his face. He looks up at the house. No one is there. He walks down into the shallow end of the pool where the surface is just above his waist. Then he looks up at the house again to be sure that no one is watching. And then he makes a kind of quick three-step run in the water letting himself fall for-ward, kicking as he takes four frantic fast strokes with his arms and tries to swim.

By the end of the fourth stroke he is going under. Quickly he stands up in water to his chest, and turns and walks back down the pool to the shallow end. There he begins again. He takes the same sluggish three-step run up and then launches himself at speed against the water, kicking high white splashes in his wake as his hands seem to be digging out the water in front of him. It is four strokes before he feels himself sinking to the bottom once again.

Each time then he does the same thing. He looks up at the house to make sure he is not seen. He walks back to the shallow end, and he tries to swim. And he does so for an hour that afternoon and many others too, trying to swim in the pool at the back of the big blue house down the dry lawn beyond the cedar trees. He tries over and over. Sometimes he gets to the fifth stroke before he sinks. Sometimes his head thrashing in the water is the image of his father's stroke, mute denials. Sometimes as he walks back through the broken wake of himself he imagines he is making progress and that within a month he will be able to swim the full length. Before Mrs Lynch or Kate return he gets out of the pool and stands and feels the momentary cool of the air. Then he picks up his suit and his shoes and his case and carries them against himself up the grass to the house where he dresses and sits on the deck and reads from a stolen book. Unseen, beyond the trees the traffic beats. The surface of the pool water below returns to a blue stillness.

*

By the end of the summer Jim Foley has no job and still cannot swim. He sometimes manages six strokes before he feels himself sink and panics and lets his feet touch the floor of the pool and make a few steps, sort of jogging in slow motion, before he kicks again. He has no concept of breathing. He cannot understand how to get or release air in water. In the evenings when Kate comes home weary from working in the garden nursery, she sometimes goes and changes into her swimsuit, and Jim walks down to the pool with her as the night is falling over the woods. He declines her offer to come in. Instead he stands and watches as she dives off the board in a graceful arc and her body glimmers beneath the underlit water. He studies her perfect form as she surfaces and begins the front crawl. How does she do that? How does she seem to move with such easeful purpose, her head turning softly to the side and her mouth wide as though she might drink the pool? She flips and turns and pushes off again and her legs are like a tail thrumming. Kate swims laps. Years of swim team have left in her this mark: she cannot be in a pool and simply float or swim haphazard curves or fluid meanders; she must do her laps. While Jim stands there thinking how peaceful and serene it is to flow through the pool like that, Kate counts her laps. She knows this pool like her own childhood, her strokes through it are laid upon others years before. She does not need to count the number of times she must arc arm over arm or glance to see the wall coming. They are within her. The wall she pushes against is the one she first encountered in a bubbly flash when her father had built the pool and filled it for the first time and she ran down the lawn and threw her towel there and leapt in to show him how brave and fast and good she was. It is the same wall she pushed hard against in morning practice before school, getting faster and faster, swimming through the broken blue water in a feverish race against an invisible opponent that could never be beaten. Her father did not stay to watch. Her brother swam and won medals and then turned to the greater more obvious glories of the football field and the track. That Kate swam first to win affection and then later, when that was not coming, to escape into that other element where pain and loss and longing were erased in the rhythm of the routine, the back and forward flow for an hour, did not matter. By the time she had joined the swim team and later was a lifeguard and later still swam for her college, the pool and she had grown so familiar that she could not get into the water without a flash of recognition, the returning flow of memories that, despite all her trophies, was bitter as much as sweet. She swims. She swims like a champion in the pool her father had built at the back of the house (arguing against the apparent show of luxury to his Irish mother in Queens that one of the kids would win a swim scholarship and thereby save him more than the expense, and then exhorting the kids to prove him right). She swims. She swims like a dreamer deep in the dream, lost to all and not least to the man who stands there holding the towel and preparing to do the thing he had promised himself never to do: hurt her.

When the count reaches its end, forty or fifty or so, like a command issued along a galley to the rowers, the stroke stops and Kate floats and turns on her back and her own momentum carries her back up the pool. Her skin is silvered, her hair flows to the sides. She draws breath and for a brief time floating is like a child coming off a merry-go-round where things have not yet slowed and gone back into place.

'You ready?' Jim says and opens the white towel in the darkness behind the lights of the pool. He has decided. *I have to tell her.* He cannot deceive her any more. He cannot pretend that he interviews in the city or that Callaghan at BBD&O has called him back for a third interview, or that Conroy at Bursten & Marsteller is seriously considering him. He holds the towel and over it looks up at the lights of the house where he can see Mrs Lynch smoking her cigarette and talking with some animation on the phone to Gerard in California.

Kate rises out of the pool and Jim enwraps her. He keeps his arms about her. She is small and thin and very beautiful and when he holds her he feels the fierce current of love that makes him feel he is both saved and her saviour. She turns her head and shakes her hair loose. He is standing behind her.

Kate, I have no chance of getting a job. I haven't been able to do any interviews. I can't face them, the people in those offices don't want to see me. I'm not what they want. I'm sorry. I go into the city but when I get there something happens, something. It sounds, I know I know, I'm an idiot.

'I'm cold. It's cold,' Kate says and shivers and moves deeper within his arms and all the words that are running through him run into the dark. He holds her and in his embrace she feels like a part of himself that he has rescued from the water. She turns her head back to see the night sky but the floodlight on the pool obscures the stars. Jim moves the towel in small motions on her back.

'You feel better?' he asks.

'Yes. But cold, so cold. I can't believe it's so cold. Summer's gone.'

He rubs the towel harder.

'Better?'

'Thanks.' Then she cocks her head slightly and says, 'Smell.'

'What?'

'Smell that.' Her face is lit like a child's with a child's wonder and she tilts back her head and inhales deeply of something delicious in the air. 'The fall,' she says to Jim when she hears him sniffing. 'The autumn in the trees. Oh, I love that. Smell it. Do you smell it?' Her eyes are still closed and the towel is around her and water is dripping from her hair. 'On a still night like this, it's just the best,' she says. Jim says nothing. 'This smell brings me back every time, when I was small, running through these woods.' She says nothing more but stands until she shivers.

And as they turn to go back up the lawn and out of the light, there is a deep beauty in the night that soothes and almost quells the uncertainty and failure Jim feels. And he takes Kate's hand in his and as they walk he silently decides to ask in one of the bookshops for a job, to get work there, even though it is not what Mrs Lynch hopes for him. It will be a start. They will move out soon into a small apartment. Yes. He holds her hand and thinks, *It will be all right yet, it will.*

*

'In a bookstore, Jim?'

'Yes.'

'In the city? But how much will you make?' Mrs Lynch pulls

a cigarette from the box and holds it on her lip. 'You'll spend half what you earn just commuting. You know that? It's silly, Jim. You've lost heart, that's all. You need another round of résumés, now that it's September.'

'I don't think so, Mrs Lynch.'

'But . . .'

'I've accepted the job.'

'Putting books on shelves?'

'And opening boxes.'

'Oh, I'm sorry, but I think that's terrible, Jim. Terrible.'

'It's just a start. I'll get something else after.'

'You haven't told Kate.'

'I'll tell her this evening.'

The smoke is shot upward. 'Well, I think it's a mistake, but . . .' She shrugs. They sit there as the shadows of early evening come swiftly over the lawn.

When Kate comes home, Jim tells her in the upstairs bedroom.

'Are you happy?' she asks him.

'I think it's a start. It's something anyway.'

'Then that's it.' She holds out her arms to him. He closes his eyes as she kisses him and he feels forgiven and blessed. After dinner they come down to the pool, where the air is noticeably cooler now. Kate swims laps. Mrs Lynch is silhouetted at the sliding door of the sitting room above. The night seems thin and edged, there are stars and a sharp slice of moon. In a week the pool will be closed. The cedars and the rose bushes will need to be wrapped in burlap against the deer. The storm windows will need to be hung.

*

The first snow falls the week after Thanksgiving. It comes one evening with darkness, thick and clotted, slanting out of the sky in slow motion. It falls so heavily that within an hour lawn and tennis court and covered pool are erased into whiteness. The trees are first fringed and then blanched in outline. Kate and Jim go outside in it. They stand in the print of themselves and look upward blinking into the twirl of flakes as if to see a source high up emptying. Kate opens her mouth and offers the sky her tongue and tells Jim to do the same. And so he does, the two of them standing, snow-blind, arms outreached, palms heavenward, the image of some winter religion perhaps, whose practice is to be attendant on the fortuitous fall of snowflakes, as if such, melting on the tongue, was a kind of grace.

And soon in fact there is grace for them. Before Christmas Jim's diligence at work in Sutherland's on East 58th Street, one of the last family-run bookstores in New York City, results in an early raise. He is to be allowed to serve the customers now, not just open the boxes and shelve the books. Kate, helping in a floral arrangement for a fiftieth wedding anniversary for Dr and Henrietta Morgan at their house in Mount Kisco, has been offered a flat in the elderly couple's grand old house above the town. A week before Christmas, they move in there. It is a bedroom and a sitting room, a tiny bathroom and a one-person-wide scullery. Around the house are extensive lawns and old trees. Dr Morgan, a benign man with a stooped neck and fluttering blue birds of eyes, has mentioned to Jim that he might help with the lawn-mowing in the spring. It would reduce their rent, he quickly added and frowned at himself for the indelicacy of his offer, as though somehow there existed a way to make it without suggesting the young couple might be short of finances. He had frowned at the puzzle for a few moments, combinations of wording passing in front of him. Then Jim said loudly across the bridge of the doctor's worsening deafness that he would be delighted.

They have their first space, their first car, their first kettle and dishes and cutlery, their first definitions of who they are and what their life looks like in the real world. On the wooden floorboards they have stacks of books, many stolen. As the cold of December grips they discover the sectioned-off apartment of the house has only one radiator that moans and knocks, so they sit in the evenings after work with heavy jumpers and bowls of thick soups or stew cooked all day in the wedding-gift crockpot. And they are happy.

In Sutherland's, Jim works from nine until six o'clock. He leaves in the winter dark before dawn and takes the train not in a grey suit but in a zippered jacket and woollen hat, reading not the *New York Times*, but John Cheever's *The Wapshot Chronicle*. He heads up Lexington Avenue and is at the bookstore as Horace Sutherland opens it. Horace at fifty-one is heavy, pie faced, pink-frosted lips. He tells Jim to get ready to hold open the second door while he goes and lends his arm to his eighty-two-year-old father, Theodore, who comes with cane and round-rimmed dandruff-snowed glasses every day. The book business is in decline, Theodore, has told Jim, reaching out and holding onto his shoulder for support.

'People don't care for books any more. This is a great book,' he says, taking down a copy of *Democracy in America*. 'Buy this, you won't regret it.'

'Mr Sutherland, I work here.'

'What?'

'I'm Jim. I work here.'

'Do you?' Through the snowed glasses peer watery blue eyes, the voice a croak.

'Yes, sir.'

'Have you read it? Have you read *Democracy in America*?'

'No, I haven't.'

'Take it home tonight. Read it, you'll sell it better. That's a tip, take home whatever you want, read it. Would you buy meat from a butcher that wouldn't touch the steak? You wouldn't. Read the books, read them.'

'Yes, sir, I will.'

The door opens and a woman with cool assertiveness in expensive shoes strides in. She wants the new John Updike.

'Who?' Theodore asks, and leans forward on his cane.

'Updike, Mr Sutherland,' Jim says. 'We have it.'

'We have it,' says the old man with a smile.

Jim goes and brings a copy, by which time the woman has had *Democracy in America* pressed into her hand.

'Here it is,' Jim says.

'Let me see that.' Theodore takes the book and holds it close for inspection. 'He's a new writer to me. You know him?'

'Yes, Mr Sutherland,' Jim says.

'Good?'

'Yes, sir.'

'Well, there you are.' He hands the book to the woman. 'I'll read it this evening myself.'

'But I wanted it in paperback.'

'In paper? Get it in paper, please.'

'But it only just came out, Mr Sutherland. It's only a week old.'

'The lady wants it in paper.'

'But . . .'

'Go and find one. We have it in the back, I saw it yesterday.'

Jim goes down to the storeroom where he first worked opening boxes from the wholesalers Bakers & Taylor and various publishers. He knows the book is not there. But he waits. He looks at sorry stacked copies of books unsold and due for return. When at last he goes back up to the front counter the woman has four other books in her arms. Theodore Sutherland is leaning on the customer. She will not get away.

'I'm sorry, Mr Sutherland, we don't—'

'We must have sold the last one.'

'Yes, sir.'

Theodore smiles at the woman. 'I'll order more and one for you personally myself.'

'Thank you.'

'Who is the publisher on that?'

'Alfred Knopf,' Jim tells him.

'I'll call Alfred myself tonight. In the meantime, you read these. Ring these up, Jim. Two dollars off the *Democracy in America*.'

'Yes, sir.'

It happens time and again. Sutherland's sells more copies of Tocqueville than any other retail bookstore in America. Whatever the customer asks for, you tell them you have it. If you know you don't, you delay, you make an order, you suggest something else.

'Nobody leaves the shop without a book, Horace,' Theodore tells his son. 'That's the business we're in, selling books. That's how I built this from a cart in the street. Remember that.'

Horace pouts pink lips to kiss the truth of his father's statement.

Despite the old man's gloomy forecast for the book business, there are plenty of customers in the shop every day. They come at all hours, spend minutes or sometimes the entire morning or afternoon. They come for specific titles, for obscure books of nonfiction not found elsewhere, or with fragments of information, an author's name someone mentioned at the weekend now part-forgotten, a title unremembered, something about doves, it was mentioned in the *New York Times*. While Jim hunts the books down, Horace sits in the back in the small office working on the accounts. His father rests in an armchair behind him, or comes to patrol the aisles, unaware perhaps of how the more regular customers, with book open, manage to move sideways around the shelving and into the next aisle as he heads toward them. Or perhaps he is not unaware, and enjoys the hunt and the exercise that keeps him alive.

'Isaac!'

'Good to see you, Mr Sutherland.'

'Wait for a minute, I want to tell you something.'

The old man tries to shuffle, stretches his arm with cane to pull in the distance, says, 'I'm not as quick as I used to be.'

'You look well, Mr Sutherland.'

'Thank you.' A wheeze, a croak, a moistening of dried lips.

'There's a book I wanted to talk to you about. Remarkable. Have you ever read *Democracy in America*?'

'You sold me three copies, Mr Sutherland.'

'Did I?' A smile lights the old face. 'Isn't it extraordinary? As relevant today as when it was written, don't you think?'

'I do.'

'Have you this edition?'

In the freeze that comes that year in January, February and March, Jim rides the morning-dark train in through the snowscape of Westchester and spends his days in shirtsleeves in the pumped-out snug of heat in Sutherland's. Theodore and Horace fear the cold like a terrible enemy; it brings aches, coughs, flu, rheumatism and more. They have the heat on high. The old man sometimes comes as far as the front window and, his head above the display of mysteries, peers out at the slush-grey sidewalk disapprovingly. He remembers a time before there was a store, he tells Jim. He remembers his father taking off three coats and fingerless gloves. He nods at the memory, he tells Horace to put the heat up another notch. And so, in winter, books and customers dwell in mid-tropical climate there on East 58th Street. The season is nothing to the authors arranged there.

It is not so for Kate. She drives their old Toyota to the nursery in workboots and jeans with a thick sweater and down vest. She stops and buys coffee in Chock full o'Nuts, and before starting work stands among the empty flatbeds and curls herself around a travel mug, two-handed, steam and breath vanishing. There are few customers or none. The owner, Jimmy Manzano, is gone to Europe. For the few employees kept on, there is the heavy work of moving and lifting, of digging out and mulching, of getting ready for spring. There are repairs to the old glasshouse to be made, new display beds to be laid out, the old and dead to be dug out and burned. In a kind of winter silence then, in the contemplative emptiness of the nursery, Kate works. In a way she enjoys the season more than the bustle of summer when the plants are too often bought as quick remedies, the showiest first, by ladies who come in expensive clothes and small cars for something in a pot or to make a display for the weekend barbecue. Here there are only the handful of gardeners and the unglamorous chores of care.

The hours of morning can pass without a word. She stoops or kneels at a gravel bed. She tries to free a root from the frozen ground. The air still and birdless and clear seems an element pure and cleansed and cleansing. Time runs away there. She stops around noontime and tells Petey she is going on her lunchbreak, but she only goes as far as the corner of the tree nursery where there is a bench by slim bare dogwoods and there she has her sandwich. She works until five o'clock and drives home weary in her bones.

*

For Kate's birthday in April Jim thinks he will write her a poem. The inspiration may be the absence of money – he earns enough only to keep them surviving in the special low-rent lawn-exchange apartment of Dr Morgan, cannot afford any of the fine things behind the bell-jingling doors in the shops of Bedford Village and Chappaqua. The poverty is relative, but it is enough to leave him feeling a stain of shame, of unworthiness, which could be absolved by the composition of a poem. The problem is he has not written anything in a long time. When he last did there were only phrases, pieces of a possible something, some rhythmic fragments that ran in his head. But the poem itself never quite materialized, as if, though he said the words and tried to sound out the feeling, no act of transubstantiation took place. He abandoned it.

Now he sits on the morning train in April and shuts his eyes to say silently the first words of a love poem to Kate. On Her Birthday. Moon and stars come and here. Moon and stars come and here in my hand be held. *Moon and stars come / and here in the hollow of my hands / be held for her whose* . . .

'Grand Central. Next and final stop Grand Central Station. Be sure to take all your belongings with you, and have a nice day. Grand Central Station.'

whose heart . . .

He walks up Lexington Avenue in the coatless crowds of mild April. Sunlight on glass and steel glints as if on armoured towers.

His footsteps beat the rhythm of phrase. Over and over he repeats the words in the only means of composition he knows. He watches the green street signs pass, getting near the bookstore without further progress on the poem. He arrives at the door and Horace Sutherland greets him with puff-pastry cheeks and black-cherry eyes of panic.

'We have to do a complete inventory,' he says, 'come on. Everything. Everything has to be done. And father is not coming in, he was ill last night. O God, I need coffee. Go and get coffee will you, Jim? And a few donuts.'

'All right.'

'Cinnamon-glazed.'

He goes as far as Blintz's on Third Avenue. He tries to find again the rhythm of the poem, but loses faith in it, puts it away in some corner of his mind until later. He brings back the coffee and begins the inventory, handling book after book in a slow patient exercise of names and numbers. In the poetry section he opens some of the volumes he takes down, reads marvellous first lines of Whitman, of Robert Lowell, Wallace Stevens. He thinks the poem he has started is appalling, soft sentiment, like old fruit saved in a drawer, greyly powdered to nothing. What was he thinking, moon and stars and such rubbish? In mid-afternoon, the bookstore in a hush and stacks of volumes out on the ground, he thinks again, Poem on Her Birthday.

Forgive me. No word or music comes / In April afternoon an ache opens.

Whether it is a real or false beginning he cannot say. The lines lie in his mind, but there are no more of them. He finishes work, the inventory not yet half done, and takes the train home. He has two days to finish the poem. But in those two days a hundred phrases are forced and each one after ten minutes or half an hour reads untrue. The night before her birthday Kate gets a call from her mother. Mrs Lynch is in a panic, she has been going over her bank account, she hasn't enough money, she will have to sell the house. Kate tries to calm her on the phone and then leaves to drive over. Sitting at the small table, Jim writes the two lines on a white sheet.

In April afternoon an ache opens . . .

Like what? Like? Like?

Like a drawer of knives.

A moment after he has written it down it occurs to him it is a phrase he has read and stolen from somewhere. Sylvia Plath maybe, or Eavan Boland. Disgusted, he crosses it out. He balls up the sheet and starts again. By the time the headlights of the car cut across the sitting-room window two hours later he has still only two lines. Quickly he gathers up the wasted pages and bins them, opens F. Scott Fitzgerald's *Tender Is the Night.*

When Kate comes in her face is drawn and her eyes full of sadness.

'Were you able to calm her?'

'When I left her she said she was all right. She was in her night-gown, but I think she was going straight back to her yellow pads. You should see the office, pages and pages of numbers, and chequebooks, and . . . oh, I don't want to talk about it.'

'Here.'

He holds her in his arms. 'Come on.' He leads her to the tiny bathroom where he runs the water and watches as she undresses. She lies back in the deep warm water and closes her eyes.

In the morning he is awake before her and has coffee and toast on a tray. She sits up and smiles to his soft singing two lines of 'Happy Birthday'.

'Here. I wanted something more,' he says, and gives her the folded piece of white paper.

POEM ON HER BIRTHDAY

Forgive me. No word or music comes.
I have no gift. In April afternoon
An ache opens, and will not close.
Screen door blows and bangs,
My unhinged love for you.

'Thank you,' Kate says.

'I tried to—'

'Thank you.'

She looks at him, and has in her eyes a kind of faith he doesn't possess.

'Write more,' she says. 'Write, Jim. You have to, you're a writer. You should be writing.'

*

But he cannot. No words come. Or rather, thousands of them come, singly, and in clusters, at all times of morning noon and night. Words he loves the sound of, words he links and plays with in his mind, making free associations. *Fractious. A vaporous smile. Imperious rain. The lustre of her intelligence.* But nothing comes of them. They wash up tide after tide on the edges of his brain, flotsam and jetsam of language, useless fragments of a supreme fiction perhaps, but without intimation of how they go together, or what he is to make of them. Sometimes Jim thinks it is because he does not sit down at blank pages and work at it. And so he does, writing phrases, poem-pieces that do not match, like a blind man's newspaper clippings. What is his subject? What is he to write about? He feels at times stricken by a sense there is something he is supposed to say, something that is his alone to write. But whatever it is is beyond him. It is as though the message has been faultily passed, or whispered and missed in the roar of traffic, the words there, but just outside the range of his hearing.

One morning spring is become summer, the city wears its shirtsleeves and slings its jacket. Along the dazzling glass towers are mirrored the beautiful. Scents of almond and coconut lie on the air. Over on Third Avenue Blintz's does a trade in homemade lemonade. On the huge half-block poster that covers the construction hoarding at 46th and Fifth is a giant supine model in black bikini and knowing smile, lying on the word 'Summertime' in scarlet letters, with beneath it the store's name. At Sutherland's the book business takes on its seasonal face, paperbacks and travel books are moved to a table near the front, picture books of New York City, maps and guides given a new sign. In the heatwave of June, Theodore does not come to work. He suffers in this weather, Horace explains.

'I mean, can you imagine still coming to work at his age?' he says, not a little proudly. 'He's something, isn't he?'

At noon Horace emerges pinkly from his backroom meeting with the sales woman from Harper & Row.

'I'm only halfway through,' he says. 'I haven't even started the backlist. Do me a favour, Jim, go to Blintz's, get a roast beef on rye, lettuce and tomato, mayo and pickles, no onion, a medium lemonade, half-ice, they put so much ice you can't taste the thing, he won't drink it unless you tell them half-ice, all right? Then here—' deep from a pocket jangle of change, Horace fishes a key – '62 East 76th, between Lexington and Park. Apartment 12. Call out as you go in the door. He'll be in his armchair. All right? She'll take me out to lunch when you get back. Tell him, it's Harper & Row and I couldn't get away.'

Jim takes the key and walks up the bookstore.

'No onion, right?' Horace calls.

Half an hour later, Jim arrives with the drink and sandwich at the apartment building. There is a spacious and elegant lobby and an air of old unquestioned wealth. He is surprised the old man lives there. But it is not until he turns the key in the apartment door and steps inside that he realizes Horace lives there as well, that Sutherland's Books does not have to make them money, and is in fact a kind of long slow drain of wealth made elsewhere decades before.

'It's Jim, Mr Sutherland.'

'Who?'

'Jim from the bookstore.'

'Yes, what is it?'

'I brought your lunch. Horace asked me to; he's with Harper & Row.'

Theodore Sutherland sits, hands on the arms of his chair,

facing the window. A book on American history is open in his lap. His eyes as he peers up are like milky blue water.

'Roast beef on rye?' he asks.

'Roast beef on rye,' Jim says. 'I'll get you a plate.'

He heads out of the room into the front hallway where there are several doors. He opens the nearest thinking it will be the kitchen, but it is a cloakroom. Another is a bathroom. The next opens on a passageway with other doors leading off it. They have the entire floor. He opens doors as he goes, bedroom, second bathroom, bedroom, and then, a large dusky room of shelves and boxes with blinds drawn. Upon one of the boxes a book title: *Democracy in America*. He takes a step further into the room, looks at another of the boxes. The same book. There must be five hundred copies of it, all of the same edition. And the shelves are filled with it too. In the half-light and dust of that room it comes to Jim Foley: lesson from America. The old man pushes the Tocqueville not because of any philosophical or ideological or literary kinship, not because he has a mission for the world to read it, or because he believes it carries a message or anything of significance or import. He pushes it because once he got a shipment half-price or giveaway and because now he can make money from it. Because he can continue even in his eighties to prove to himself an adage older than his own father, older than when they changed their name to Sutherland: Son, in this country you can sell anything.

Jim finds the kitchen when he has gone in a half circle through the rooms of the apartment and realizes there is a door from it directly to where Theodore is sitting sucking lemonade with a straw.

'Half-ice,' he says. 'This is good. They put in too much ice to make the lemonade go further, you end up paying for ice. It's hot out there?'

'Yes, Mr Sutherland. Very hot.'

'I can't stand it. Makes me feel I can't breathe.'

'You're better here.'

'You mind bringing me my sandwich?'

'No.'

'Tell Horace you can bring it every day.'

When Jim leaves and is waiting in the hallway for the elevator to rise, he notices a sign on the far wall saying 'Pool' and an arrow indicating the stairs. Moments later he is standing at the end of an ancient narrow blue rooftop swimming pool, its waters perfectly still and inviting.

The following day when he brings the sandwich, he brings his swimsuit. He slips into the water in the shallow end. He makes six strokes before he sinks. When he returns to the bookstore his hair is still wet.

'You're sweating,' Horace says, 'this heat is something, isn't it? I hate the summer in New York. Hate it.' Later he comes down the history aisle. 'Thank you for taking my father's lunch, Jim. I'm going to give you a raise.'

*

The summer passes. There is the mowing of the great burnt lawns around the house in Mount Kisco, the growing of tomatoes on canes in a small plot opposite the apartment, impatiens in window boxes, Saturday barbecues on the deck of Mrs Lynch's house in Westchester where she sits with smoke and coffee ever more worried about the frailty of her world. Alimony payments are well over now and she does not see how she will have enough money. She will have to sell the house. It is too big for her anyway, she says, blowing away the anguish of the decision in smoke. Gerard is working in California and won't be coming back. The upkeep of the place is too much. Just too much.

When they drive away, Kate is quiet, the roads around her childhood slipping back into darkness, but leaving her burdened with the sad image of her mother in the doorway, watching the tail lights fade over the crest of the driveway, before turning inside to go over her figures once more.

'There is nothing I can do for her,' Kate says.

After summer goldsmiths work the trees. In the burnished

season on the back flap of García Márquez's *One Hundred Years of Solitude* Jim writes:

> *What skyward creature lets fall*
> *Such copper wings?*

But he writes no more than that, only such fragments now. He is too tired after work. He cannot imagine his own name ever appearing on a book. He handles hundreds of them every day, and sometimes unpacks a box of a new title and holds a book in his hand as if he could study the secret of how the writer got himself inside its pages. He sniffs the book and turns its leaves, feels with the tips of his fingers the quality of the paper, the firmness of the covers, the binding, the physical thing itself with captured spirit. No, he cannot imagine it. Or perhaps can only imagine it. Some trigger of faith, whereby desire becomes action, is missing.

It is winter then. In the frozen nursery Kate falls into depression. She cannot explain it, she says.

'I love you,' Jim tells her.

'I know that.'

She asks for space. They sit in the two separate rooms of the apartment until midnight. Kate smokes curled in an armchair looking out on the dark.

'I feel we've given up,' she says one night, when the lights are out and she lies still in the bed beside him.

'We haven't. I love you.'

'Don't say that. That's not the answer. That you love me is not the solution to everything. You always say that.' A hurt silence. A voice of thin despair, 'We've given up.'

He says nothing. They lie there. Outside the night is whipped by an ice wind.

*

A week after Christmas Mrs Lynch goes to hospital for tests. She says Dr Weinstein has explained she needs to go in for investigation, that's all. Kate is not to worry.

'I have pain,' Mrs Lynch tells Jim in the library. 'I have pain all day and all night. I've been to six doctors. They have me on Percocet every four hours. I can't sleep.' Her eyes look wild and frightened. 'Now you're not to alarm Kate, Jim, you mustn't. I don't want her worrying. I'll go in and they'll find out what it is. I'm not concerned, Jim, really. I'm more concerned about the insurance. I don't understand it. They won't renew it. I've written to them three times. Can you imagine, you can be with one insurance company your whole life and then when you get older and something happens to you they can just drop you. It's incredible.'

The tests become more tests. She is in hospital for one week, and then a second. And then a third. When Jim and Kate visit she looks suddenly very ill, as though once outside the domain of her home the stays that kept together the appearance of her health have now fallen apart.

'I must look terrible,' she says.

'You're in hospital, Mom.'

'Kate, will you? Look in my bag there somewhere.'

While Jim stands by, Kate fishes and finds a brush and sits to groom her mother's hair. Then she untops a lipstick and leans in and with a kind of infinite tenderness makes her mother's mouth red as a rose.

'Thank you, dear. That's better.' Without warning a great weariness descends. Mrs Lynch closes her eyes, is asleep in an instant.

'She has been suffering a very long time,' an Indian doctor tells Kate in the corridor. 'It is in her bone marrow,' he says. 'The worst kind, if there is a worst.'

Two days later Gerard arrives from California. He is tanned and calm and sits beside his mother's bed and holds her sleeping hand. He stays a week, ten days, two weeks. In the white glare of the cafeteria downstairs he tells Kate, 'She has no money. The house is mortgaged to the rooftop, she has no insurance.' He shakes his head. They sit with styrofoam cups of weak coffee, take turns keeping vigil by the bedside. One evening Michael Lynch arrives and sits in the chair and bows his head. He stays a long time and seems slumped there a figure who has known outrageous defeat and whose eyes are cavernous with regret for things irretrievable and perished. When at last he comes from the bedside he holds Gerard's shoulder. 'Send me the bills,' he says softly as he goes.

Mrs Lynch dies in the night. Kate cries upon her chest and holds onto her and will not rise or let go.

*

There is another spring and another summer, and Jim and Kate Foley live a life of unremarkable struggle. In New York City it is a time of yuppies, of MBAs, of inflated salaries, trophy CEOs, white-collared-and-cuffed blue shirts and five-hundred-dollar suits. On the train into Manhattan one morning Jim has the impression that all of the other passengers have somehow pulled away, been fast-forwarded five years – five years of pay rises and stock options – and are now in the comfort of a kind of wealth he will never know. In the five years they have strangely all grown younger-looking and their smiles whiter. In Sutherland's there is no such transformation. Horace has brought him up to $5.25 an hour, but can afford no more. It's a hard time for books, he has explained. Theodore is still coming sporadically to the store, and in the heat of summer taking his meals delivered in his armchair at home. Jim Foley feels lost, a character inside a long chapter where the reader is grown tired.

One evening with the air cooling in late September he comes home up the hill of Carpenter Avenue to find Dr Morgan waiting for him on the front deck with Henrietta by his side. He can tell by the way the doctor is twisting his hands that the old man is caught upon the spikes of a dilemma and unsure if he can free himself. Henrietta prods him as Jim comes up the driveway.

'Jim,' he booms out and smiles and waves a hand in such a way that you cannot be sure if he is waving you by or over to him.

Jim waves back. Three days before, the doctor had reminded

him about the lawn and he still hasn't got around to cutting it. As he goes on toward the side door, Henrietta prods away like crazy at the doctor for him to say something. His big hand lingers in the air by the side of his head. His smile turns baffled and sad.

'I will be cutting the grass this evening,' Jim calls back, and the doctor nods delightedly; by this simple thing his dignity is saved. Jim pulls open the screen door and goes inside. *Soon the storm windows will need to go up*, he thinks, *he will be waiting one evening to tell me.*

'Kate?'

The old yellow Toyota they own and which Kate takes to work is parked alongside the garage where Dr Morgan keeps his powder-blue Oldsmobile.

Jim comes into the bedroom. Kate is lying there crying.

He goes and sits on the bed beside her. He strokes her hair and says her name. In the silvered light of the room his mind flits like a moth, hunting solutions, he thinks, *grief comes from not living your own life. We are not the people we dreamed we would be or in the place we imagined in the night streets in Dublin.* He realizes only then that love is a more difficult reality than books make it seem. He is not earning enough money to afford them any kind of free-dom. Not enough to free Kate from watering and weeding chores in the nursery, to fulfil silent promises he made when he held her and swore to repair all that he saw broken in her eyes. In Dublin he had told her she was a painter. He had watched how she saw the detail of the world, the smallest of blossoms, the minute touch of colour in a hedgerow, and seen her sketch these things in note-books. He had told her she must paint.

But such things seemed easier then. Then you only had to say the thing and it seemed it would become true. In America, he has no means to make it so. Kate put away the paints and the easel. He did not speak of writing a book.

Now on the bed in the dying September evening she raises her head.

'I'm sorry,' she says.

'Don't.'

'It just . . .'

'Kate, it's all right. I am the one who is sorry.'

She closes her eyes.

'It's all right,' he says again. 'It'll be all right.'

And for a time says nothing more. Nothing more seems sayable. Kate lies below him in his awkward embrace. Through the window he can see leaves yellow and brown come in a constant falling from the old trees. The season is turning. The light thins out of the sky quickly. From the end of the driveway he hears the garage door being electrically opened and knows that Dr Morgan is there huffing and blowing and taking out the mower. Jim moves the hair from around Kate's face and asks her to come with him.

'There is something I want you to see.'

'What is it?'

'Just come with me. Come on.'

She goes to the bathroom. Jim watches the doctor go back inside. Then they leave, driving the car out past the unmowed grass and the window in the sitting room where Dr Morgan's face looms. They drive from Mount Kisco toward Bedford and on to Wapaqua. They stop at the end of the gravel driveway of the old house that has been sold to a vice-president at IBM.

'Come on.'

'We can't go up there.'

'They're not there yet. Come on.'

He takes her hand. They go up the hill in the darkness past the woods.

'It's here,' Kate says, 'what you want to show me?'

'Yes, come on.'

Around the back of the unlit house they hurry now, down the halfmoon-shadowed slope of the lawn past the cypress and the cedars. And beneath what stars there are, Jim winds back the pool cover so the water slaps darkly.

'Now, watch,' he says, and stands and takes off his clothes, comes to the pool's edge and dives.

The water is an instantaneous shock of cold. He crashes down through the nightblue glass of it and is briefly blind in the bubbles of himself. His eyes are wide and the chlorine burns. For a fraction of a second he sees Kate standing, her hands to her face watching. He digs into the surface and pulls, aware of the absolute and finite musculature of his body from toe to fingertip as his swimming is a kind of equal agony and joy both. He is a white slice of moon or man or fish, fallen in that water. He progresses halfway up the pool without touching the tiles of the floor. He kicks from the shallow into the deep end, feeling the bulk of water below him now, the unseeable bottom. He sees Kate and mistimes his breath and his mouth fills with water. At once he panics. He chokes and coughs, kicking on, his face the face of a man crying. Then the diving board is over his head and the wall comes for his fingertips and gives him the solid world back again.

Jim is hanging on there and coughing when he hears Kate clapping. He looks up and she crosses her arms and lifts her dress over her head and dives into the pool. She swims up to him and kisses his lips. They cling to each other in the cool of the night where what light there is breaks on the water about them in diamonds and squares.

*

Perhaps a week later, sitting on the train home out of Grand Central, Jim discovers a short story by Brian Friel in the *New Yorker*. It is set in a small townland called Corradinna in Donegal, and as he reads the story he loses his place on the Harlem and Hudson line. The towns beyond White Plains are announced, the ticket collector comes and goes and punches tickets, but Jim does not see or hear any of this, he is away back in Donegal, a part of Ireland to which he has never been. When he looks up from the telling of the story he sees the Westchester sky through smudged train windows, but to him it is the swift changeable sky above the ruined house where the character, Joe, has returned to revisit his childhood. Joe remembers playing in the bower with his sister and going down to the chestnut tree and swinging and laughing there, and crossing the little river and wandering up through the blue-bells. There is no rain falling in the story, but Jim sees it, sees it falling in the brown valleys at the foot of the Bluestack Mountains, falling in the soft boglands where soundlessly it seeps into ground that melts underfoot. The rain that makes run the rivers of Donegal, greens the fields where the cattle stand in the part shelter of the stone walls.

The rails rock and soft-clack their steady hypnotism. Across from Jim men with rolling or fallen heads, gaping mouths, loosened ties, sleep themselves free of their workday. *New York Post*s are splayed on their laps, centre pages slipped free and trampled on the floor. Jim reads on, reading himself back into Ireland, or rather into the Ireland of Brian Friel's story, an Ireland that is both imaginary and immediately recognizable. He knows the place without ever having been there, knows the farms and the farmers thereabouts, the small fields and the hundred weathers of cloud and rain and rainlight. To say he imagines himself there is to suppose a distance he crosses in his mind. But in fact it is not like that; it is not that he reads the phrases of the story and makes any effort of imagination. Rather it is the combination of phrase and rhythm and voice, the turning and tuning of language, the note of sadness and loss, that is at once most familiar and compelling. *I am listening to the story I am telling to myself,* he thinks. *And I am there in Donegal.*

He is sitting in the train as the towns of Chappaqua and Pleasantville pass by outside the window. Men and women step off and hurry away in the blown rain with briefcases over their heads.

Slowing, like a reader deep in a novel who regrets the thin fewness of the pages still unread, Jim does not want to arrive in Mount Kisco. The train pulls out of Chappaqua and no more than five hundred yards out of the station it stops with a jolt. Heads roll and startled faces turn upward. Dry mouths are tongue-circled and yawned free of stiffness. The train is more than half empty now, and populated with a kind of ghost after-presence of passengers departed. Above, bars of light flicker and hum, and then go out. There are curses in the dark. Jesus Christ is called and God is damned. Then there is nothing but the emptiness of the carriage and the scattered dark shapes of the ten or twelve men and women separated out on the vinyl seats.

Low-glow emergency lights come on. Jim holds up the magazine and finishes the story. Its ending is wistful, Joe finding that his past cannot be refound, but can be repeated in a way through children.

Over dinner Jim tells Kate.

'It is a wonderful story,' he says.

'Tell me.'

'About a ruined house and a man who had moved away and wanted to return to see it with his family. It had a . . . I don't know . . . a sort of powerful sense of place. You could sense the quiet, the beauty of it and yet how it had changed from its past, from the place he carried in his head. When he arrives there, Friel slips him right back into his memories. It's seamless. There's nothing much happening, nothing dramatic, just this quiet movement, like a gentle current. I can't really explain it.'

'I'll read it, after class,' Kate says. 'Leave it out for me.'

After dinner she goes to an oil-painting class Jim has given her. It is late when she gets back and later still after a bath when she picks up the magazine. Jim falls asleep while she is still reading it.

The following day Jim leaves Sutherland's on his lunch break and goes to the Irish Bookshop on 580 Broadway. When he left Ireland he left his books behind too. Now he goes down the stairs and under the street into the bookshop where the same editions sit on the shelves. He looks for Brian Friel's short stories, but only his plays are displayed, so Jim moves along the rows of Irish authors, taking down books he has owned and read, studying familiar titles and covers. He reads a few lines of a book and hears its voice as if for company. Standing there for over an hour he reads Frank O'Connor, Liam O'Flaherty, Maria Edgeworth, Ben

Kiely, Brian Moore, John McGahern, Edna O'Brien. Before he leaves he slips inside his coat a copy of Patrick Kavanagh's *Tarry Flynn*.

Three days later he does the same thing, this time leaving with *The Green Fool*.

He is sitting up reading it and far away in the black hills of Monaghan when Kate comes from class carrying the canvas of her first oil painting. She keeps it turned from him as she closes the door.

'It's wet,' she says, 'and it's just finished. Although you never know when it's really finished. I could keep going on at it, and never be happy. But–'

'Let me see it.'

'Wait.'

She goes and turns on the overhead light, and stands by her grandmother's grand piano in the centre of the sitting room with the painting facing inward to her body.

'I don't want you to be disappointed,' she says.

'I won't be.'

Kate turns the painting toward him. It is her self-portrait, painted in thick bands of colour upon a deep green background. It is a picture of sorrow and survival, but no joy. Within it, the bones of her face are painted like pale planes of fallen light. Her hair is tied back and is no longer blonde but streaked with firelike tints of orange and red and silver. At her brows is bruised colouring of purple and blue, the same blue that reoccurs in sad purses beneath her eyes. Her cheekbones are high angles of white and cadmium yellow with thin strokes of a slightly flushed pink, her lips together, held. But it is her eyes that most arrest Jim. They gaze out from the painting with a kind of fixed interrogation, a look that says what the eyes have seen is the full and varied compendium of life's disappointments and asks if this is all there is.

The painting is truthful in a way words can rarely be. Kate holds it in front of her and Jim looks from the picture to her face and sees the beauty of the girl he met in Dublin.

'It's wonderful.'

'Really?' Her face is that of a child's.

'No. Not wonderful. Extraordinary.'

'You thought I could be a painter,' she says.

'Yes.'

'Well, here is my first painting.'

'It's . . . I don't know what to say.'

'Say it again. Tell me it's wonderful.'

'It's wonderful. It's wonderful, wonderful.'

'I thought you said it was extraordinary.'

'Extraordinary, extraordinary.'

And he takes the painting from her and finds a place for it on the dresser, supporting it with a flowerless vase on either side. Then he holds Kate in his arms and touches the delicate skin of her face and with his lips traces the contours he has seen revealed in the colours. But as they kiss, enfolded in one another, his loving is made desperate by what flows beneath it. It is as if no touch, no gesture or embrace, is free of his desire to make it something more than it is. As if the love he would make then should be a compound not merely of kiss or caress or even in any manner corporeal, but rather of a substance of spirit and fire. He dreams a loving that can rescue them both, lift them out of the separate despairs and secret loneliness of their life and be, for want of a better word, transforming – always the plot of rescue. He chases with mouth and fingers the means to make Kate happy, as if happiness is a construct or some elusive figment that can be captured and held and undiminished by time.

He and Kate lie together on the couch. The bay windows hold deep blue parcels of the night sky. Wind comes and goes through the trees in the garden and takes down their last leaves in a furious undressing. There is no moon. In the stillness that falls after love what peace comes is frail and light and too shortlived. They lie wordless in the swirl of things beyond saying, their breathing soft and low and listened for against the whirling of the outside. Sometimes a car brings its headlights up the street and across the glass of the breakfront and the portrait looks out with brief and beautiful sorrow before dark closes over it again. Kate is in Jim's arms. Neither of them moves nor wants to move again, or wants to hear the clock pulse across the quiet.

'I've lost you,' Kate says.

'What? No. I'm right here.'

'What are you thinking?'

'I'm thinking you are a painter.'

'Really? It's good, isn't it?'

'Yes. Yes, it is.'

'I feel it's the first thing I have ever done in my life that I am proud of. It sounds silly but it's the first thing that wasn't done for someone else or someone else's idea of me. It's really me.'

They hold each other still. The old sash windows in all the rooms in Dr Morgan's house rattle in the age-smoothed casing of their grooves. A screen door flaps and bangs. An upstairs light comes on as Doctor and Henrietta awaken, throwing a pale parallelogram onto the lawn, and then the door opens and the floor creaks with some business of bathroom or house amidst the arrival of a storm. There is the thin high call of Henrietta's voice shouting, *Thornton! Thornton!*, reaching into the doctor's deafness to keep contact with him after fifty-two years of marriage. He comes down the stairs in heavy slippered steps and clicks wall light switches. Henrietta is still calling to him from upstairs. The doctor opens the back door and a breeze rushes in and through all the downstairs rooms and beneath the dividing door of the main house and the apartment. Jim and Kate hear the doctor pull the screen door tight and click it closed. He must stand there a moment doing nothing for there is no sound. Perhaps he watches the night. Perhaps he thinks it will be his last winter. Or wonders why Jim has not yet put up the winter screens or how he will ask him tomorrow. Then he moves again and there is the slow shuffle of his return up the stairs to the bedroom once more. It is a brief interlude, a business ordinary and private and uneventful in the night. It should mean nothing. But when the upstairs light goes out Jim is filled with sadness.

'Are you all right?' Kate asks. Her voice is a whisper at his chest.

'Yes.'

'Tell me,' she says.

And whether because of the love or the painting or the darkness, or perhaps because of the Friel story or the books he has been reading, or somehow because of the lonely journey of the doctor to the door of winter, he does.

'You should be painting,' he says. He speaks so low he is not sure Kate hears. 'You should be painting.'

There is what we call silence but is in fact the noise of air, of breath and thought and dream and heartbeat. Then Kate lifts her head.

'Go on,' she says.

'We shouldn't be living this life. I don't want you to go back to work in that nursery. I want you to paint.'

She sits up. She has the blue-tasselled throw drawn around her.

'To paint?'

'Yes.'

'What if I'm not any good? What if this was just . . . I don't know, luck?'

'It isn't. You're a painter.'

'I don't know.'

'I do.'

'How can you?'

There is a pause, then Jim says, 'We have to leave here.'

Wrapped in blue against the deeper blue of the night, Kate's hair falls pale and long, and just then, when Jim thinks he is the one rescuing her, she rescues both of them.

'Well, I'll tell you what I have been thinking,' she says. 'I'll tell you what I thought when I read the story.'

'The Friel?'

'Yes.' Kate moves closer. She holds the unsaid thing in her

mouth until the sweetness of its taste becomes too great and she smiles upon the words. 'We should go.'

'Go?'

'Go back to Ireland. To the west. To your home.'

The moment she says it Jim sees the house as he last saw it, sees the kitchen narrow to nothing as he slowly shuts the door, hears the click in the lock as he turns the key. He sees the house and the rumpled fields about it and the wind bringing the rain. And he is afraid to say yes, afraid that his imagination is not large or powerful enough to change real life. To return to the west of Clare and remake a life there. He lies in the half-dark not knowing if this is a moment of victory or defeat, advance or retreat, and says nothing and Kate reaches and touches his arm.

'Imagine it,' she says, 'I will paint, and you, you will write.'

*

Innocence is recovered so.

And in part then because of a story – and themselves like characters in a story, like ones who arrive on some quickening moment of the plot and find themselves in the quickly turned pages – in the following days they get ready to leave America. There is a little cluster of scenes. Jim tells Horace in Sutherland's who turns bright pink and thinks Jim has been offered another job.

'Five dollars seventy-five,' he says.

'It's not about the money.'

'Six dollars, my absolute best offer. You have to understand, Jim, there is no money in the book business. No money at all. You do it for love.'

In Mount Kisco Jim cuts the lawn as close to the ground as the mower will allow. He mows through the fallen leaves he has not raked and leaves mud scars in the damp green. Dr Morgan comes out on the deck in his sweater and his coat and woollen hat and blinks away watching. He waves, perhaps for Jim to stop. When he has finished Jim goes up and sits beside him and loudly tells him they are leaving.

'Oh?' he says. 'I see.'

His pale sad face looks out at the streaked bare lawn.

'It's nothing about here, about the house, Dr Morgan; we are going back to Ireland.'

'I'm sorry?'

'To Ireland,' Jim says even more loudly. 'I am going to write, Kate is going to paint.' For the first time Jim hears the words with their unreal sound, and even as he is saying them he is at first unsure of where they are leading or what happens next. But then curiously, as if he is listening to the story he is telling, he comes to find that he believes in it.

'I'm sorry,' Jim says. 'I'm sure you will get someone else.'

Dr Morgan says nothing and looks at the scars on his lawn and Jim is not sure if he has been heard.

Blackbirds come hunting on the grass. The cool of the year's dying is in the air.

'Will you be able to put up the winter screens?' the doctor asks at last.

The more they tell the story the more they believe in it. The words come to have a reality of their own. Jim looks at Kate in the tiny kitchen and says, 'We are leaving,' and they are. They are the ones in the story of the man and woman who stepped out of the lives that were not their own lives. Jim can imagine the next months as if they are chapters, telling them to himself and in that way finding faith. He believes completely in the words. Only sometimes, when he utters out loud a sentence or hears himself say *happiness* and how strange that sounds, as if the very sounding of the word is a kind of unluck and tempts doom, he feels a shiver run and the air of the room change. Briefly he imagines all manner of fates stir in a cavernous dark and cock their ears and come forward to hear the foolishness of this announced ambition. Figures of doubt, they come and in Jim's mind, schooled on the novels of the nineteenth century, assume the shapes of characters familiar, of Heeps and Pumblechooks, Bounderbys and Squeerses. Men with pale or plump faces in ruined ragged gentility, with narrow eyes that have seen the full compendium of vanity and hope and ambition and taken sour delight in the variety of ways in which Pip or Copperfield or Chuzzlewit failed.

They crowd forward. They press their cold hands together. They pass crooked grimaces one to the other when they hear Jim Foley say, *Because I am going to make her happy*, and then nod with raised eyebrows and downlipped mouths, acknowledging that, yes, here upon the market is a new investor in a stock so long devalued as to have been all but forgotten. What plot, what twists, what rise and fall they will witness here now again! What sentimental folly will be here! What dusty themes of Love and Money will here emerge in the timeworn story of flight from city to country! From some gallery in Jim's mind their breath blows out in mixed awe and anticipation: oho! it is a long time since they had this. They take their places and wait the last few days while Jim and Kate's leaving begins.

Their life fits in five suitcases. They step a last day outside the door of the apartment in the old house. A winter wind blows.

The figures in the gallery in Jim's mind rub their hands together. Go on, they whisper, turn the page, begin the chapter.

Three

There is a rhythm to the mornings. It is a simple thing but I feel if I get it wrong I risk some collapse in the frail centre of our life and we will not be able to carry on.

This wet spring morning, I was lying on the bed roiled in dream and worry and wakeful imagining when I heard Hannah enter the kitchen downstairs.

'Good morning, Hannah.'

She made a small nod. 'It's raining,' she said. Her black hair makes her complexion more pale, her eyes despondent.

I looked out at the sorry combination of grey and green, the overgrown and bent-over tangle of the bare fuchsia hedge, the mottled blotch of sky.

'Yes.'

'I'm not cycling,' Hannah said.

'No, it's all right. I'll drive you. Is Jack awake?'

'I didn't hear him.'

She opened the fridge and stood looking into it. I switched on the kettle. I knew enough of the morning rhythm now not to pry into how she was feeling. I knew that it was important to put aside the desire to try to remedy anything. And yet at the same time I felt the undercurrent of guilt that I was reneging in some way, taking the easiest option, and that in a couple of years Hannah would be gone into the world and I would be left surrounded by whole libraries of things I should have said to her. She took out a yogurt and closed the fridge.

There was no sign of Jack. I have been trying lately to give him some responsibility for his own waking. I am not sure if I am right or wrong, if he is still too young. We have had mornings when I have woken him gently, sitting on his bed and talking him around to getting up, waiting the ten minutes more and the five minutes more and patiently encouraging him from the warm hold of the blankets. I have brought him into the kitchen an hour before school, only to have him eat his breakfast and be ready in fifteen minutes and then sit growing more and more angry that he was woken too soon. We have had mornings when I laid out the bowls and cups and filled the sugar bowl and the milk jug and set the kitchen like a scene ready for some gentle domestic drama. But on such mornings Hannah could say she did not want anything but juice and was taking it to her room while getting ready, and Jack could say he wanted his breakfast by the television. And I have not had whatever is required of fathers to insist their children sit with them at the table. I know that insistence can bring only anger and tears, that Hannah will sit stony and silent and eat nothing anyway and that Jack will cry. I have argued with myself that their world has already been so fractured that everything must now go the way of repair. So, I have come to know a certain rhythm, a way of being together in the mornings that gets us through the time. I do not ask Hannah what she wants or offer to cook her anything. I do not comment on what she eats or how her uniform looks. I can speak to her about school, or what classes she has that day, but only by way of information and not to enquire any more closely; such questions are not for the mornings. With Jack I have recently taken the step of buying him his own alarm clock. We had an expedition together to Jimmy Brohan's in Ennis to select one and afterward I sat with him and we spoke of him being very grown up now and more in charge of himself, and I showed him how to set the alarm for eight o'clock.

It worked for three days. Then for two nights he pushed off the alarm button after I said goodnight. On the third night I came back up to his room when he was sleeping and reset it, and the following morning he would not speak with me, and I drove him scowling and white-faced to school.

So it has been. We are not trying to be perfect here, I have told myself, only to carry on, to get by.

This morning then, while Hannah took a yogurt and turned on the news on the radio, I went to the door of Jack's room and listened to his sleeping. I needed to wake him to bring him with me while I drove Hannah to the school. It was the simplest of everyday situations. But outside his door I hesitated, as though the way ahead was in some way precarious. I write this down knowing how absurd it seems, the everyday problem of waking a child for school. And yet, there I was, wondering if I should wake him now and have him dressed and breakfasted quickly, or if I should lift him from the blankets and carry him through the house into the car at the last minute.

I left him for a while and went back into the kitchen.

'Is he awake?'

'No.'

'Dad, why didn't you wake him? It's half past.'

'I know. It's all right. We have a little longer.'

'I'm going to brush my teeth and then we have to go.'

'Yes. That's fine.'

Hannah walked to the door and stopped.

'Do you want me to wake him?'

We have had experience of this before, this scene where, in the absence of a firm adult, Hannah becomes transformed into a kind of stern mother, and Jack explodes like a water balloon on my chest. It is not a role I should force her to play.

'No, don't. Thanks, Hannah. I'll do it.'

'Half past.'

'Yes, I know. Go on.'

I took out the bowl and the spoon and the cereal. I got the carton of milk. On the news was another expert on terrorism; I lowered the volume to a murmur so that Hannah would not listen to it.

'Dad!'

'Yes, I'm getting him now.'

I went back to Jack's bedroom, where he was still sleeping. I thought, you think you can protect your child, you think you will be

a wall and grief and hurt and loss will crash against you and not pass.
But you are not a wall, you are only a witness.

'*Jack, Jack, wake up now.*'

The warmth of the bedclothes was extraordinary. When I passed
my hand down through them to rub his back the heat of him rose
into me instantly.

'*Jack, good boy, time to wake up.*'

His head turned on the pillow but his eyes stayed closed. I did not
really want to wake him. I didn't want to be the one insisting he rise
and face the day and that he do so because that was what was called
for, was expected, and that he should take his place in the columns
and files of schoolchildren everywhere going through the gates of
schools. That this made me a weak and ineffectual father did not
really matter to me. I didn't want the role of enforcer. If he wanted
to sleep the whole morning what did it matter? What would he miss,
some sums, spellings, some Irish? A confusion of these thoughts ran
through my mind as I stroked his back. He could stay at home, I
decided. But I still had to wake him. I couldn't leave him in the house
alone while I drove Hannah. So, with the hand that had rubbed his
back and was warmed to the heat of him, I turned him gently over
and his eyes opened. He has the bluest, most beautiful eyes and when
they looked at me in that first instant of wakefulness I felt an
unsayable love.

'*Jack.*'

He reached his arms up and they came around my neck. I craned
back then and so he was lifted and let himself be lifted from the bed-
covers, his face smiling. And in that moment then the scene I had
feared did not arise but passed like others we only imagine, and Jack
hung from my neck and laughed. I held out his clothes for him and
he dressed himself, and then I said, 'Jack, we have to rush, OK?
Because of you-know-who.'

'*I know who.*' *He smiled and opened wide his eyes, and made an*
exaggerated grave nodding and a comic face of his sister.

'*Come on, my man.*'

We raced together into the kitchen, where Hannah was standing waiting.

'Morning, Jack,' she said.

'Morning, You-Know-Who.'

'Right, let's go.' With Jack beside me I opened the door on the cool air and the falling rain, and turned back. 'Are you ready now, Hannah?'

She didn't exactly smile. But almost.

Half an hour later, after no resistance, I had dropped Jack at school and returned to the quiet of the cottage once more. The quiet was such that it seemed less to do with sound and more to do with space – a quiet that left only the feeling of emptiness. So, although there were all the small outward signs of life – chairs askew at the table, bowl with half-eaten cereal, yogurt container, peeled foil lid, used spoons and small stains beneath them, Hi-Lo milk carton with mis-torn beak, soggy tea bags leaking brown on the lip of the sink – all seemed doleful and weighted with an unsettling feeling of vacancy. I tidied up and tried not to think of you. I turned up the radio. There had been more cases of anthrax discovered in America. Two postal workers were critical. On the morning programme that followed the news a minister for state was being asked about our National Emergency Plan. Under the pointedness of the questions he seemed to waver and fluster. What should we do, he was asked, if there was a nuclear disaster at Sellafield? If terrorists targeted that, and there was a meltdown, what should the Irish people do? What was the government's plan?

There was a stunned pause before any answer.

'Well, for one thing,' the minister said, 'stay indoors. Definitely.'

I turned off the radio and drove through the rain to the sea.

The country we fly to is the country of memory and fiction, an amalgam of the place of my childhood remembered and the country I have been travelling back to in the stories and novels I have been reading in New York. Neither are real places. I know this, but, sitting in the sky, tell myself no place is real beyond our perception of it. The house that I grew up in was perhaps a different place altogether to the one my fevered imagination recreated even as I was sitting at the wooden table in the kitchen or lying later in my bed. Did imagination not always stand between me and reality? So as I sit there in the plane that flies through the night I am unsure of how it will be to arrive. To drive back into the village, to pass the shops and the post office, and go out the little stretch of the road to the house that is empty and so full too. To open the door.

In the early morning the hostesses come through the plane and the blinds are lifted on the oval windows as we descend over the west coast of Clare. The green of the country as it lies below us is startling and looks like the unreal pictures in books of Ireland. There are exclamations from tourists and photograph flashes and the small nods and smiles of those who lean and take just a quick glance at their own country as if it is an account balanced in their favour.

Kate is awake and suddenly anxious. 'I can't believe we are doing this,' she says. She says it in a whisper, as though we are engaged in a subterfuge of sorts, or are secret renegades, fugitives from the life of commuter train and office. 'Tell me how it will be,' she asks me.

'We are going to land.'

'Tell me.'

She closes her eyes and her head leans in against my shoulder. And so I do. I tell her the story. There on the plane coming down from the high places of the sky, and moments before we land on the ground, I tell her the story once more. I tell it to reaffirm, to make believe, the way a man might say a prayer over and over until the thing he is willing God to make happen happens. And if it doesn't he will not relent. He will suppose he has not amassed enough prayers in his coffers yet, or that the balancing of books in heaven is differently calculated to methods used on earth, and he will pray and pray on, feeling the bones of his fingers lock as the flesh falls away from them, feeling the balls of his knees press into the ground while the prayers ascend. I tell the story to make it happen.

I tell Kate that in the house we will have rooms for books and paintings. I will begin writing my first novel straightaway. We will go to Ennis and buy stretchers and canvas and oils and an easel and she will begin to paint. We will remake the garden and grow vegetables in the field out the back where one light day my father thought a pony should run. He thought this would get my brother outside in the air, but when asked Matthew said he didn't want one, and the idea passed out of my father's expression like sun going behind cloud. The field remained wild and unkempt, and in it ran only the horse of the Deerhunter Hawkeye or the Apache Geronimo or other such that crossed through the high grasses of my imagination. In that field we will make something real now. We will make the house anew. 'And we will have children there,' I whisper, in those few simple words healing all the past, as if nothing before was written in our lives and there was now only to be this simple story where the end was something out of the marvellous.

'It will be wonderful,' I say, not thinking then of the burden of dreams or what would happen if it weren't. It would be. At least for as long as three thousand dollars would last.

*

It is seven o'clock in the morning and the roads we drive are all but empty. There is a strange desolate feeling in the green fields and the sleeping, shut houses and the few cars that follow their headlights with windscreen wipers going. At intervals there are single figures standing in broken shelters awaiting the first bus. Others, men with woollen hats and small gear-bags, shuffle at front gates looking down the rain for their pick-up to bring them to the site. The dawn sky is grey and as we arrive in Ennis and turn west out to the peninsula, the day that comes up comes with little light through the paste of cloud. It is not the weather of stories, nor the setting of any but doleful dreams. It has a dampened low-spirited melancholy, a kind of dour unforgiving that falls and makes the distance between ground and sky an illusory nothing, as if there is no up there, no place other than the cold jail of the rain. We drive within it. Kate sits beside me and whether out of half-sleep or fallen spirit says nothing. We drive on the rising road out of Ennis and into the open country of small fields of ragged shape loosely fenced between crooked stakes of ash branches. Cattle stand in the mesmerism of rain, and seem to me the same cattle since forever, the same animals standing witness to my comings and goings, the constant journeying of all my attempts to escape. I have no energy for announcement, to declare that this time I am coming back to make a life. For in some silent part of me I am too afraid, and on the road to home too entangled in the briars of memory. Here I am sitting in the seat behind my father on the way home from the library. Here I am holding books on my lap. I am reading their titles, handling their plastic-sheeted covers and anticipating what lies within them, looking out of the side window at the rain and the cattle in the rain and already away somewhere else, in that place where no pain can be felt nor love asked of me. And none given. Here I am on all those journeys back and forth from home in the time after my father's stroke. I am the student sitting on the bus looking out into the dark fields, thinking of a dead sister or lost brother or the purposeless laceration of grief, and opening the pages of a novel to read by the yellow light, and, by doing so, looking away from all that suffering.

Or so I excuse myself and explain my flight into books.

Now I pass the cattle in the fields on the way back in the morning rain. We drive on past Darragh and Lissycasey and the horses waiting by the fenceline, and turn off the main road to cut up by Moriarty's and Lorigan's and along the narrow way past the boglands where deep brown pools appear. Here there are old houses that are built along the side of the road, that hunker there and hold the families of sons who live where their fathers and grandfathers lived. There is the first smoke of turf fires rising as we pass by. The smoke is sweet and full of the triggers of memory and hangs low and heavy in the rain. Further along we come upon an old man crooked and sideswaying in large wellingtons and rain-darkened brown coat as he follows a herd of cows up the hill to the milking parlour. I slow the car to the pace of his walk. He gives a half-glance over his shoulder to acknowledge us and raises his stick of rubber hose and calls to the cows that move on without noticeable haste. On we go like this at walking pace in the early morning rain. The cows know their way and need no herding. Their udders are full, bloated bags dripping mud and milk both. It is a scene out of a thousand I have witnessed before, the farmer bringing the herd along for milking, the slow knot of the animals in the narrow road. But this time, the car loaded with our suitcases and the considerable burden of our great expectations, the aged figure of the farmer alone and the sense of his being almost a fixture, a part of that landscape strikes in me a chord. He belongs in a way I have never done. And as he turns the cows in along the gravel to the open gate where his wife is standing waiting and turns back to us his raised stick salute of thanks, I am wondering if I can find that belonging here now.

We drive on up the hill of Greygrove and through the thickening rain.

'I wish it wasn't raining,' Kate says.

I look over to her and see her anxiety and wish I could make the weather change. She has never seen my house, or seen it only through the stories I have told her of what it was like to grow up there. Now, in winter, in the rain-run road with no flowers in the hedgerows and the wind-slanted trees bare above the weeping stone walls, I think no story I have told could have captured this, and wonder if her silence in the seat next to me is already regret.

'I do, too.'

'It feels like a mistake,' she says.

'Don't say that. It isn't.'

But of course I already think it may be; I just cannot say so.

The low sky lies grey upon the road. We pass through puddled corners and paint the grass with mud splashes. Farmhouses with shut doors, yellow light burning in kitchens and first smoke rising, have their backs turned on the ruined morning. The first children are getting ready for school with coats and books and bags, sandwiches and drinks. Tea is being poured, radio news switched on. But all of this is within, leaving the road still a bare ribbon rising and falling and winding westward toward the village.

When we come to Hayes' cross I slow the car to a stop. Although I know there is no traffic coming or going, for a moment I wait there. We are less than six hundred yards from the house now. We are at the meadows I have walked in and even sometime worked with a hayfork, the fields I have bounced across standing on the back box of a tractor or just lain down in with a paperback book. In the morning rain there is a grim unwelcome in them now. I see the dark slates on the roof of Mick Hehir's farmhouse, the fairy fort on the top of the hill field, the place where through the tangle of whitethorns is the Blessed Well. All the coordinates of this familiar place come rushing back to me, becoming real there just beyond the rain-streaked window.

'Well?' Kate says. She turns to me. She knows my heart better than I know it myself. 'It's here?'

'Over there. You can't see it from here. Behind the trees.'

The car idles and the fan races. The wipers come back and over in a smear. We wait, watching the nothing of the scene, rumple of fields, ragged line of wire, stand of pine trees, aware that upon this landscape now we are placing ourselves like ones in a story. I want to write that the clouds moved, that the obscured sun lanced through, that there was a token offered or a gesture however small that prompted us forward. But none such happens. Nothing comes or goes. If there is a sign I do not see it. I turn the car into the crossroads and drive the broken road to the house. Its ditches clogged, rainwater runs in two black streams along it, pooling in potholes and flowing on. The hedgerows are high, bare fuchsia and thorn bush entangled, disappearing altogether to fragments of old stone wall. My mind takes in all of it, seeing it through another's eyes now. We come to the front wall of the garden where now the privet hedge is eight feet tall and long wiry fingers of it have entwined across the inside of the small rusted front gate. Only the slate roof of the house and the dark unpainted chimneys can be seen.

'It's here,' I say foolishly.

Kate is already getting out into the rain. 'Come on.'

Then we are standing before the gate, and I am pulling at the hedge with my hands, tearing loose a green confetti and snapping the small twiglike branches before turning and pushing my way in backwards to the front garden. There we stand, our hair flecked with leaves and diamonds of rain, and look at the house. It is a squat two-storey building painted by my father in the yellow my mother chose ten years or so before and not repainted since. The salt west wind from the Atlantic has since stripped away whole scars of it and, like fragments of a map into the past, revealed a grey beneath. In the line of the roof there is a sagging by the eastern chimney, in the pattern of the slates three separate places where you can see the black felt beneath. Clumps of grass have grown in the gutters and dam the rainwater to overflowing at either end. Although the house is bordered by the garden and the high hedge that screens it from the road, the six double-paned windows facing front all have a faded mouse-grey net curtain strung across the lower sash, screening the view inside and lending the house a grim privacy. Looking at it I think of my father, of pride and silence, and how a house can take on the personality of its keepers. As it stands, all of it is in a state of reduction, of being turned back into lumps of stone just as the garden is returned to wilderness. The raised flowerbeds that were already unruly in the last years of my mother's life are now vague mounds of weather-burnt stalks and dirt, forlorn graves that rise in front of the house.

Kate is beside me looking. The rain is falling steadily.

'I'm sorry,' I say. 'It's not what you were hoping. It's . . .'

'Shut up, come on.' She takes my arm. 'Where is the key?'

We go up the grass, and I lift the stone where last I left it. It leaves an imprint. Before the front door I am hesitant and fearful, a ghost of myself returned to the dread of crossing thresholds, before doors into past and future alike. I stand, frozen. Kate waits and does not say anything. She presses her lips together, hair rain-running now, face pale. The key slips inside the lock and I try to turn it, pulling the handle to me, releasing the pressure on all that keeps the house closed. We hear the click of cog and bolt and open the door inward on what might now escape. My heart is in the base of my throat. I pause on the point of entering where so much has departed. Whole parcels of time return and are relived. Past me comes the small coffin of my sister Louise, the mourners tramping on the Christmas-time frost, my father head-low en route to the post office, my mother carrying the bag of her sewing, Matthew with schoolbooks, and myself, aimless freckled boy with a novel to read in the grass. With such traffic of ghosts I neither move nor speak. I can see inside the modest hall where the coat hooks on the wall are empty and further to the open kitchen where a pool of grey light falls. But I cannot step in. Kate holds my arm. I want to fall down and shout out, to roar the long cry of all remorse and pity and loss and grief that I did nothing to try to heal. I want to tear myself open, to free myself of all of it, to take my hands and pull apart the caving of my ribs and release the heavy blood-dark birds of regret, wide-winged and beaked, and let them climb out of me beating the air and letting drip to nothing the rose-red clotted stuff of sorrow. But such means of redemption are beyond me. Kate steps past into the house.

I see her, a shadow among the shadows, as she goes. She crosses from the kitchen to the parlour while I am at the door. To gather myself, I turn and look down the garden and across the hedgeline at the valley. The morning is made of a quietness I had forgotten, so still and hushed it is impossible to imagine anything of significance is happening. Across the fields of Clare no time at all exists, nothing of change or moment, only a long singular season of soft weather and wet grass.

Kate comes to me.

'It will be fine, Jim,' she says, and reaches and takes both my hands and draws me to her inside the front door and kisses me there. 'We can be happy here,' is a whisper at my ear, as though she, like me, fears the air of the unpropitious, the doom and bad luck that cocks its ears and sits up on such announcement. I bring my hands to the sides of her face, cool and damp, and hold her to me.

'Yes.'

'Come on.'

We go slowly together through the rooms of my childhood, rooms that are smaller than I remembered and contain a faded, vanquished air of must and weariness. The eight-day clock of Eustace in Kilrush is stopped at five minutes to twelve, noon or night-time unknown, the pendulum a still brass eye. Upon the dresser is blue-patterned ware stacked and displayed with a gravely enduring optimism, attendant upon guests that never come and never came, for my father seemed without friends and my mother unable to escape the prison of loneliness in which she found herself. Below the ware are photographs of all of us but Louise. We look out from the frozen instants with a stiff and unnatural regard. Within the frames we are caught, in doomed essay of family cheer, standing in front of the house as though knights of a kingdom, defendants of a realm whose crown is cracked. I cannot look at them. But in fact everywhere in the house are old deposits of the past, minute fragments of time that have fallen and gathered like dust: the cracked brown linoleum underfoot, its curling corners; the painted and over-painted and peeled gloss of the banister; the latches and knobs and handles that have my family's fingerprints upon them.

In grey rainlight Kate and I move among the many ghosts. She doesn't say anything. She stands at the door of the room where my mother's Singer sewing machine sits on the table and she puts her hands to her chin and bites at her lower lip. There are spools and needles and cloths of different textures and colours, two silver thimbles, and – rolled neat and tight – her measuring tape. I have told Kate of the clothes my mother made compulsively, and the stillness of the room now without the whirr of the wheel, the rising falling jab of the needle, is deep and desolate. And suddenly I cannot bear it. Some trivial detail – tape, cloths, thimble – snaps the thread of my composure, and I go into the room and lift the sewing machine and carry it out the front door and throw it in the garden.

It lands with a soft clunk in the wet earth.

'Feel better?' Kate asks.

Not yet I don't. Relief or rage needs more, and I return and take up the narrow wooden chair with the sugan seat, the small transistor radio, and from the wall the picture of the Sacred Heart. All of them I hurl out of the door and come back for more. I move with fixed and clear purpose, like a knife removing disease. At first Kate stands watching. She watches me go to the dresser and reach for the large plates and the bowls and stack them in my arms, and she says, 'We have no dishes, you know.' But she does not stop me as I go out the door with them.

The shattering crash is a rent in the green stillness of the morning. But nothing more. The broken pieces lie placid in blue and white crescents, half-moons and slipped smiles. I go back. Teacups, saucers, the cutlery drawer, beside it the drawer of little everythings, stuffed assortment of oddments, string, glue, screws, keys, pens, I pitch out there. From above the fireplace two china dogs, a small statue a gift from some visitor to Lourdes, *Far East* religious magazines, the *Clare Champion* from the week my father died, then the armchair he sat in. I come in a sixth or seventh time. Kate says, 'Well, if you're going to throw out everything, I'll start here.' She has the food cupboard opened; in sad display are jars and bottles, packs and packages, half-finished and saved foods of years before powdering, mouldering and filmed in rat-grey fur. For an hour, we criss-cross the kitchen with armfuls of the past. We gather up and throw out what our hands touch. We are caught within a frenzy of destruction, and it is as though we are engaged in a battle against the house itself, as though its past life is an enemy too great or large or long undefeated to let lie, and will, if not vanquished now, overwhelm us. I cannot otherwise explain how we come to tear down the curtains, drag all of the furniture through the house and pile it on the grass, how I go upstairs and into my parents' room and pull down the pictures on the walls, snapping the cords, and throwing them out of the window. I clear all manner of memorabilia cluttered on the bedside tables. In the chorus of crash and rattle, the thin arrhythmic timpani of things, I am without regret. I throw all away. Sometimes, even as my hand is reaching for something, or my eye picks it out in the otherwise kaleidoscopic jumble of glass and plastic, I am snagged as if by thorns on the memory held there. Here are the pills my mother thought would cure my father. Here are the rosary beads that were entwined in his hands. But I stop for only an instant.

Until I come to the small stack of books I stole for him.

My breath catches in my throat when I find them beneath the bed. I had not put them there. I pick them up and sit down. What remedy, what confused hope and healing I had once invested in them, is turned to chalk in my mouth. These books made nothing happen. What did I think I could have repaired in stealing them? In the pale bare light of the bedroom I am paused with the books upon my lap. I am filled with loathing. Then I take the first book firmly in my left hand and with my right tear down the centre of its spine. I tear it in half, then rip the pages across and take the next one and do the same with it, ripping faster and faster, with jagged effort pulling apart the spine, then across the cover, then fistfuls of pages, until I have destroyed them all. Then I go to the window and push up the sash and fling the pieces out over the garden. Birds of printed white fly everywhere.

In two hours the house is emptied, its insides out in a sprawling heap upon the grass. We have kept nothing. No furniture that could be moved, no picture or photograph. With the last armful of towels and bed-linen added, Kate and I stand outside. The rain is soft drizzle now and the damp untidy mound will not let the flame catch though I try several times. So in the end we just stand with the quiet of the countryside about us. Our breaths mist and fade. In the fields across the valley black cows move in slow file toward the gate. Turf smoke rises from Dooley's chimney. A tractor sounds along the road below us and stops and idles when it reaches the hedge below.

Then, in cuff-down wellingtons and tattered tweed, Mick Hehir is coming in the gate and up to us. He looks at the great mound on the grass, but he doesn't stop or pass remark.

'Well,' he says, extending his hand, 'you're home so?'

*

We sleep that night on the floor of the empty house on a rough bed made of clothes. The fire in the wide hearth goes out and the cold comes under the doors and through the frames of the windows and we cling and turn and ache and sleep and wake with dreams coming and going like fever. Rain falls down the chimney and what ghosts there are shuffle and stir from the fireplace and stare at the figures on the floor. They assemble, these Dickensians, these fellows with faces narrow and long in black coats and finger-less gloves, with mouths downturned and eyebrows arched, shambling through my dreams until I think to meet them, when they move off soft and silent as motes before a breath.

The night is long. A dozen times or more we wake and turn to the window and the deep unstarred blue is framed there and beaten with rain. Kate moves close against me but is restless and far away, I think, travelling some of the long distance it takes to get away from the past. Still the morning will not come. The house creaks and groans. Upstairs in Matthew's room the ceiling bleeds a large rain stain that spreads until it drips on the floor-boards above us. It continues some time after the rain has ended and intrudes into the quiet that comes around the house. I lie there and hear the steady dropping, and think of my brother and where he might be and fall into frowning sleep then and do not wake until I have the sensation that a grey creature has just run across my chest.

I sit up with a start, but see no mouse. The morning that has broken is frail and uncertain and of a weary washed-out light, as if it arrives across the fields only after great struggle with the night that retreats towards the sea. At the window I look out upon the sad, wet wreckage of the house, a sorry island mounded above the weeds. Kate stirs on the floor. What have I brought her to, I am thinking. I have no faith we can make a life here and I feel sour defeat, as though the story I had hoped to write is suddenly absurd and weak and the characters outlandish and false. For it strikes me that this is what we are hoping: to script our life and be the ones turning its plot. But in a moment the enormity of this, the effort of creation, and the iron belief needed, is a crushing burden and the vanity of it buckles me.

'Well?' Kate says softly. Her head is raised slightly and her eyes puffed and pursed with poor sleep.

'At least the rain has stopped,' I say.

'Come here.'

I cross back and crouch down to the bed on the floor and she reaches and kisses me. And perhaps because she tastes my disquiet, or because she wants to banish the grey spirits of the house, or because there is in her something that loves the hopeless, doomed, innocent and childlike and even childish sense of our arriving there, her hands hold my head and draw me down to her. We embrace on the hard bed of the floor and kiss until the heat comes through our clothes and we undress quickly the way lovers do.

Later we lie there on the scatter of our belongings and stay close against the coolness coming on our skin.

'We are here,' Kate says, looking away into the white turf ashes.

'Yes.'

'Can you believe it?' She doesn't look at me. Her voice is dreamlike and may be addressed to anyone or to herself.

'Yes, I can believe it.' I feel the need to be the carrier of hope, even at times when I have none. 'We are going to make it work,' I say. I am turned on one elbow looking at her. Her head rests on a pillow of jumpers and the high beauty of her face with its fine lines and bones is perfectly serene. She says nothing. She, unlike me, has known love to fade away and die, and there is in her at all times a shadowing sorrow that can come about her in moments. I speak to keep it away.

'We can begin on the house right away. Now that everything is out. I just couldn't otherwise. I couldn't live here. We'll be able to start afresh. I am going to set up a room for each of us, for the painting and the writing.'

She turns and looks at me and smiles, and I am aware that she is older and wiser than me and has in her regard sometimes a fond-ness for the foolish, for all in me that is naive and simple and credulous, just as sometimes it is the quality that most maddens her.

'You're always full of dreams,' she says, 'but I'm starving.'

We drive down into the village where the news of my return has arrived ahead of me, but is evident only in the slightest look, the side-glance at the rented car and the man I have become in slept-in clothes and white runners. The single street of shops is grown smaller than the one in my memory. The shopfronts are shades of beige, the buildings squat and crooked, and some are derelict. These, with glassless gaping windows and faded weathered names painted above their doorways, stay like stubborn reminders of a time when the village was busy with traffic of carts and horses and my father a young man. I show Kate the post office at the top of the street. We go inside where the interior is now changed completely, the space of the switchboard now taken by two computers, a display of information brochures where my father's old armchair sat.

Margaret Liddane, big and breathy and dough-faced, welcomes us.

'You're above again?' she says.

'We are.'

'That's great. Welcome home. Not many come back these days.'

'I suppose they don't.'

'No, then.' She pauses. 'I hope that you'll be happy there,' she says to Kate.

'Thank you.'

There is a moment in which she looks at us then, as if she is gauging by her own weights and measures what chance we have, what lies in our favour and what against us.

'I'll send any letters up so,' she says.

We leave and head along the street, passing buildings that have such an intense familiarity to me that I might be walking within a recurring dream. I know these places as if they are inside me. I know the crooked street of shops from the days when I was a fretful boy and carried an inexplicable dread of them, afraid of what normal robust life went on there. We come past butcher and chemist to the main shop of the village, owned and run still by Mrs Brady. She operates from a chair now behind the counter and has a freckled wing-eared boy who runs the aisles for her. Her husband died on the day of their fortieth wedding anniversary and for reasons peculiar to her own twist of mind she took this as his bitter joke on her and soured overnight. Now she watches the comings and goings of the village for the strange pleasure of seeing its population age and lie down before her and be carried to the cemetery behind the dispensary. She shushes the customers and stalls the sale if they appear in front of her as the death notices on the radio are being read.

She sees us enter and narrows her eyes as if aiming. I do not greet her and take Kate behind a row of cereals and juices, and think that perhaps Mrs Brady will not recognize me. For I am that first morning burdened by the difficulties of being back in a place I left so readily, and so often, leaving behind my ailing parents and the house and then the country, as if nothing had claim on me and I could be free of it all. I am burdened by the sense that I have betrayed this place in some way, and have a grey guilt and shame scurvying along my skin. And yet, in an acid Irish paradox, I know too that in the village they believe those who go to America do not come back, and that my return will be read as evidence of a kind of failing. None in the village will think it a place worth coming back to; none would believe us if we said we came to make a new life. They will think there is another story beneath, and one beneath that.

Such thoughts are with me as I go through the cramped little shop with Kate. By the time we come to the counter Mrs Brady has me.

'Young Jim,' she says in a triumphant wheeze.

'Mrs Brady, how are you?'

'Young Jim,' she says again, looking up from her chair and working some slowing mechanics in her mind to deliver all she can associate with my name. Whatever she finds causes her to smile and nod, and across the glaucous gaze of her eyes I can see myself a boy.

'Not so young,' I say. 'This is Kate.'

'Oh, yes?' says Mrs Brady, and places her hands on the armrests to prop herself and then lean up and offer her hand. 'Hello, dear.'

'We've moved back into the house,' I tell her, to move her squint from Kate.

'Is that right?'

'Yes.'

'Is that right, indeed?'

'Yes.'

'Well, I hope you'll like it, dear,' she says to Kate.

'I'm sure I will.'

Mrs Brady stops as if caught on something. 'Is that an American accent I hear?'

'I'm from New York.'

'Is that right?' She smiles and nods, as if here is a story worth hearing and telling.

'Yes.'

'I see. From New York. Well now.' She pauses, her eyes stay on Kate. 'So this will be a big change, dear.'

'Yes.'

'Oh, yes, a big change.'

Perhaps I imagine it, or there occurs here another moment of measurement and judgement, of the careful calculation of a spirit, as Mrs Brady considers the facts. And in the moment it happens, I fall through a door into the past and think of how my mother must have felt and how foreign the west must have seemed to her, and of the parallels of plots and stories and how they all meet in the end. Even before Mrs Brady has finished her calculation I am resolved that this time it will be different. There comes to me again, with greater clarity than before, the realization that what we are engaged in is a plot to heal the past, both mine and Kate's, to make things come out differently. I take Kate's arm.

'We have a lot of rain, you know, dear,' Mrs Brady says, bagging the groceries and punching the prices on the old till.

'I've seen.'

'Oh, that's nothing, I'm afraid, to what we get. Has he not told you?' She stops and looks at me as if I am engaged in deceit.

'We don't mind the rain, Mrs Brady,' I tell her.

'Ah no,' she lets herself back down into her chair, 'ones in love think they change the weather, sure.'

We exit into the morning. There are low clouds along the sky. Kate takes my arm and walks me quickly down the street, laughing.

'Change the weather for me, Jim, will you?'

'Well, let's see,' I say. 'That morning as they walked down the street of the village the clouds lifted and the sun shone like something smiling on them.'

The rain teems. We run for the car.

*

Mick Hehir comes with a can of petrol and stands beside me to watch as the mound in the garden is set alight and a high tower of flame climbs and snaps and twists with tongues of black smoke. Things of glass crack angrily amidst the pop and hiss of foodstuffs and coloured containers that had been in the house since my earliest memory. I see the fire peel back layers of things. I see photographs in their frames that I shouldn't have thrown out and watch the images bubble and retreat into the dark. The heat from the blaze is huge and for a time it seems the fire will run out of control. It has been set too near the house and while we stand guard we suddenly see the paint cracking and falling off the front wall, shards of colour rising on the wave of heat and flying upward into the smoked-out sky.

Mick moves about the edge of the blaze with a shovel, banging embers into the weeds.

After, when all is smouldering and a charred unconsumed plateau lies in the grass, Mick says to join him.

'Breda said she'd have the dinner ready for us. You're to come on.'

We go in the back box of the tractor, bumping over the road. The Hehirs' is a small old farmhouse next to the road. It has three windows in the front and, down one side, a line of low cabins built before the famine. When the tractor pulls in, Breda is at the door to meet us. She is fair-haired and soft-spoken and wears an apron against which she brushes her right hand before coming with it held out to greet us. Her smile is warm and her eyes kind as she takes my hand.

'You're welcome home, Jim,' she says.

'This is Kate, Breda.'

'You're welcome, very welcome.'

'Thank you.'

'Come on in now. It's just something very simple but I thought you would be hungry after. Mick told me you had a share of clearing-out done.'

We follow her into the kitchen inside the front door and there is a plain deal table beautifully laid.

Mick picks up a napkin.

'What are these for?' he asks with a grin.

'Those are napkins, Mick Hehir, as well you know.'

'Oh, righto.'

'This is lovely, thank you so much,' Kate says.

'Oh, it's very plain, I'm afraid,' Breda tells her, 'and getting cold, so sit down now wherever you like.'

From the top of the turf range she brings a pot of soup, and then some of their saved potatoes from the year before and carrots and cauliflower and from the oven succulent lamb. We sit and eat in that small kitchen by the heat of the range, the front door open on the road where no cars come or go and there are the sounds of the country only, bird, breeze and beast. Breda is up and down from the table. She is spooning out more on our plates before we can refuse and taking a deep satisfaction in seeing us well fed.

'Whatever you need above now, you tell us, Kate,' she says. 'There's only the two of us and we have any amount of blankets and linens and things. Whatever you want, all right?'

'You're very generous. Thank you.'

And she is. And I am filled with gratitude to her and think of how insufferably high and haughty I must have seemed to her before, never calling at their house as I came and went from my parents', never thinking to enquire of them, my head lost in books. I think too of how the personality of my father must have closed them off from him, how he was the postmaster, and how to them our family must have seemed in another country behind the high hedge and the wall. And perhaps there is in Breda's welcome too something of regret for how it worked out, the missed opportunities and failed relationships which now, at the table, in the simplest of ways, she can begin to repair.

The warmth of the welcome humbles me. We sit on wooden chairs after the meal and Mick offers his cigarettes and lights one when we decline.

'So, two calves?' I say.

'Yes, two so far. It's still early yet. There isn't growth for 'em, Jim. Rest will be due in a month or so.'

'That's good.'

'Time enough for 'em.'

'Yes.'

There is a pause; he draws on his cigarette and shuts one eye. 'Ye're thinking of farming yourselves?'

Kate laughs. 'You're kidding.'

'No, no, you could rent the few fields now and get started. I might know of somewhere.' Across Mick's face slips just the flicker of a grin. 'What do you think, Breda?'

'You're a terrible man, Mick Hehir,' she says, picking up the plates.

'Jim a farmer?' Kate says, getting up to help.

'Oh, certainly. And why not? Wasn't he reared with it all around him?'

'I'm not sure it made much of an impact,' Kate says, carrying dishes out after Breda.

Mick smiles as she goes and quiet falls. Thin sunlight at the window behind him makes a pale and grey skein of the smoke.

'You didn't need to come in and help at all,' we hear Breda say, and then the rattle and clack of dishes in the deep sink and the rush of the tap water.

'Thank you, Mick, for having us down.'

'Glad you came. There isn't much above, sure.'

'No.' Both of our chairs are turned now toward the open front door where we can watch if anything comes or goes, and there is the still calm feeling of the grass in the fields and the stone walls and the hedgerows and the slow traffic of clouds.

'I felt I had to throw everything out,' I say.

'Oh, yes?'

'To begin again, for ourselves.'

'Fair enough.' Mick pulls on the cigarette. He is not looking at me. 'There was a share of sadness there all right,' he says.

'Yes.'

After another while: 'Any news of Matthew at all these days or where is he?'

'No. No news. I'm not really sure. England, I think.'

'He was a brilliant fellow, Matthew.'

We watch the fields. Two birds dart and cross low above the grass.

Breda comes back with Kate carrying tea mugs and cuts of a currant cake.

'Kate's a painter, Mick,' she says. 'Did Jim tell you?'

'He didn't.'

'She's going to paint pictures above. Jim's going to write a book.'

'Is that so?' says Mick turning back to the table and taking a mug. 'Ye won't be needing my fields so?'

'Not yet anyway, Mick,' I tell him.

'Well, here's to writing books and painting pictures,' he says, and raises the tea for his toast. 'Whatever else, that ye may be happy.'

'Please God,' says Breda.

*

That afternoon we walk back to the house along the road. The air is mild and the fields gleam in the sunlight that comes and goes from beneath swift Atlantic clouds. Cows are moving head-low in slow westward grazing. Behind them blackbirds land and stand and fly small distances into bare trees of ash. As we walk, the valley falls away to our left in the green slopes of Hehir's farm. Below, the river is thick and dark and swollen with rain. Where the fields rise up on the far side are the farms of the Keanes and the Dooleys and, plain in sight, the old roofs of the houses of the parents and the newer slates of those their children built alongside. There are red haybarns near both and the low farm buildings of the yard. An older country still lingers here, in its last days without knowing it. We walk back. The food and the warmth of the welcome, the dreamlike quality of hush in the landscape and the frail sense of spring, all combine to imbue us with hope.

At the house we open all the doors and windows. I scrabble some turf from the back shed and light a fire in the hearth. Mick comes in his tractor and appears in the doorway.

'Maybe you'd give me a hand?' he says.

Out on the trailer are chairs and a table and an iron-frame bed.

'I bought a farm of land there, and what they call Buachaill's house, do you remember it? Came with all this stuff inside of it. There's whatever ye want now. You only have to say. Breda has the world of blankets and sheets and things. She put some in this bag for ye, but if there's more needed, well, that woman has it.' He flicks back his head and takes our thanks and calls it a thing of nothing and, once the furniture is carried in, lights a cigarette and stands to survey the scene.

The bed is set before the fire in the main room; I cannot quite imagine sleeping in the bedrooms of the house yet. It is as if we can first occupy only the small space around the hearth that we have claimed already that morning. So we place around the room whatever we carry in, and when Mick has left and the light is quickly retreating out of the sky, it is there we sit and drink tea and eat thick buttered wedges of Breda's griddle-bread. We have no radio. The house fills with quiet and is then more silent than any place I have ever been. The soft flap of a flame sounds, stirred to life by the tongs. Smoke grey and white climbs against the black of the chimney. The windows of the house now are night-curtained on the outside. Dark deep blue is garden and hedge and sky. The bare light bulb that hangs above us gives the room a glaring brightness that Kate dislikes so I shut it off and we sit within the pale amber glow.

'Here we are,' Kate says.

'Here we are.'

We hold each other and watch the fire grow low. I wish I knew words to say, verses to recite. In my head slips half a line: *on such a night did Lorenzo and Jessica.* But it escapes me, as does a fragment of Diarmaid and Grainne.

'What are you thinking?'

'Of lovers.'

'Tell me.'

'They never come back. They are always running away. Happiness is always elsewhere. There are no Irish stories of homecoming. No happy ones, anyway. It's all banishment, emigration and exile and sorrow.'

'Well, we will have to write this story ourselves, then.' Kate takes my head in her hands and kisses my forehead. And for then and in the night we allow ourselves to believe that, that all can be changed, that the past is passed and nothing that has been is of any significance. We love slow and warm and tender in the bed before the fire, keeping away fear or disquiet. We sleep and wake cold by the white ashes in the grate and lie closer together awaiting the dawn.

In the morning I make tea in the back kitchen and bring it to Kate in the bed. Her eyes are small and her hair tousled. Her face looks washed in a clear sadness.

'I had a terrible dream,' she says. 'You died.'

I sit beside her. Her head lies on my chest.

'Don't die,' she says.

*

In the bright wind-buffeted morning I go to the shed alongside the house and take out my father's shovel and spade and walk into the tangle of the garden. Kate studies the overgrowth and what were the raised flowerbeds. She looks back at the house as though painting an imaginary garden, as though in the movement of her hand is revealed the promise of spring and summer, and beds and borders and such are all equally made real before her. It is the gardener's annual act of faith, the covenant of the possible.

'I'll begin here,' she says, and takes the spade, her hair blowing around her face. 'You have to start with that.' She points to the charred lump near the door.

It takes the morning to barrow it away. I dig and fork the blackened ends of things, some still recognizable, others nothing but dark distortions, twists and melts of metal and plastic and wire. The garden is run around with breezes. They come through the thin parts of the hedge and over the roof of the cabin. The sycamore trees in the grove are still unleafed and their limbs make a heavy slow swaying. We work without words at remaking the garden. I cross down to where Kate is hacking at a bramble with the edge of the spade, trying to trace it back and fork it out. Such little victories are ours then. We dig away the top surface of weed and open a brown rectangle of earth in the green. The soil is poor and full of stones. I pick and throw them behind until there is a steady dull clatter. We dig. Kate works more diligently than I do. When I stop and stand and look, pressing my hand into the small of my back though the ache is unreachable, she is working on. Not with desperation or impatience, but with what occurs to me is joy. I watch her awhile.

Down in the village the church bells ring. We have forgotten it is Sunday. Since the death of my parents, and even before, I have stopped going to Mass. I am guilty of all sins of pride in relation to God, and have wanted since I was a boy for a personal answer. A message, a sign of what I was to do. We are not talking at the moment, He and I, I have told Kate. But that morning in the garden as the church bells ring I feel something almost sacramental. The clear notes fly out across the fields near the village. I allow myself the sentimental fancy that even the cattle pause and the birds hold their song. I look at Kate who is stopped and back-handing a fallen strand of her hair.

'Do you want to go?' she says.

'No.'

'Are you sure?'

I am.

'This is going to be a beautiful garden,' she says, and turns to it and digs on.

And I take the shovel in my hand again and bend forward to angle it in. But even as I do, pushing the blade down the earth to meet stone, I find myself making a silent prayer. The words are in my head without my saying them. They are less than whispers and offered with tentative care as though the muscle used is deeply bruised and its tissue remembers the blow and the suffering. I pray to myself, not to God, pray that this is right, that we are right to be here, that the desire for happiness and our own beginning is not arrogant nor conceited nor of an outlandish and futile vanity, but the simplest and oldest longing dared. *That ye may be happy*, Mick Hehir said.

We eat lunch outside and lean our backs against the front wall of the house. Along the palm of my right hand are four suns blistered open and brown with dirt and ooze.

'You poor thing,' Kate says. 'First time you've been in a garden this long.'

'I used to lie in it. Read books in it. But never really . . .'

'. . . thought about how it all happened.'

'I can hear the lawnmower going, my father pushing it, while I am up at that window reading something.'

The ghost of the moment passes. Kate smiles at me and says, 'Well, you will be able to push it soon for him and he can listen.'

We sit in the tremendous quiet of the Sunday noon. The country is bright, polished by the breeze, and white clouds cross the blue of the sky swift as thoughts. Blackbirds come from the high branches to the ground we have opened. The air is filled with the heavy damp scent of clay. Wet clumps of it cling to our boots. We back-heel them against the path but the earth remains and thickens as we go back into the dug ground for the afternoon.

The work is long and slow and hard. Once I supposed that in work such as the digging of a garden a mind would be free to wander. I believed that in the repeated mechanics of muscle and sinew a natural rhythm would emerge and I might be thinking of books or poems or such. But it is not so. Digging is digging. I am too tired and too in need of concentrating on each push of my foot on the back of the spade, each press of forearm, swivel of shoulder, to think of anything else. But there is in the work nonetheless a kind of peace. Even if it is only felt in the afterwards, when we stand at the top of the plot of brown earth we have opened in the weeds and survey it – this act of faith, this declaration of our belief in beginnings, in returning spring.

That night Kate writes a letter to her brother. She writes that it is like arriving on a shore after a shipwreck.

I go upstairs to what was my bedroom and where now nothing is left but some books. There are books there I have read three or four times. When I take them in my hand I can feel the hands of my younger self on their covers and the pure intensity of my reading, the fire that was in my head. There are the books that are part of me. There is the copy of *Sons and Lovers* that burned itself into my mind, *The Rainbow*, *Absalom, Absalom!*, *The Sound and the Fury*, *Light in August*, *The Brothers Karamazov*, *Crime and Punishment*, *The Death of Ivan Ilyich*, *The Overcoat and Other Tales of Good and Evil*, *Persuasion*, *Madame Bovary*, *Le Père Goriot*, *La Cousine Bette*, *Germinal*, Tolstoy's *Boyhood*, *Childhood*, *Youth*, his *Resurrection*, *One Hundred Years of Solitude*, *The Great Gatsby*, *The Good Soldier*, *Jude the Obscure*, *Tess of the D'Urbervilles*, *Brideshead Revisited*, *Mrs Dalloway*, *To the Lighthouse*, and, of course, the tattered dog-eared copies of the old reliables: two of *David Copperfield*, two of *Bleak House*, a *Pickwick*, *Dombey*, *Nickleby*, *Dorrit*, *Drood*, as well as, there, the old stolen library copy of *Great Expectations*.

I pick it up and open it, touchstone to so much. The due-back page I have torn out long ago, but the title page is still stamped, 'Ennis, County Library'. With earth-stained, nicked and blistered hands I flick the pages and release the scent of time and words and all that is captured there. Here is Pip with Herbert Pocket in London, here he is with Wemmick and the Aged P, flick the pages and here he is again on the return to the forge and Joe and Biddy and the sorrow and sense of loss that builds there. And so here too am I myself, joined into the pages of the book. I take it downstairs with me.

'What did you find?' Kate asks.

I tell her, and tell her then the story of how I stole it and how my father defended me at the library desk and how I hated him for it. After, we sit together on the bed and watch the fire.

'Read to me, will you, Jim? Read me something from it.'

And I do. For the first time in that house I read out loud the words. I read of Pip meeting Magwitch and being turned upside down and shaken, just as everything that follows in his life will be. I read the vivid opening scenes there before the low turf-fire in the hush of the house where the wind makes blow-downs of the smoke sometimes and we sit and wait and watch a pall unfurl and float up through the ceiling. Then I read on. I read us to the edge of sleep.

Kate lies down beneath the blankets in the dark.

'When will you start?' she says, softly.

'Start what?'

'Writing. Your own book.'

I am unsure what to say, how to say I am afraid to begin, afraid to sit down and discover I have no talent when we have risked so much upon it.

'Soon,' I say, 'the next rainy day, maybe.'

*

And for a week none comes. The country falls into mid-winter spring, days bright and blown into which the first daffodils raise their heads and dance in the wind. We work in the garden, we clear away the roots and weeds in the flowerbeds and open them to the air. We slash at bramble and nettle root and pause and unbend and feel the ache of the work, raising our heads into the breeze. We are complexioned with wind and earth and brief Irish sun. We are visited by Mick Hehir in his tractor and go and sit along the deep window sills at the front of the house and survey with him the progress. He brings sometimes Breda's griddle-bread or a tied cloth of warm scones, and we eat them there with hot mugs of tea while birds tentatively arrive on the earth apron of the garden.

'Leave my worms!' Kate shouts down at them, sometimes getting up and brandishing tea mug and watching as the birds rise and wheel and alight in the high branches once more.

It is a time of such ordinariness, a time of work, of the innocence of gardeners. Potato ridges are dug down one side in the front of the house, and beds for cabbages and carrots and onions.

One afternoon, when we have kicked wellingtons free at the front door and come inside in socks and sat in the weariness of a day spent digging, I feel for the first time some clearance has happened inside me. I feel a lightness in my spirit that was not there, like entering a familiar room in yourself and finding the heavy furniture gone. Something has changed, and I tell Kate so, coming from the sink with the towel in my hands, and then surprising myself by telling her that I am going down to the graveyard.

I have not been there since the day my father was buried. It is a small graveyard at the crossroads of the village behind where the old church used to be. There are tombstones from the famine and weathered stones of jagged edge whose carved inscriptions are long erased by salt and wind. They tilt at odd angles to the ground. Some graves are weed-grown and walked on, others have plastic flowers in plastic domes and white stone chips turning green with moss. I walk along the passageway between families of the dead. Old names of the parish are gathered there: Considines and Kellys and Conways, Morriseys and Morans and McCarthys. And down the way a little bit: here is ours, our corner of the dead. There is the small grave of Louise I was brought to visit after Mass on Sundays until I said I would not go any more. There my mother knelt often, and often unbeknownst to me, I think now, and my father stood in the stolid disillusion and grief that were his and waited to bring her home. Next to the grave are those of my parents. I read their names on the marble tombstones, as if for me it is always words that make the thing real. The cold of late afternoon is inside my clothes. The sky is heavy with clouds of lead. I stand there, alone and bowed and thinking of what to say – for words seem called for. It seems without them some element of repair, of reconciliation, is impossible. I should say a prayer then. I should say out loud an Our Father or a Hail Mary or an Act of Contrition. But no matter how long I wait to begin I don't seem able; I stand as though waiting for something to happen, some portal to open or to feel a soft tap at my shoulder and turn and know that I am in the presence of their ghosts. But in that small and desolate graveyard in west Clare there is only the long emptiness of the westerly wind and the first coming drops of the rain.

And perhaps it is that which finally prompts me. The rain comes like a curtain. I can see it away over by Mescalls and the hills of Ayahah before it begins.

'I felt today—' I say, and stop myself and swallow some dryness in my throat and raise my eyes to the sky to contain tears. 'In the garden, I felt today that you had forgiven me.'

I say no more. I stand there until the rain falls.

When I go back to the cottage I sit with Kate and read to her the last pages of *Great Expectations*. And after, we drive together through the rain to Ennis and park and go inside the yellow-lit late opening of the county library, and I bring the book to the plump cheerful woman at the front desk.

'I stole this some years ago,' I say. 'I have meant to return it.'

*

The rain that began falling in the graveyard is falling the next morning still. We sit inside the window and look out on the garden and the veil that drapes it.

'It will rain all day, won't it?'

'It could,' I say.

'Well, then.' She lifts her eyebrows at me.

'Yes?'

'Well, we can't watch it all day.'

'No?'

I turn from her face and look out at it. I could watch it all day, I think. There are a hundred ways for rain to fall and a hundred ways to watch it. It drizzles this morning in grey sheets of thinnest gauze falling so softly as to appear a substance lightly suspended in mid-air. It has a slow soothing, like a cool moist balm against forehead and temples. It makes nothing of time, of day or afternoon or evening, as sun and light and shadow are all put away and changeless hours of grey only endure.

Kate is looking at me.

'You have to start.'

'I know.'

'You should try. I will. I am going to set up in the sitting room if you will light a fire for me.'

And so, within an hour, we are sitting in separate rooms inside the great quiet of the house, Kate sketching and I staring at a yellow page in a pad brought from New York. I sit with my back turned to the window, the pen in my hand. What am I to write? Now that I have arrived at the place imagined, at a table in the middle of the morning, with nowhere else to be, nothing else to do, what words do I put on the page? There are a hundred books I wrote in my imagination before this. A hundred times I have sat in a room and laid down the book I was reading and let my mind wander for a time among the characters and along the plot, supposing I could invent such a story, believing the characters so real in my mind that I could invent others of their ilk and had only to follow them with my pen.

Or so it had seemed.

I sit there in the pallid rainlight. I look up from the yellow page and across at the wall, the rough texture of the plasterwork, the way it is stippled in places and brushed and scored, how the wall itself is not straight but bulges slightly towards the floor. I have not noticed before that dark unfaded square on the linoleum, nor how where the water pipes come through the floor is the thick grey-white webbing of a spider. I look at the crack in the ceiling where the electric wire lets hang the bare light bulb. Lines, shapes, stains, smudges of paint where the brush carried cream onto the window's white, cracks, nail holes, fragments of dirt and dust, the minute gathered detritus of living; all things tempt me. The page itself, and the pen too, my hand holding it. My mind is in sharp focus on the real. The concrete world of objects and surfaces is like a cage around me as I try to find a place for imagination to enter. But for an hour I cannot.

I get up and walk across the room and look in vain for the spider. I listen at the door for the sounds of Kate working in the other room and think in the stillness I hear the soft scratch of charcoal cross-hatching shadow. I go and sit down again. I smooth the smooth page with my palm and then hold my forehead on my hand until I recall my father in the same pose.

The drizzle still veils the garden. There is the noise of a car, then a tractor passing. Then nothing. The country is a hushed scene awaiting.

What fears and doubts twist and coil and knot in my insides makes the writing of the first word impossible. I find the excuse of getting turf for Kate's fire, and go outside then across the yard to the stack. The hedges are dripping. Leaves are surfaced with rain-pearls and diamonds. The sods are black and damp and I move some aside to get the drier ones beneath. I come back with my arms full to the door of the sitting room.

'May I come in? I got you some more turf.'

'Sure.'

She is sitting with a sketchpad and working a still-life of the window and round table and the garden beyond. On the floor are three or four sheets, pencil and charcoal versions of the scene upon them, each one more true than the one before.

'How is the writing?'

I bend and load the fire.

'Just beginning,' I say.

When I return to the table and sit down I take up the pen as though the words are at its tip and bursting to be released. I bring it to the paper and write, *My name is Nicholas Copperly.*

But nothing more. Just that. By noon I have written the same sentence four times on four different sheets of paper. I have moved the margin, written Chapter One, just One, just the numeral, and then only an asterisk. Perhaps it is enough, I think. Perhaps there is need today only to have the name and to imagine him then, this character on the page. *Nicholas Copperly.* I stop and have lunch with Kate of tea and sandwiches before the fire. The rain is still falling. I ask her if I can look at the drawings she has made.

'They're only practice,' she says. 'Don't.'

In the afternoon I return to the yellow page and read aloud the sentence written there, as if in reading the words when I come to their end I will know what comes next. I read it as if it is a story I am telling, and being told, as if I am writer and reader both. I say the name over for its rhythm and sound. I say it for the many associations I can find in its music, for Copperfield of course and Nicholas Nickleby, but also for others more obscure, for Saint Nicholas, for the magic of transformation, of miracle, and this combined with the dull unprecious metal of copper, for elements Christian and pagan both. I say the name and think of some hoped-for alchemy, some plot of redemption that will befall this character. But in the dead and failing light of the long afternoon I cannot find a way forward. Instead my pen draws boxes on the margins of the page, and then makes x's across them. Perhaps the rain seeps into me. Perhaps it is the dull unborn day outside, the drear of season, the sealing hood of grey sky that makes me lose my will and put down the pen and then just sit.

I hear Kate in the kitchen.

Don't get up, I tell myself. Stay here, stay. And I do, sitting perfectly still in the chair until at last I pick up the pen.

My name is Nicholas Copperly, I write again on a fresh sheet.

But who are you? Where are you?

'My name is Nicholas Copperly,' I say out loud to whatever ghosts or figures grim are gathered to listen, and then louder still: 'My name is Nicholas Copperly. I walk about these streets in the rain.'

*

For a week it does not stop raining. By the end of it I have fourteen pages of *Nicholas Copperly*. He lives in London and walks in the rain. He comes to the aid of an elderly man who suffers a stroke and falls in a puddle in the street. The man owns a bookshop off King's Road and Nicholas gets a job there.

I have never been to London except in books. But now, in the rain of west Clare, in the house where my imagination grew up, I am there every day. I imagine the bookshop. I call it Stafford & Sons. It is the kind of bookshop where the books are set out on old tables and the tables themselves crowd together and make narrow passageways for the customers. It is not the kind of bookshop where you can find things easily. There is little apparent order or arrangement to the table-top volumes other than the whim and taste of Mr Stafford, who this week puts a new hardcover by the young writer Ian McEwan alongside some old orange Penguin editions of Graham Greene. Next week the Greenes may be next to Patrick Moore's *Astronomy* or Lawrence Durrell's *Balthazar* or the teachings of Teilhard de Chardin. Only in the shelving is there traditional order. The customers, the bald and stooped Mr Stafford tells Nicholas, come for discovery, for the pleasures of browsing, as if they are walking through a company of the most fascinating people.

'Imagine it, Nicholas. They are all here.'

In Stafford & Sons a book does not get pride of place just

because it is new. Sometimes it is because it is old. But always it is because it is good. Old Mr Stafford likes Nicholas. He likes the care he sees in him. He likes how Nicholas carries the books from the storeroom, how he carefully arranges the small stacks Mr Stafford likes along the staircase as it curves upward.

'A Joyce, a *Shane*, two Dickens, a history of India, and a *Vicar of Wakefield*?' remarks the old man, looking at a stack on the stair. 'Wonderful, Nicholas. Who could walk up these stairs without stopping for these?'

But as it happens, many do. By the time Nicholas Copperly has been at the shop for two months he is hearing the clunk and ping of the old till sound through the bookshop less and less. There are customers all right, lunchtime browsers, Saturday-morning readers, men and women who stand for an hour or more over the tables handling the books. But sales are slow.

It does not seem to bother Mr Stafford unduly, but by the fourteenth page of the novel Nicholas has already decided he must do something to help.

And while I figure out what that is, I work outside with Kate in the sodden garden. In the rain-drenched week, she too has been working, drawing time after time the same set scene of window and table and garden. I am not supposed to look. She is not ready to begin painting yet, she tells me.

The spring that has come is wet and heavy and makes of the soil a clammy thickness that quickly turns to mud. We seed pota-toes into furrows and fork in manure. We mound up ridges and watch the birds come and go along them, curious and hungry for the life we have stirred. Quickened breezes blow, bringing with them swift showers of rain, sometimes lasting no longer than the time it takes to set damp saddle-stains across our shoulders. We set rows of summer cabbage plants, and onions, and make a fence for peas, and are all day out there in the garden, in the simplicity of that, like figures in a naif painting.

But after, in the evenings, in the deep weariness we both fall into before the fire, we lose faith and wonder what we are doing and have to talk ourselves back into it.

'It will be all right,' I tell Kate.

'Will it? Are we not just playing?'

'No.'

'Sometimes I think we are. I don't even know what's going on anywhere, what's happening?'

The fire hisses a few raindrops.

'Nothing is happening.'

It's not true of course. The country is then a grim place of strikes and cutbacks, of employment freezes and whispered political scandals. There are men in grey suits and frowns outside government buildings. There is talk of help from Europe, of betrayal by Europe, of the case of the farmers, of how the future of the country is at stake. But I am thinking of none of this, only of the two lives that can be rescued here.

In the bluster of sunlight that comes the following day, Kate takes her oils and a canvas outside. Facing the house, she leans the canvas against a chair that is set into the uneven ground. Behind her are the pair of wild holly trees, their glossy jagged leaves glistening. She begins to paint the scene from the opposite side she has drawn it. I go upstairs to *Nicholas Copperly*. I am stuck, without an idea of what he should do, and idly watch down from the window into the garden where the wind keeps catching the canvas like a sail and blowing it forward. Kate saves it twice, a third time it flies off, wheeling over onto the dirt. I watch her stand there, still looking at the space where the canvas has been. Then she goes and picks it up and walks up toward the house where I think she will come in now and give up. I wait to hear the latch on the kitchen door, but it doesn't sound. Instead there is the tapping of a nail, another, then Kate, her arms wide as on a cross, is carrying the canvas back down the garden and with yellow baler twine tying it against the back of the chair. When it is secured she stands back from it, paintbrush in her hand. The wind comes and makes fly blonde ribs of her hair. She raises her hand to them. They blow free again. Leaves, twigs, seeds, dry dead figments of winter are teased out from under hedges and fall from nests. Birds dart. The blue overshirt Kate wears rumples and wrinkles with the gusts going through it. But she stays there painting. One time the wind takes canvas and chair and all and she reaches the brush-hand and catches it in time, and then, as if pressing down a shovel, she puts her boot on the crossbar beneath the seat and digs the legs down into the ground, down and down until at last the painting is firm in the earth.

*

In a clear April evening dying into early night as the stars climb above the cabin roofs, we sit across from each other reading. Then I tell her: 'The money is going quicker than I thought.'

Kate lowers her book.

'Really?'

'I didn't want to tell you.'

'How much? Jim, how much quicker, how much have we left?'

'I'm going to work something out.'

'What?'

'Something.'

'How can you say that? There are no jobs here. There's nothing. We thought it would last another six months.'

'I know. The things for the house . . .'

'Jim!'

'. . . the furniture, the car, I didn't count on them, didn't think that I would have to get rid of everything. I shouldn't have. It's my fault. I'm sorry. I am an idiot.'

We sit and the quiet of the house is heavy and the heat from the fire too much in my face.

In the morning I go into the village to the post office. I wait while an elderly woman finishes her business at the counter. She moves to one side as she puts money in her purse. I wait, not wanting to step forward, to be overheard. Margaret Liddane smiles at me and waves me to come on.

'Well, Jim? How are you getting on? I hear ye've great work done above.'

The woman at my elbow is slow and folding her banknotes and stops to look at me to see who I am.

'We have a beginning anyway.'

'That's wonderful, so it is. Fine weather will be coming in soon now too. So, what can I do for you today?' Margaret's face is broad and innocent and welcoming and across it passes her emotions easily visible. I see her disappointment when I lower my voice and tell her.

'I need the forms to sign on the dole, please.'

She can say nothing straightaway.

'Thank you, now, Mrs Brogan,' she says quite firm and loud. 'Jim, would you maybe get the door for her?'

I do, and in that time, Margaret has a moment to gather herself. She brings her hands together on the counter. She presses her lips tight. I stand before her but am hardly listening to what she tells me. I am filled then with lumps of crimson shame, sour and curdled. I stand where I have stood as a boy waiting to go out into the street when my father unlocked the post-office door, in the place where the world came and went through him for all those years, where he connected the calls. I feel shivers on my spine.

'There's a form there, Jim, but you have to go to the office in Kilrush. To be assessed.'

She says more but I do not hear it. I leave with a slip of paper and drive out of the village to Kilrush.

There I sit before a thin man in a pale room with a grille upon its window. He looks at me through large glasses.

'What kind of work would you be looking for?' he asks me.

'I am a writer,' I tell him.

'Yes, but you have to be looking for work.'

'I am.'

'In what line is that?'

'Writing.'

'I see.' He makes a grimace of a smile. After a time he asks, 'You're married?'

'Yes.'

'I see. Your wife is working?'

'She is a painter.'

'A painter, good.'

'An artist.'

'Oh. Well, does she sell her paintings?'

'She is working on her first one.'

'I see.'

We wait there, figures in an empty room.

'You are the son of Tom Foley, the postmaster?'

'Yes.'

'And come back home now from America?'

'That's right.'

Another wait, another eternal duration in which shame thickens in my throat.

'You'll get sixty-five pounds thirty pence a week,' he tells me at last.

I stand up. I feel like a beggar.

'Thank you.' I say, 'I won't be needing it for long.'

'No?'

'I'll have my novel finished.'

'Oh yes.' The grimace smile comes again. 'I forgot.'

That evening I sit upstairs in the bedroom and read back the pages I have written of *Nicholas Copperly*. What does he do now? I watch him there on the page, standing alone in the empty bookshop as afternoon light slants in on the stacks. What does he do, this Nicholas? How can he help Mr Stafford? He stands there in the grey beam of falling dust and the soft susurrus of traffic in the London street outside. He walks along by the tables and runs a hand upon the covers of books he knows well. That day only two have left the shop. He is eaten by worms of anxiety. He goes then to the shelving where he knows books will not be missed and he takes down three copies of Dickens, four of Hardy, two Brontës and he brings them to the back storeroom and puts them in a bag there beneath his coat. That evening he hurries off through the streets with them before Mr Stafford locks up.

*

Soon there are potato stalks above the ground. The green world comes again. Fields let up grass that is thick and sweet and soft and moves in the bright breezes with waves like water. Leaves tremor in the sycamores. The high branches sway and there is sense then of all unfurling. The fists of the roadside ferns open. Birds and flies and insects innumerable are everywhere crossing the air. Tractors noise along the road where none came before. They come with cone spreaders of fertilizer and bounce through gateways into the broad open places of meadows below. All day then there is the buzz of activity, and the irresistible force of what runs beneath the ground and now is propelled upward beneath the high blue cathedral dome of the sky. Down in the valley the river silvers and turns like a tongue in the deeps of the banks. The days stretch toward the night and move it backward, as though more hours are needed for the dalliance of sunlight on seedling.

The garden transforms, its growth and leafing a green act of faith I come to realize I did not believe in. We live on the sixty-five pounds and thirty pence I collect each week in a line of older men at the post office. Sometimes I bring Mick Hehir in the car because he has the trailer hitched to the tractor or something loaded in it. He gets in beside me and compliments the car. Always he asks if he can light a cigarette and then smokes with it held just below the open window. We agree the weather is wonderful and the spring something.

'Isn't it just, though? Isn't it something?' he says.

'It is.'

'Mighty altogether. Mighty.'

And driving along toward the village I think of that, and let the word mighty echo inside me and find the simple resonance of force and an uncontested belief in it, in spring and renewal and the movement of all things toward rebirth.

*

Night after night Nicholas Copperly steals the books of Stafford & Sons. He steals a hundred volumes before he knows what he will do with them. The books stack up in the small room he rents at the top of a house in Kilburn, while Kilburn itself is populated by all the grim figures my imagination has stored over the years. I put them all in there. On the streets, in the shops, in the stairwell of the house Nicholas Copperly meets every shade of sallow stubbled faces, with crooked tooth or red hair and thin twisting hands, fellows with a bush of eyebrow, or purpled tulip bulb for nose, squints, twitches, rashes, scars and scabs – all the released Dickensians of my mind.

Meanwhile, in a parallel plot, there is a squat bull-headed man who cheats his customers with reused parts in the appliances of JG's Electrical.

One warm evening in the beginning of summer, as the cuckoo dementedly sings, I sit in the upstairs room and out of pure chance have Nicholas break into JG's shop and rob it. For the money he takes he leaves behind four Charles Dickenses, three Thomas Hardys and a Tobias Smollett.

All hardcovers.

The money he puts into the till at Stafford & Sons.

Two weeks later he robs the same business again. He leaves behind three Jane Austens, four Ford Madox Fords, a Waugh, a Wodehouse and a copy of *Waverley*.

Nice hardcovers, with stitch binding and flypapers.

'What kind of lark is this? What the blazes do I want books for?' JG asks the policeman.

*

There are paintings now in the front room. Kate calls me in to look at them. She stands to one side with her hands together in front of her as though in prayer. They are scenes of the garden and the house, painted in strong colours so the earth is sometimes purple and sometimes blue and takes into it streaks of green and yellow like cables of current pulsing just below the surface. They are pictures alive with the ordinary and have a sense of wonder that will be called childlike, because it seems improbable that an adult could see the world so simply or have such an unbroken sense of joy. I look at them for a long time and in some part of me I know that here is an answer. Here is a response out of all the days of doubt and unbelief, out of the meanness and defeat of penury and need, a voice saying yes, we are right, there will be paintings and books here.

I stand there and am too long without speaking.

'Are they any good?' Kate asks.

*

In the evenings we go walking along the road west of the house to where it rises over a broad view down into the village below. To the south the church spire climbs above the rooftops. To the north the land runs scraggy and poor with wet fields of rushes turning to the brown of bogland. Ahead of us as we walk is where the land rises at Kilkee and falls into the ocean. In the clearest of light you can see the thin silver glimmer of the Atlantic.

We walk toward the sunset. Cows stand and turn momentarily then graze again. Young cattle nose the wire fence restlessly and press and shuffle. One lifts its head and snorts loud breath and twists away and runs and the rest follow, charging down the field with back-kicks and great shoulders tossing. They run themselves out and stand and blow in the warm air of the evening.

Kate takes my arm. We talk of our life as a thing we are making. Of the garden and the paintings and the novel. And sometimes of the loneliness we feel.

'Is love enough?' she asks. 'I sometimes wonder.'

To such questions there are no true answers, but I make some nonetheless. Kate smiles, knowing more than me. 'You are a true believer, the last innocent,' she says.

'I am.'

We walk only as far as the high point of the road and will turn back before it drops down to curve into the village. When we reach it we stand by the stone wall and the brambles and survey all that lies below. Kate looks at me.

'Jim,' she says, 'what kind of father will you be?'

Here we are, then, in the pages of a book. That I want to be something more than a book. I think that out of collapsed faith, out of hurt from the absence of response from God Himself, I write the words the way I used to say prayers, that something may happen, that the pages and their words be a kind of redemption. It is outlandish, I know. I would not say it aloud. I want a book that is not paper and print and board but is in fact a quiet kind of sacrament, a slow ritual of telling, of confession, say, and offering and consecration, that brings communion of a kind and grace with it.

Or something like that. Imagine.

Last night I wrote the scene and returned to that summer moment on the high road here where you took my arm and asked me. I read it over until I was there again, until so too were you.

'I have loved you more than anything or anyone in the world,' I said out loud.

The dog it was who lifted his ears and looked at me.

I went at last then to the shelf above the fire and for the thick sweet syrup of nostalgia took down the old copy of Nicholas Copperly and read that first line: 'My name is Nicholas Copperly. I walk about these streets in the rain.' And remembered the excitement of that, of going back to the office in Kilrush and signing off, of holding the book in my hand for the first time, and of course the terrible reviews that followed, 'derivative and cringe-inducing' I remember, the hurt you felt for me. In the photograph on the back I am a young man with hair on my head and eyes full of determined hope. From inside the pages I took out the two cards I got from Matthew afterward, when he came across the book and read on the sleeve that I lived in the house where I grew up in west Clare. One is from Nice, one from Gibraltar. Sent three years before I met him again, that uncomfortable half-hour when he came as far as the Old Ground Hotel in Ennis, and had a gift for Hannah, but couldn't face coming out to the house. He had lived in a string of places across Europe, always unsettled, always with the air of a problem unsolved. In France he had found some company in the south among the easeful wealthy straw-hatted English, and after been into Africa. 'Maybe I was looking for one of those dresses she made,' he said and gave a small laugh at himself and drank his whiskey.

I put the book back on the shelf among the others. All of them so unreal.

What a poor magician I have been, the fellow come to a country hall in old battered and purple-sprayed Volkswagen, thin music blaring, unloading baskets of old props and hauling them in the dark doors, readying for the act. My tricks are old as time. See, there is nothing up my right sleeve, nothing up my left. Here, watch how I make believe the plots work out all right.

Not this time. This time I write only to bring you here with me on these pages.

Tired of resurrection then, today after the children were in school, I took the car and drove aimlessly the winding back roads through Cree and Doonbeg, wandering in and out of small townlands hunkered there in the bluster of the Atlantic. Down behind the church I took the road to the sea, the wind terrific and the white caps coming fast on the tide. All along the sea road, not a car not a person, just the edge of the country and the salt gale sweeping in over it. I stopped there and got out into the buffeting, feeling the texture of wind and sand like pumice on my cheeks. I left the car and walked and walked until I felt my spirit lifted in a way, perhaps by the harsh beauty, the foamy tide, or maybe only the enduring of myself in fierce wind.

After, I drove back to the village and in the shop was asked what news I had of Mick Hehir.

'News?'

'Isn't he up near you, Mick Hehir? He is. You haven't heard any news?'

'What do you mean?'

'After the attack he had Monday.'

'Attack?'

'Heart, I'd say. You didn't hear? He's in the County, went by ambulance.'

'He was better yesterday,' a woman said from down the counter. 'I was in visiting Mrs Halvey and stopped over to check on him, I say he's over the worst of it, if it doesn't get you straight out, you can recover all right with the heart, so they say anyways.'

I left the shop and drove to Ennis, stopped at Sean Spellissey's shop on Parnell Street and then over to the hospital. I found him upstairs in the men's ward sitting up in striped blue pyjamas.

'Hello, Mick.'

'Jim, you're very good, there was no need to come.'

'How are you?'

'I'm right as rain, sure. I cut out on the way over and they started me again.'

I sat on the stool next to him. I asked him about the food and the nurses; he asked me about the children and then the weather and if I'd noticed Paddy Hayes checking on his cattle for him. When the questions and answers ran out we sat a while longer in quiet company. Then Margaret Liddy, widow, weekly hospital visitor, husband-seeker, appeared.

'Oh, God, not that biddy,' Mick muttered under his breath.

I stood up and gave her the stool.

'Well, you were very good to come, Jim. Thank you.'

'Tell them to call me when you need to be brought home.'

'I will so.'

'Here.' I gave him the brown-paper bag.

'What's this?' He fingered out the paperback book and smiled. 'Louis Lamour! How well you remembered.'

247

Margaret Liddy leaned in to look. 'What kind of book is it?' she asked him. 'I love romances.'

*

Today, your birthday, when Hannah came down for breakfast in her school uniform I announced that we were going to take a few days off.

'Why?' she said.

'We need it. Just a break, for a few days, just us.'

'And what about school?'

'School doesn't matter. You'll catch up.'

'Dad, it's April. It's cold.'

'I know. Take some jumpers. A warm coat. I'm going up to wake your brother. Get changed.'

I went through the cottage in a flow, the way the words fill a page on the current of an inspiration. Here was the way things could be. For a few days we would step out of the pages of our life and close the covers. I was smiling as I laid my head down beside Jack's in his bed.

'Good boy, Jack, wake up now, wake up.'

He turned on the pillow, and, without opening his eyes, reached to hug me.

'No school today, Jack. We're going to have a holiday.'

He opened his eyes and blinked, and within instants then was standing and dressing himself in the jeans I am never allowed to wash.

And so, band of escapees, father and son and daughter and dog drove out the roads of Clare where the school buses passed in the opposite direction. I had no exact destination in mind, I followed the instinct that always brings me to the sea. We turned at Cree and took the long gentle ribbon of road to Quilty. The day was dull, the sky a wet grey cardboard hung to dry. Wind shook the car. Still, it didn't matter what the weather was, I said. It was our own holiday.

'Holiday, Holiday!' Jack cheered in sing-song and I nodded back to him, warmed by the childlike simplicity of things when they seem right, fitted, composed.

The Atlantic made a blowsy show of wave and surliness. The grey tide came against the sea wall and sent small shoots of dirty spray upward. The windscreen wipers worked the salt away, and we drove on along the coast, out by the beach at Spanish Point where the sea was more flamboyant and the curve of sand spotted with islets of foam.

'Where are we going?' Hannah asked.

'Away, just away for a few days.'

'Are we going to a town?'

'We'll see.'

'Everywhere along the sea will be closed. It's...'

'I know. April.'

She reached and turned on the radio. As we drove by the empty white holiday bungalows that dot the sea road, the airwaves were filled with callers still outraged at the apparent lack of any real National Emergency Plan for Ireland. Each home has been promised iodine tablets in the post, we heard. But it will be six months or so before they are ready.

'Find some music, Hannah.'

'No, I want to hear this.'

We drove on through the empty seaside town of Lahinch where the bright colours of the houses had a dowdy desolate air and the boutiques were closed for the season. Liscanor, Doolin, Fanore, villages facing the Atlantic and America, all of them like places asleep or turned inward, listening for news. Sometimes we came up behind a delivery lorry lumbering its way down the centre of the road, and slowed and followed for miles, as though being led. On the radio a priest was speaking about the meaning of Easter. Out by Black Head, on the road that is like a skirt to the sea, we lost reception. The mountain towered up on our right, on our left the Aran Islands greyly painted into the sea. For a little while we drove on in the static with the wavering voices coming and going. They might have announced the ending of everything, or the beginning of something extraordinary, and we would not have known, moving by sea and mountain and seabirds. We drove on. Hannah gave up and turned off the radio. I felt then a deep contentment, the kind you feel in a warm car on a cold day when the journey is not hurried and the simple momentum *implies some sense of destination and arrival. It was the most hopeful thing. If there were signs I should have seen, I did not see them. If there was something other than the quiet in the car, some fracture that occurred and that I should have noticed, I didn't. I think I thought for a moment we were almost happy. You drive on down the road staring ahead and some part of you is seeing the road and nothing else, and some part of you is far away not even dreaming the place you are about to come to.*

After a while we stopped at a fishing place along the road and got out to walk down the rocks to the sea. Jack was carsick, we needed air. There was nothing else. There had been no row, nothing. We got out. Huckleberry circled around sniffing and peed against the back wheel. The wind came at us wildly, and I reached and took Jack's hand. I tried to put up his hood and he resisted and I told him he had to cover his ears but he shook his head and I gave up. His laces were open. I bent down to them. By then Hannah had already gone far ahead. She just got out of the car and went straight toward the very edge where there was a sharp fall into deep water. I called her back but whether she did not hear me or did not want to, she did not come. I tied Jack's laces, the dog beside me.

'Double knots, Daddy,' Jack said. 'I don't like them to be loose.'

'Yes, double knots,' I said. I was not afraid yet, only feeling the flickering anxiety of a parent when a child seems to slip outside the safety of your reach. And in the back of my mind I could hear a whole catalogue of Hannah's previous recriminations to me: as a father I am too controlling, I have no trust, I won't let things be. I am always trying to make everything safe and right, scripting the moments before they even happen. Relax, Dad, I have heard her say to me so often. But things happen in instants. I cannot relax. Perhaps it is the constant engine of my own imagination that does not let me see the moment, the real thing, without also seeing the next one and the one after that, and the fear rose up in me. I was kneeling to tie the laces but glancing up and over to the sea's edge where Hannah was.

'Hannah, wait, come back!' I called again, and when she did not hear me I stood and left the second lace undone and took Jack's hand

to go over the rocks after her. The dog ran lightly ahead, and then he began to bark.

'It's not done, it's not done, Daddy!'

'In a minute, Jack. Come on.'

'I'll trip.'

'You won't. I have your hand. Come on.'

The sea was huge and loud and came in a powerful wash over the rocks about us. Further ahead I saw spray climb high in front of Hannah and the sides of the coat she would not close fly out like wings. The dog was barking over and over, and then backing away as the waves came, and then inching forward to bark again.

'Hannah!'

She was still twenty feet ahead of us and did not turn back to her name. Across a crag Jack nearly slipped and twirled on my hand and cried out that I had hurt his wrist with the tightness of my grip.

The rocks were slippery and dark and he sat down on them and felt his arm and I told him he would get wet there but he said his lace was undone and he would trip again and that he had told me so before.

'All right, wait a minute here, just wait, OK?'

He was cross with me and said nothing. I was on the point of turning from Jack to go after Hannah when I saw the widening of surprise in his eyes and his mouth open to say something that he stopped himself from saying, because it must have seemed impossible, something so unlikely he knew it could not be. And so there were no words for it. He said nothing at all. The surprise blanched his face. The spray came up and over us and as I turned from him I just then saw Hannah, whether step or leap or fall, disappearing from the rocks and down into the sea.

*

I want to write that I ran. I want to write that I ran and dived in at once and rescued Hannah. That it was a freak accident and she had slipped and now swam to me in the water. I want to write our life as a story in which things turn out all right. But sometimes I am

251

not sure what all right means, sometimes the plot does not move as you expect it to, and sometimes the one you are rescuing is yourself.

I stood there too long beside Jack looking at the emptiness of the space where Hannah had been. I stood there and seemed frozen in inaction. And meantime all manner of things transpired within me, flashes, fragments of thought, fear. Was she gone? Was she gone like you into the dark, the emptiness? Did she fall or had she jumped? Was there a sign I had missed? Were there many?

It was an age before I got to the edge. The water, dark and deep and swollen, slapped and then surged and broke into spume against the rocks. I looked frantically but could not see her, the face of the water sullen glowering and impenetrable murk. Where was she gone? I think I called out her name. Hannah! Hannah! As though I could save her with a word.

She was gone. She did not break the surface. The dog stopped barking. I want to say that within a moment I was prepared to dive in but then Jack was over at my side and I was shouting at him to go back and sit down, and he was crying. I was turning from his face to the sea and caught between leaving him there and first returning him to a safe place further back. I shouted at him.

'I told you to stay back. Go back there, it's dangerous!'

He did not move. He looked at me and cried, his face wet and his eyes in smudges, small and hopeless as the morning I went to him to tell him that you were gone. And seeing him so I hesitated. I lost the plot, rescuing neither one nor the other of my children, standing there in the gale on the sea-washed rocks with the dog looking up at me and I looking straight at the face of grief. I might have wished for a wave for all of us. I might have been happy to surrender to that, the sudden bitter salty embrace.

But something carries us forward, something always does, and instantly I have lifted Jack and am hurrying back fifteen feet with him and the dog is following. With every second passing, I think my daughter is drowned.

'Jack, go back to the car,' I told him. 'Take Huckleberry back! If a car comes, wave, Jack, see if you can make them stop. Good boy.'

Something like that I said. I can't remember. I ran back then. I pushed off my shoes and threw my glasses on them and vaguely noted that they missed and hit a rock, breaking the lens, as I jumped into the water.

The cold of the sea took my breath away. The cold, the sheer grip it seemed to take on my heart. I felt the shock of it, the ice claw in my chest. How it skinned me. I plunged down through the dark and saw nothing but the bubbles of myself escaping. Then I was pulling and kicking my way back up to the surface and wanting to shout out Hannah's name underwater as if to ward off what water sprites and demons might be coming for her there. I hit the air and gasped, then kicked and flailed and looked about, swimming the stroke I knew from the summer long ago. I dived again, no more than six feet down into the blind world where nothing could be found or rescued.

I let my air escape and floundered there under the dark waters. If I tell the truth I cannot say I made a decision. Maybe I kicked, maybe I had learned to swim so that at this moment I would not drown. In the deeps of the water I heard a voice inside myself say, Please, God; say, Pray now. And for another instant I didn't, I wouldn't, whether from pride or fright or faithlessness. Pray. Say a prayer. Where is she? Where? God. I moved my hands, not quite making a stroke. I went down further, without bubbles now, the weight of water crushing my chest, and out of whatever reflex of hope or love or faith heard a fragment of prayer cross my mind.

I kicked. I came to the surface and I saw Hannah. I saw her make her way toward the edge of the rocks, saw the bent-elbow crook of her stroke and the sideways O of her mouth above the sea.

After that, the blur of moments that made up the rescue, hers and mine. All of ours. The shouting, the waving across the water, the dog barking, Jack jumping up and down at the edge and the spray hitting him and I fearing he would in a moment be swept away.

I called out to Hannah, my voice small and lost. I swam in the sway and fall of the waves until I was next to her and we washed up against the rocks and banged there until at last I could get a fissure hold and pull her up beside me. We clambered up on the rocks on all fours, coughing, spewing, gasping.

'Thank you, God,' were the first words I said, and said them without thinking, and only later, much later, thought back on them, as though faith was found there or I could see the Saviour Himself on the rocks of the west coast of Clare and knew that He was just then departing the scene.

And after that the whirr of moments that come after shock and that seem to concertina together and make a music of their own. Cries, embraces, breathless words of no import, glittering salt tears, silent thanks said over and over, a reel of many repeats.

I was not sure Hannah could stand or walk and when I stood to help her my head spun. I swayed as I bent down and got my arms about her. Up the rocks then, with Jack and the dog and Hannah in my arms and the sea wind screaming.

'Your glasses are broken, Dad,' Jack said, holding them in his hand. 'Can you see?'

'Yes. Thanks, Jack, good boy. Come on.'

'I'm all right, Dad,' Hannah protested as she sat into the seat, but her face was white and there were blue lines below her eyes and about her lips. I turned on the engine and the fan heater. I went to the boot and took out towels and my overcoat and wrapped her even as she fussed against me. My hands on the wheel were shaking badly, my teeth chattering.

'Are you all right, Hannah?'

'Yes, Dad, I am.'

In jagged, lurching motion then I brought the car about and hurried us along the sea road to Ballyvaughan. I stopped at the first house and the soft-voiced elderly woman who came to the door brought us inside at once.

'Goodness,' she said. 'Goodness me.'

And now here we are, in a large bedroom upstairs in her house, darkness fallen and both of the children asleep in the same large bed. Before she fell asleep I asked Hannah about what had happened.

'What?' She looked at me with eyes red and weary.

'Tell me. What happened?'

'I'm too tired. I want to sleep.'

'You fell, right?'

'Dad, I want to go asleep.'

'I just want to . . .'

'Dad.' She half waved, half protested a hand between us, and got shakily to her feet. She had a blanket around her. Jack was watching without speaking, the covers up to his chin where his small fists appeared holding them.

'Hannah, please,' I said. 'Tell me.'

And across her face passed the first crease of emotion, then her chin lifted and her eyes were glittering with fierce pain. I stood and had my arms about her as she wept. Her body shook.

'I don't know, Dad, I don't know,' she said. 'I went down there, I didn't think I was going to. Then . . .' And I closed my eyes as the grief of her went through me and I said it's all right it's all right over and over as she sobbed and shook and released the tears so long held inside her.

She wept and could not stop for a long time. I held her in my arms and rested her on the edge of the bed still in my embrace, and after a time Jack sat up in the covers and then crawled across and put his arms around both of us so we were an island there in the strange bedroom where the sea sang in the wind outside.

After, Hannah spoke to me and told me of her sadness, and how she missed you. And I think in telling it she found some kind of peace and at last lay back on the bed where I put the covers over her, and Jack curled close, and I said to them, 'We will be all right. We will. We will all be all right.'

And they slept.

And are sleeping now, and their faces in sleep, I think, have the serene and calm look of those who know they are saved.

Or so I believe tonight.

I stay here awake. Downstairs our clothes hang before the turf range. The dark sea batters the rocky shore across the road outside.

I had promised myself I would not write for a few days, but

tonight, here in this room, within the hearing of the children's breathing, I think I will finish now. I have a small notepad and a pen. Beneath my hand I smooth the page and, for the last time, begin.

The cuckoo comes in May, and soon the early mornings and late evenings of June are filled with his call. The branches of the sycamores are heavy with leaves that twist dark and pale and in front of the house the garden becomes rich and dense with green growth. Lustrous ivy climbs the cabin wall and through it tangles soft wiry clematis with flowers of purple trumpets. Down in the valley the meadows are filling or full, a pale brown-yellow against the green of the grazing fields. On cutting days, the tractors in the distance move as in slow motion, concentrically painting in the darker lines of the mown ground and leaving the stubble that remains. The Keanes and the Dooleys and the Downes are there, their faces dry and embrowned with hay-dust and sun and pollen. Stretches of fine weather come. A buzz of midges like a thinly darned patch of air hangs in the garden. Swifts return and nest in the roof of the cabin as they did in my childhood. They dart in and out, one, two, three, or more, flickering one after the next up and out of sight.

The days are long then, and of a timeless kind of beauty where it is possible to think the world a place still pastoral and Arcadian.

I write *Nicholas Copperly*. Kate works in the garden or sets up the easel we have got for her, or sits sometimes on the grass before the irises or the poppies and with soft oil pastels makes pictures. I watch her from the window. I have Nicholas fall in love. In the middle of the day I come downstairs and make rough sandwiches from brown bread and cheese and the hard tomatoes Mrs Brady sells and we eat them outside the front of the house on a bench we have taken from the old school at Clonigulane.

Sometimes Kate speaks of her mother and the sadness comes over her, the loneliness for how things could have been. We sit there in the steady hum of the summer garden, and slowly the moment passes.

'There will be our family now,' she says.

'Yes.'

'Things will be new.'

Mick Hehir comes, his wellingtons cuffed down in the warm weather, but his jacket still on him.

'On a fine day like this you want to get up on the bog to that turf that's cut,' he says.

'What turf?'

'Turf that's cut above for you,' he says, trying to hide his smile though it shines in his eyes. 'I cut for your father before and footed it too when he told me he wouldn't ask his boys to do it. You and Matthew were for the books, he said. But you'll go up to it now, I'm thinking.'

'We will. Thank you, Mick.'

'Advice: take a flask of tea, it's thirsty work.'

And so we do. We leave the house and go out across the back meadow where the grass is to our thighs. We go over the stone stile in the wall and into the hill field where a pheasant rises suddenly with great clattering, its wings beating madly. The way is along a crushed grass track made by the tractor. It rises steadily up out of the meadows and into ground more rocky where thistles grow and blackberry brambles in blossom tangle. The growth, the richness, the sense of full summer is a kind of deep luxuriance, of overabundant and carefree creation. We come up around the curve to the scattered rock places on the crest where we can stand and look out over the country. There is Kerry to the south and the mountains, there to the west the Atlantic.

Behind us then across a small wet field of rushes is the bog. The turf is cut and laid out in brown lines of sods. Sprigs of stiff heather are between them, and sometimes the feather-white tips of bog cotton. The work is slow. We must lift each piece that was wet when cut out of the ground and now has a wind-crisped skin and stand it upright against others in small clusters or *grogans* so the summer will dry it. In August we will bring the turf home for the fires of long winter.

We bend and lift and stand the sods. Up there on the bog a wind always blows. It is quiet. An hour passes, two. We bend and unbend, standing to press our hands into the small of our backs. I stop sometimes and watch Kate and watch a long strand of her fair hair fall down in front of her face and she blows at it and it goes away and comes back again. She works on, and works the hardest of us and is there on that bogland an image of trust and faith, of a bond believed between man and land and providence. We lift hundreds of sods and stand them upright, stippling the ground with standing brown stacks. In mid-afternoon we stop and sit on the edge of the bank on a coat and drink the tea from the flask. It tastes good, and better perhaps for the fatigue and the thirst and the bluster of the air.

'There are times,' Kate says, 'when I am very happy. When I can't imagine being more so.'

We sit there. A hare stands and runs not thirty feet away.

We get up and work on, until at last I call across to her that I can do no more for today.

'I've already done twenty more than you!' Kate laughs.

'I know.'

All the way down the hill fields we can see the house below us. I carry the old coat over my shoulder and Kate carries the flask. The summer evening light is golden. We come in the back door of the house and almost fall to sit in front of the low burning of the fire, our feet out before us. We are exhausted and unwashed and full of a contented kind of love.

'I'm so tired I could fall asleep here,' Kate says.

'Do,' I say.

'I couldn't.'

'Why not? Go ahead.'

She pauses.

'I don't want to lose how good I feel,' she says. And then after a little while: 'If I sleep, will you promise to stay awake?' she asks me. 'Or at least not fall asleep until after me?'

'Why?'

'Just. I'd be too lonely without you.'

Her face is very beautiful and her eyes tender and deep and knowing of the frailty of things. 'Will you stay awake while I sleep?'

I reach and take off her boots.

'I will,' I say.

Afterword

How does the real get into the made-up?
Ask me an easier one.

'Known World', Seamus Heaney

Now I sit at the long table in the cottage and watch while you go down through the summer garden for the post. The day is brilliant. The dog follows you down and back, fooled into thinking you were taking him on a longer walk. You come in the door, and because you can tell from the expression on my face, you ask me, 'Well?'

'It's finished.'

'Really?'

'Yes.'

'That's wonderful.'

You stand at my shoulder and look at the last pages.

'You call me Kate in this one?' you say, and put a hand on my shoulder and then stroke once the back of my head.

'Yes.'

You stand there beside me like that a little while in the peace I have then, knowing that I have written all these pages to face something in myself. To face the fear that washed through me like a foul tide in the month of September. The fear of losing you, of losing my life, that lay within me through autumn and winter. It is what writers do, imagine and feel the pain of others, sometimes perhaps at the expense of feeling their own. Here, then, in these pages is mine, the fear of death, of loss, of unexpressed love. Here is the truth told in a story. And in the telling of it perhaps I have found some way to have courage, to believe.

I have said the words and, for now at least, am healed.

'Is there a rescue?' you ask me.

'Of course there is.'

'Good. I like that.'

You bend down and kiss the side of my face. 'Tea to celebrate?'

'Yes.'

'Come on, then. Here. There's a card from your brother.'

'Let me see.'

'Huckleberry, Huckleberry, stop. Sit.'

The dog noses the hand that holds the letters, and then turns when told and lies out along the inside of the door. I get up and leave the stack of the manuscript and go with you into the kitchen. At the sink by the window you fill the kettle. The sky behind you is wide and blue. Sunlight touches your shoulders. I stand as if across a threshold. The kettle begins to warm. The children will be home soon.